INVESTIGATING THE DUKE

Suddenly a Duke Series
Book Eight

Alexa Aston

ARE YOU SIGNED UP FOR DRAGONBLADE'S BLOG?

You'll get the latest news and information on exclusive giveaways, exclusive excerpts, coming releases, sales, free books, cover reveals and more.

Check out our complete list of authors, too!

No spam, no junk. That's a promise!

Sign Up Here

www.dragonbladepublishing.com

Dearest Reader;

Thank you for your support of a small press. At Dragonblade Publishing, we strive to bring you the highest quality Historical Romance from some of the best authors in the business. Without your support, there is no 'us', so we sincerely hope you adore these stories and find some new favorite authors along the way.

Happy Reading!

CEO, Dragonblade Publishing

Additional Dragonblade books by Author Alexa Aston

Suddenly a Duke Series
Portrait of the Duke (Book 1)
Music for the Duke (Book 2)
Polishing the Duke (Book 3)
Designs on the Duke (Book 4)
Fashioning the Duke (Book 5)
Love Blooms with the Duke (Book 6)
Training the Duke (Book 7)
Investigating the Duke (Book 8)

Second Sons of London Series
Educated By The Earl (Book 1)
Debating With The Duke (Book 2)
Empowered By The Earl (Book 3)
Made for the Marquess (Book 4)
Dubious about the Duke (Book 5)
Valued by the Viscount (Book 6)
Meant for the Marquess (Book 7)

Dukes Done Wrong Series
Discouraging the Duke (Book 1)
Deflecting the Duke (Book 2)
Disrupting the Duke (Book 3)
Delighting the Duke (Book 4)
Destiny with a Duke (Book 5)

Dukes of Distinction Series
Duke of Renown (Book 1)
Duke of Charm (Book 2)
Duke of Disrepute (Book 3)
Duke of Arrogance (Book 4)

Duke of Honor (Book 5)
The Duke That I Want (Book 6)

The St. Clairs Series
Devoted to the Duke (Book 1)
Midnight with the Marquess (Book 2)
Embracing the Earl (Book 3)
Defending the Duke (Book 4)
Suddenly a St. Clair (Book 5)
Starlight Night (Novella)
The Twelve Days of Love (Novella)

Soldiers & Soulmates Series
To Heal an Earl (Book 1)
To Tame a Rogue (Book 2)
To Trust a Duke (Book 3)
To Save a Love (Book 4)
To Win a Widow (Book 5)
Yuletide at Gillingham (Novella)

King's Cousins Series
The Pawn (Book 1)
The Heir (Book 2)
The Bastard (Book 3)

Medieval Runaway Wives
Song of the Heart (Book 1)
A Promise of Tomorrow (Book 2)
Destined for Love (Book 3)

Knights of Honor Series
Word of Honor (Book 1)
Marked by Honor (Book 2)
Code of Honor (Book 3)
Journey to Honor (Book 4)
Heart of Honor (Book 5)
Bold in Honor (Book 6)
Love and Honor (Book 7)
Gift of Honor (Book 8)

Path to Honor (Book 9)
Return to Honor (Book 10)

The Lyon's Den Series
The Lyon's Lady Love

Pirates of Britannia Series
God of the Seas

De Wolfe Pack: The Series
Rise of de Wolfe

The de Wolfes of Esterley Castle
Diana
Derek
Thea

Also from Alexa Aston
The Bridge to Love (Novella)
One Magic Night

PROLOGUE

London—Christmas Day, 1798

SHELBY SLADE AWOKE with a start, on edge, as always. Then she took a deep breath and forced herself to relax. She would not be in a rush today. It was Christmas.

Her twelfth birthday.

For some reason, it was important to her that she keep up with the date. Four years ago, she hadn't a clue she would live to be this age.

She shifted, lying back against the sack of flour she used as a pillow in the storeroom of Griffin's Inn & Tavern. Not that the owner knew she did so. She had learned to pick a lock at a young age and liked the location of this place. Mr. Griffin kept the storeroom swept and clean, though it was a bit of a hodgepodge. It gave her almost a sense of permanency, coming here each night to bed down. Or actually, in the wee hours of the morning. She would linger in the alley behind the tavern and wait until the Griffins went up to bed, some of their customers doing the same, having taken rooms at the inn, while others left for their own homes.

Then Shelby would ease open the lock with her picks and hide in the storeroom, pulling out the small blanket she kept hidden, and stretching out to sleep. Griffin kept the door to this room locked at all times, and she felt it gave her an added bit of protection. She never felt safe on the streets and certainly could never let down her guard. For a few hours, though, the storeroom allowed her to relax and rest in peace.

For some reason, she wanted to see Mum today. Not that her mother had ever cared to see her only child. Mum always had chosen a man over her daughter any day. Shelby had no idea who her father was, only that he had up and left when he found out a babe was on the way. She had grown up with a string of men coming and going in their one-room flat. She had learned to keep out of the way and stay quiet, not drawing attention to herself.

That had changed shortly after she turned six. The latest in the parade of men had noticed her presence and let her and her mother know he was not fond of children. He began shoving her out the door and locking it, telling her not to come back for a few days. It was when she first started becoming street smart, having to learn how to survive the best she could. She learned how to beg. How to live on scraps of food tossed out by others. How to keep herself small so that others on the streets did not notice her.

But all the time, she was learning.

At seven, a different man had replaced the one who had tossed her out, and Shelby spent a short time at home. He had seemed nice, even giving her a peppermint once, making her feel as if she might come home for good and they could become a family.

How wrong she had been.

His smiles only hid the malice in his heart. He soon began beating Mum and then Shelby herself for the slightest infraction. Once again, she fled to the streets, rarely coming home. When she did, she would linger outside, waiting for him to leave before she went in for a quick visit with Mum. Her mother usually sported a black eye or two, not to mention bruises and even broken bones. Mum was nervous whenever Shelby appeared, always worried her daughter would be caught there—and both of them would be punished.

Finally, she stopped coming around, realizing Mum dreaded those visits.

She learned more about survival on the streets of London. Which churches gave out meals and clothing. How to fight with her feet and fists. The ways to choose a mark and pick a pocket. Then one day she heard that her mum had taken up with someone new, her former lover having died in a tavern fight. Once again, Shelby ventured a visit home and found the new man to be handsome and kind. He encouraged her to come home for good, telling her that he had always wanted a daughter, and they could be a family. She decided to test things out, trying her best to live a normal life of an eight-year-old. She even got a job selling flowers, coming home and giving money to him.

But not all of it. Her instincts told her to hold some back in case some emergency happened. In case he wasn't the good man he seemed to be.

And she was right.

Shelby had heard of predators like him on the streets and how to avoid them, but she had never realized they groomed their victims with kindness and attention. She let her guard down around him and almost paid for it with her life.

He did what she guessed others like him did. Lulled both her and her mother into a false sense of security. One day, Shelby came home, handing over her coins as always. This time, though, she had seen a glint in his eyes which had been missing before. It was as if he had become a totally different person, one she had never met. One she was afraid of. One she knew would do her harm.

She had asked where her mum was, worried that she didn't see her. The man told her Mum was feeling poorly and had gone to the apothecary for something to soothe her stomach.

Something in his tone didn't ring right with Shelby. She told him she would go in search of her mother. Then she made her biggest mistake, turning her back on him so she could make it to the door. She was reaching for the doorknob when he latched on to her elbow, his grip like an iron vise. Then he had slapped her so hard that she saw stars dance before her eyes. As she lay on the ground, too stunned to move and yet cursing inwardly for being so foolish, he had lifted her and placed her on the pallet she slept on each night.

His hands began touching her body, skimming over her chest. He had held her down, using his hands and body to keep her against the ground, and kissed her. At the same time, his hand went under her dress, and his fingers skimmed her thigh. Even now, she could feel the surge of panic she had felt that day. When he had plunged his tongue inside her mouth, she had come to her senses and bitten down hard on it, all the while reaching for the sharp blade she had carried in her boot. One she had taken off a dead man in an alley. He hadn't needed it anymore—and Shelby had known it would come in handy one day.

When the man shrieked in pain and jerked to a sitting position, still straddling her, she saw anger flashed in his eyes. He raised his hand to slap her again—and she slashed him across the throat.

Shelby would never forget the look of astonishment on his face and the line that turned red.

Pushing hard on his chest, she scrambled from beneath him as he started to pitch forward. It was only then she saw the lump in the corner, realizing it was Mum. Rushing to her, she blocked out the gurgling noises coming from the other side of the room as her attacker drowned in his own blood.

Her mother lay curled in a tight ball, beaten savagely, her face almost unrecognizable as a mass of bruises developed. One eye was swollen entirely shut. Mum opened her mouth and Shelby saw her teeth had been shattered. But she had spoken. Mum had whispered one word.

"*Run . . .*"

Shelby had done just that. She did not want to hang for murder. She knew the authorities would neither listen nor care about what this man had done to a defenseless woman and her young daughter. She also knew she could never come back here again. She had gently kissed Mum's brow and then returned to the body. He lay unmoving, face down in a spreading pool of blood. She wiped her knife on his shirt and then left.

That had been four years ago. Shelby never spoke to her mother again. Oh, sometimes, she hid in the shadows and watched Mum come and go, her looks fading even as a new group of men moved in and out. Finally, two years ago, she learned Mum was gone. In that time, Shelby had honed her street skills. She could filch items with the best of any of the pickpockets working in London. She also could clean up nicely and beg in the better parts of town. She stole when she had to, be it food or clothing. She had tried working for her living, first as a chimney sweep, climbing up flues to sweep out soot and put out fires. It was filthy, exhausting work. Then she had gone to work in a mill, quickly giving up on that after seeing three children close to her age losing limbs in accidents. Two had died in agony, while the other had lost his arm and been fired. Besides the filthy conditions and meager pay, Shelby hated the confines, spending sixteen to eighteen hours a day in cramped conditions. She would rather be on her own, making her own way, answering to no one but herself.

Snuggling back against the flour sack, she raised the blanket to her chin, relishing the thought of not having to be gone immediately. Usually, she was out of the storeroom by six o'clock each morning, folding the thin blanket and hiding it behind a barrel. With today being Christmas Day, however, she had time to luxuriate. Over the years, Shelby had learned the Griffins would not be serving anyone until mid-morning. She supposed they went to church before returning to the tavern and feeding their guests.

Rising an hour later, she stifled a giggle, feeling as if she were a lady of leisure for one day. She left the storeroom, relocking the door behind her as always, and headed to church herself. She had learned over the years which ones gave out things to the poor, whether it be a hot meal or a warm coat. This time, she got both, handing over the coat she wore, which was getting too small for her, and slipping into a new one. It was slightly too large, but she didn't care. It was clean, and she would be able to wear it this winter and probably next, as well.

Her belly full now, she walked a long way to a field where the poor were buried, ready to visit with Mum now. Her mother's grave did not have a headstone, but Shelby counted the graves and stopped when she found the correct one. Sitting on the ground, she placed her palm flat. This was the closest she would ever be to Mum.

"I just wanted to come and say hello," she said softly. "Happy Christmas, Mum. I miss you."

Shelby sat for an hour beside the grave, telling her mother what she had been up to since their last visit. Her legs grew cramped sitting for so long, and she finally rose.

"I'll be back, Mum. Someday. I don't know when, but you haven't seen the last of me."

She left the graveyard and went to Hyde Park, her favorite of the parks in London. It was where the toffs' grooms exercised horses each morning in Rotten Row. She loved watching them put the beautiful beasts through their paces and told herself that one day she would be rich enough to own one. She would ride it everywhere, handing out coins to the poor, and people would think she was a great lady. Today the park was empty, thanks to the holiday.

Wandering down to the Serpentine, Shelby sat on the bank, pulling a bag of leftover chestnuts from her pocket. She ate them slowly, thinking she would take a day off from working the streets. Not that many would be out now. The day had grown colder and even more bleak, the wind biting, stinging her cheeks and turning her fingers numb. Others would be in their homes, celebrating the holiday with their loved ones, so there would be no pockets to pick or strangers to beg for money.

That was all right because three days ago, she had picked the pocket of a fairly ordinary-looking gentleman, only to find she had struck a windfall. What she had earned from that single outing would keep her comfortable for a month or more. Shelby had even gone to a bathhouse and taken a long, hot bath, washing her extra set of clothes as well as herself. The first thing she had learned on the streets was to dress as a young boy. Females were seen as weak, no matter what their age, and she always wore a shirt, vest, and trousers. She kept her hair short, pulling a cap low on her face to hide her feminine features.

Her only problem was she now had breasts. At twelve, she had grown long and lean, stronger than other girls and even boys her age. She had heard talk about girls bleeding and had spent a coin a month ago in a brothel, asking for information about that. The tart who had talked to her explained what her monthly courses would be like and how to handle them. Shelby dreaded the day when they came. It was already hard to pass herself off as a boy this past year. That situation would only complicate her life.

She rose and left the park, going back to the streets of Mayfair and wandering them for a few hours, looking at all the pretty houses. Most were unlit since toffs liked to go to the country this time of year. Still, it helped to keep moving since the temperature had dropped even further, the brisk wind chilling her to the bone.

When she reached a street that had some foot traffic on it this late afternoon, she instinctively began looking for a mark. Shelby saw one coming. He was about thirty, well-dressed but not conspicuously so. Looking straight ahead, she timed it perfectly, bumping into him, mumbling, "'Scuse me, sir," and then walking away. A lesson she had learned was not to rush from a mark because it left them suspicious. Neither did she tarry, though, merely moving at an easy gait.

She walked a few blocks and then turned into an alley to see the pocket watch she had taken, hoping it would be a piece which would fetch a pretty price. As she viewed it, though, she sensed another presence in the alley. The hairs on the back of her neck stood up, and she jammed the watch into her coat pocket and whirled.

It was her mark. The one she had bumped into blocks ago. He must have followed her. Blast! She thought she had warmed her fingers enough from the cold to make a move. Obviously, he had felt something and given her chase. Cursing inwardly at her carelessness, she was disappointed that her instincts had let her down. Or her sheer laziness. She knew better. To always be on her toes and alert to everything about her.

"I am not going to hurt you," he said, holding his hands away from his sides, palms out, indicating to her he held no weapon.

Her survival instincts hummed now. Just because a weapon wasn't visible didn't mean this man didn't possess one. She had underestimated him. He might even be someone who moved as quickly as she did.

Her eyes darted about, looking for a way to escape.

"I said I wouldn't hurt you, and I mean it," he said convincingly, "but you must give back my pocket watch. It belonged to my father—and his before him. It is my most prized possession."

Still, she hesitated. Doing so would admit guilt. He might hit her. Knock her down. Grab her by the hair and drag her off to where she'd be thrown in prison. Or worse.

"I don't know what—"

"Oh, do me the courtesy of telling me the truth, young lady. I will accept a lot from someone. But not lies. If you are worried I will go to the authorities, rest assured that I won't. Simply give me the watch. It is mine. Not yours. I will have it and have it now," he said firmly.

Reluctantly, Shelby pulled the watch from her oversized pocket and tossed it at him. She had learned never to hand something to a stranger because he could lock on to your wrist. Bad things could happen. They had to her. It was a lesson Shelby would not forget.

He nodded approvingly. "Thank you. Now, would you like to come home with me and have a hot meal?"

His words surprised her—and she was rarely surprised.

"I am not someone who wishes to rob or hurt you. I have seen you before on the streets. How long have you lived on them?"

Something about his kind, brown eyes made her want to tell the truth.

"Six years, sir, though the first two I bounced between home and the streets."

"So, four solid years—plus a little of learning how to care for yourself before that. Do you have parents?"

Again, it shocked her that she wanted to give him the truth. Her truth.

"No, sir. My father left before I was even born. My mum . . . died two years ago."

"And you have no one else now? No brothers or sisters. No aunts or uncles who might take you in?"

She shook her head.

"I know you have no reason to trust me, but I am going to ask you to come home with me. For that hot meal, even if it is all you wish. If you want more from my wife and me, we can give it to you."

Shelby shook her head violently and began backing away from him. "Stay away." She bent and pulled her blade from her boot, the boots she had taken off a dead man a month ago and stuffed with newspapers so they might fit better.

"Stay away," she repeated, the warning low and deadly. "Don't think I won't use it."

He nodded, almost in approval. "I've no doubt you can do so with some expertise."

She wasn't familiar with the word. Moreover, his manner confused her.

"My name is Boyd Franklin," the man told her. "I am a Bow Street Runner."

She knew of the runners. All London did. They solved crimes for pay. They had a reputation for being crafty and determined.

Persistent to the point of annoyance.

"I see you know of us. I work to help others. I find thieves and the objects they have stolen. I hunt for missing persons who might have absconded with money not belonging to them. I know you have no reason to trust me, but I want to help you. What is your name?"

"Shelby. Slade," she said begrudgingly.

"Well, Shelby Slade. It is Christmas, and I have just wrapped up an important case. I am on my way home to Mrs. Franklin. I promised her I would be in time for supper—and she promised me roasted goose. We would be happy to share that meal with you. What do you say?"

The thought of goose made her mouth water. He hadn't harmed her so far. Bow Street Runners had a reputation for being a bit rough around the edges, but were known as hard workers and good men.

"I suppose I could eat a few bites of it."

"Excellent," Franklin proclaimed. "Come along, then."

He turned and began walking briskly down the alley. She liked that he didn't turn to see if she followed him. Shelby did so. At a distance.

A quarter-hour later, he turned the corner and then went down three houses. He paused and looked to his right, waving at her. She caught up to him.

"This is our home." Pride was evident in his voice.

He removed a key and used it in the lock, calling out, "Dearest, I have brought home Shelby Slade to dine with us."

A woman close to thirty appeared, golden hair piled atop her head. She was tiny, short in stature and with delicate bones.

"Why, hello, Shelby. I am so glad you've come to share Christmas dinner with us. Of course, as late as it is, I should call it Christmas supper instead. Come in and wash up."

She did so, still wary as her eyes roamed the place, seeing it decorated with Christmas greenery.

Mrs. Franklin set another place at the table, and they went to it, taking their seats.

"Hat, dear," the woman reminded her gently.

Grabbing it from her head, Shelby slipped it under her thigh.

Mr. Franklin carved the roasted goose, giving her a more than ample portion. Mrs. Franklin encouraged Shelby to fill her plate and she did so, covering the goose in hot gravy and piling foods she did not recognize next to it. The smells were delicious, though, and she savored each bite she took.

As they ate, the Franklins talked about themselves. Where they had met and when they'd wed. Mrs. Franklin then paused.

"We had a child once. He died shortly after I gave birth to him seven years ago. They have told me I can have no more. That his birth was too traumatic to my body."

She paused. "We had a room for him. A room that has never been used. If you would like to stay the night, you are welcome to do so."

She didn't want to leave this warmth. This home. These people. For the first time in years, tears filled Shelby's eyes.

"One night," she said. "Only one."

Something told her one night would become many.

Shelby Slade had finally found a home.

CHAPTER ONE

Edgewood, Hertfordshire—New Year's Day 1814

JASPER LINCOLN LOOKED out over his congregation, concluding his sermon by saying, "And so in this new year, my friends, it is important to be the best version of yourself you can be. The Lord has given us a new year—and a blank slate. Write upon it with the joy and love good Christians should always hold in their hearts. Love one another as Christ urged us to. Forgive each other seven times seventy, as Our Lord asked be done. Do unto others as you would have them do unto you. If you do so, this will be the most satisfying year of your life."

He left the lectern and returned to his seat, giving time for his words to soak in and glad to have finished his sermon on a positive note, as he always tried to do each time he addressed his congregation. Rising again, he asked his parishioners to join him in song, and turned his attention to the organist, who also served as his sexton. Mr. Orr nodded and the strains of *A Mighty Fortress is Our God* began.

As Jasper sang in his rich baritone, knowing all the verses by heart, he thought about his own life and what it would be like in this coming year. He had settled into the living at Edgewood, thanks to his father, the Duke of Edgehaven. He had been serving here two years now, after the death of Edgewood's most recent clergyman, and it was good to be home again. Having recently turned thirty years of age, he knew that it was time for him to finally settle down and find a wife. He had no lack of candidates. Ever since his return to Hertfordshire from his previous post in Kent, ladies in his congregation had been placing themselves in his path, left and right.

Jasper was not looking for some great love match. He didn't know if he truly believed in them. He would simply find a woman with a kind heart, one who would be as Eve to Adam, a good helpmate. Well, perhaps someone a little better than Eve had turned out to be. As the hymn's last chorus came to an end, he chuckled to himself. Eve had tempted Adam, causing the First Man to lose his place in the Garden of Eden. Jasper didn't need a vixen such as that to ruin him. No, he was dedicated to his congregation and his family.

It was time, however, for him to create an earthly family of his own. Perhaps that would help hold the loneliness at bay. While he led a full life and filled his waking hours, it would be nice to have someone to talk to about his day and to watch his children grow.

He would be seeing his parents later today when he traveled to London. He had always been close to his father, who got along famously with everyone he met. The duke and his three sons had been inseparable until the boys reached adulthood and had gone their separate ways. Jarrod, Earl of Sutton, now resided in Sussex with his two daughters, Sylvia and Fanny. Jarrod's wife had died in childbirth less than two months ago, in another attempt to try to give her husband the heir he so desperately wanted.

At five and thirty, Jarrod was becoming anxious about an heir. Jasper believed his oldest brother would partake in the Season this coming spring, cutting his mourning period short so that he might find a bride, one young enough to provide him with the heir he so desperately desired. He couldn't blame his brother. His wife had lost numerous other babes over the years. If he didn't produce an heir, the title would fall to the middle

Lincoln brother.

Jude, the second son of the duke, served as a colonel in His Majesty's army, fighting under Wellington. Wellington's troops had finished their long mission in Spain and Portugal and had moved on to France. No letter had come from Jude since late-October, and the family was becoming anxious. Jasper prayed for his brother's safety and health every night.

Once again, he approached the lectern and led his flock in a closing prayer to end the service. Once it concluded, he reminded his parishioners, "I will be traveling to London in order to spend some time with my family these next two weeks. I won't be with you next Sunday, but I should have returned by the following one. Keep safe and God bless you all."

He exited the church and waited outside, greeting the congregation as they left. As always, it took longer than he'd hoped, thanks to the many women who simply had to get a word in with him, married or not. He knew he was handsome but had never traded on his looks. Jasper wished, though, that he favored his father. Jude was the only one of the three brothers who did so, having the duke's blond hair and green eyes. Jarrod and Jasper favored their mother, with both having russet hair that appeared brown indoors and yet had strong red highlights when out in the sun. They also had the duchess' deep blue eyes and the tall, athletic build of her father and two brothers.

He returned to the vicarage, thoughts of his mother troubling him. Of all the Lincoln brothers, Jasper was obviously his mother's darling. Her favoritism was blatant and had been awkward the entire time the boys were growing up. Nowadays, Jarrod and Jude merely teased their younger brother about it.

Although he was close with his father and considered the duke to be his best friend, Jasper had never warmed to his mother. The attention she lavished upon him smothered him as a child and overwhelmed him as he grew to manhood. He did what he could to distance himself from her when the duke and duchess were in residence at Edgehill. That would not be possible during his stay in town, however.

Most couples remained in the country until March or April, only returning to their London residences when the Season was ready to commence. The Duchess of Edgehaven loathed the country, however, tolerating it from Season's end until the new year began. She had always insisted they return to town shortly after Boxing Day. Jasper loved his father but had thought the duke should have put his foot down years ago and have them remain at Edgehill. Then again, his mother would have sulked. Pouted. Finally, railed against the decision. He supposed to keep peace in the family was why the Duke and Duchess of Edgehaven returned to town earlier than most of the *ton*. At least his father's closest friend, the Earl of Darrow, did the same. Jasper suspected Lord and Lady Darrow did so simply to keep the duke company.

Lord Darrow had been as a father to the three Lincoln siblings, often accompanying them and the duke as they hunted. It was Darrow who had taught all three boys to fish, the duke having no interest in the sport. The same was true of swimming. Lord Darrow was an excellent swimmer, and he made certain all three young Lincolns were, too.

As Jasper finished packing, he wondered if Lord Darrow would be in town. Lady Darrow had passed in mid-October, her heart weakening after a fever. Jasper didn't know if the earl would remain in the country to mourn his wife or if he would return to town in his usual pattern. He hoped the earl would come to London.

Because Jasper was worried about his own father's health.

The duke had been quite robust his entire life until the past several months. While residing in the country, his father enjoyed riding every morning, as well as hunting and shooting in the afternoons. But when the duke had returned from the Season, he appeared thin to Jasper. The weight continued to fall off Edgehaven until the point of the duke being downright gaunt. Jasper had insisted their local doctor call at Edgehill and examine the duke.

Dr. Davies said he could find nothing physically wrong with the duke, telling Jasper that when a man hit his mid-sixties, things were usually downhill from there.

He could not imagine a world without his father and best friend in it. It renewed his desire to find a wife and start a family as soon as possible. He needed his children to know their grandfather.

A knock sounded at his door, and he answered it, finding two Edgehill footmen on the other side.

"Is your trunk ready, my lord?" asked one.

"Yes," he replied. "It is in the bedchamber."

Though he never used his courtesy title of Lord Jasper, his mother insisted their staff continue to address him in that manner. It made him uncomfortable, but his mother was the single most stubborn woman Jasper had ever encountered. Once she had something in mind, there was no use trying to change it. While he looked forward to the time he would spend with his father during his two-week holiday, he knew he must put up with being around his mother. He hoped to limit his time with the woman.

Jasper climbed into the ducal carriage, and they were off. The journey from Hertfordshire to London usually took a little more than two hours. He found his thoughts drifting, and then he must have fallen asleep. Looking out the window, he saw the bustling streets of London and within a quarter-hour, they had arrived in Mayfair.

Bowen, their longtime butler in town, greeted him enthusiastically. "Good afternoon, Lord Jasper. It is delightful to see you once more. How does your flock at Edgewood fare?"

"As of this morning, all of them are in good spirits, with one being in labor with her third child. I pray for a safe delivery and will christen the babe upon my return."

"I have your old room ready, my lord. Tea is about to be served in the drawing room."

"Then I will head straight there, Bowen. Thank you."

Jasper had spent summers in this townhouse, leaving school each term and coming to town with his two brothers. It was unusual because most parents of the *ton* sent their children to the country while they were participating in the Season. His parents insisted, though, that their three boys be with them. He knew his father did so because he enjoyed being around his sons. He believed his mother only requested their presence so she might be with her youngest child.

Still, London was a familiar city to him, one he always appreciated visiting. He, Jarrod, and Jude had ridden early each morning in Rotten Row as boys, a groom always accompanying them. They had gone to museums and bookstores with their father during the day and taken tea with many a noble couple since the Edgehavens entertained frequently while in town. The boys were even allowed to sit in the gallery and watch the dancers at the ball hosted by his parents on Midsummer's Eve each year. He had attended a few of those balls himself while he was still in university but had not done so since then. He had trained to enter the church and been assigned to a parish in Kent, where he had stayed until the living opened at Edgewood.

Entering the drawing room, he tamped down the disappointment when he saw his mother and no one else. Dread filled Jasper as he crossed the room and went to her, bending to brush his lips against her cheek.

"Hello, Mama," he said, taking a seat opposite her. "Where is Father?"

Irritation filled her face. "He is napping, Jasper. His health is not much improved since we last saw you at Christmas dinner."

It had worried him when his mother had entered the church on Christmas Day alone. During the entire sermon he gave, his worries had increased. After the service ended, Mama had told Jasper the duke had wished to rest up for their Christmas dinner, which was held at three o'clock that afternoon. Jarrod had not come to Edgehill, sending word that he and the girls wished for a quiet Christmas this first year since the death of his countess.

When the duke had entered the dining room, leaning heavily on his valet's arm, Jasper had been shocked at how frail his father looked. He'd eaten very little, though Jasper had encouraged him to try almost every dish available.

He now asked his mother, "Is he worse off than he was on Christmas Day?"

"I believe Edgehaven's time on earth is limited, my precious boy."

"Then you never should have returned to town," he snapped. "Father did not need to be traveling. And you know he prefers Dr. Davies to any physician here. I think you should return to the country at once, Mama."

The duchess studied him a long moment. "You have always defended him, Jasper. You have been a good protector of your father over the years. I do not believe, however, that Edgehaven is well enough to travel at this time. He needs to regain his strength before undertaking even a short journey. We shall remain in town for now."

He eyed her as he began pouring out for them. "Will you return to Edgehill with him, Mama? Or stay in town, as you prefer?"

"Jasper, you are old enough that I should be able to speak to you candidly. It is time you knew the truth."

A chill settled over him. "What truth?" he pressed.

"Edgehaven and I have barely tolerated one another through the decades."

There. She had admitted it aloud. He and his brothers had suspected it for years. His parents always spoke cordially in front of their children, but in his heart of hearts, Jasper thought his mother despised her husband.

"We have put up a good front all these years, but I am tired of all the pretense. It wears on me. I cannot stand the sight of Edgehaven, while he is indifferent to me."

"Then why did the two of you even wed?" he demanded.

She handed him a cup and saucer, shaking her head. "You

have no idea what it is like to be a woman. Women are merely chess pieces moved about a chessboard by their families." She paused and then softly said, "I fell in love when I was a young lady making my come-out."

He watched as her face softened. No longer was she the haughty Duchess of Edgehaven. Instead, Jasper caught a glimpse of the young woman she had been. One in love.

She stared into the distance as she revealed, "I loved a viscount with all my heart. He had offered for me. He asked me first, before going to my father, and I had accepted him with enthusiasm."

Her face darkened. "When he called on my father the next day, however, he left Father's study looking bemused. I had been lurking at the top of the stairs and rushed down them to him."

Mama's mouth hardened. "It was then that he told me I already had a betrothed. That my father had arranged for me to marry the Duke of Edgehaven, and the marriage contracts were to be signed later that day. No one had shared a word of this with me."

Her eyes met Jasper's, and he saw hate glittering in them.

"Immediately, I went to Papa, demanding to know what he had arranged behind my back. He told me while a viscount—who would one day be an earl—was a suitable husband, a duke was much higher in rank. That the union between our families would be good for both sides."

She frowned. "I had been introduced to Edgehaven, of course, soon after the Season began. I had not even danced with the man, much less held a conversation with him, though." Her eyes narrowed. "He was weak, allowing his own father to force this union upon us. And I have never forgiven him for it."

These revelations had Jasper reeling. Still, he tried to calm his mother's anger. "Mama, there are many women who marry candidates their fathers have chosen for them. Surely, you knew this going into your come-out Season?"

"Of course, I did," she said bitterly. "But I was in love."

"I am sorry you had to be parted from your sweetheart. On the bright side, Father gave you three wonderful sons. Are you not even a little happy that you have us?"

A slow smile spread across her face, and she reached for his hand. "Of course, I am, my darling boy. I live for my children. *Especially* you."

He pulled his hand from hers. "Mama," he said sternly. "I have asked you not to be this way. Your preferential treatment of me has got to end. It caused trouble between my brothers and me growing up."

"Pish-posh," she declared. "You are grown men now. You have a brother who is an earl and one who fights for his country. You rarely even see them. At least I am lucky enough to see you more ever since you came back to Edgewood."

She reached out and brushed a fallen lock from his forehead.

"See!" he said angrily, jerking back. "You still treat me as if I am a child. I am a grown man, Mama. I have a profession. And I will soon be seeking a wife."

Alarm filled her face. "Oh, you do not need to do so, Jasper. Not yet."

"Why should I wait? My parishioners expect their spiritual leader to be wed. I also wish to have children and certainly need a wife for that."

Her gaze pinned his. "Promise me you won't do anything rash."

He cocked an eyebrow. "Have I ever been known to be rash, Mama? I am likely the most deliberate man you have ever known. I have decided, however, to take a wife and will do so by the end of this new year."

She breathed what sounded like a sigh of relief. "Keep me apprised, Jasper."

He didn't say that he had no intention of doing so. Any name he mentioned to his mother wouldn't be good enough for her. She would toss out that he was a duke's son and should wed someone within his own class. In truth, he was a poorly compensated clergyman and needed a wife who was not from the *ton*. A woman who would be willing to put in the hard work beside him in leading their congregation. He already had three candidates in mind—but would keep that to himself.

Bowen appeared, bearing a silver tray. "This came for His Grace, Your Grace. I thought I would leave it with you, Your Grace."

"Thank you, Bowen," the duchess said dismissively, and the butler exited the drawing room.

She began to break the seal, and Jasper said, "Wait. What are you doing? Bowen said it was addressed to Father."

Before she could reply, he heard a cough and looked up, seeing the duke being led to tea by his valet. Immediately, Jasper came to his feet and hurried across the room.

"I'll take it from here," he told Watson.

Guiding his father to a settee, he eased the older man onto it and sat next to him, shocked at how much his father's health had deteriorated in the week since Jasper had last seen him.

"Father, you look gravely ill. Have you seen a physician since you arrived in town?"

"No, Son. Dr. Davies has found nothing wrong with me. Neither would anyone else. I am simply growing old." He coughed again. "I fear my end is drawing near."

"Don't say that," he admonished gently.

"A letter came, Edgehaven," Mama said sharply. "Shall I read it to you?"

The duke sighed. "Go ahead."

Jasper watched her break the seal and skim it. She glanced up, looking flustered.

"What is it?" Jasper asked.

She swallowed. "It is news. News of your brother."

A sinking feeling filled Jasper. He took the parchment she offered and quickly read its contents to himself.

15 November 1813

To His Grace, the Duke of Edgehaven —

I regret to inform you that your son, Colonel Jude Lincoln, was killed in action during the Battle of Nivelle, fought on French soil these past four days. This defeat of Soult would not have been possible without brave men such as your son.

I had the pleasure of working closely with Colonel Lincoln and personally saw to his burial. He was a bright, courageous man. His contributions to Britain's war effort will not be forgotten.

Sincerely,
Sir John James Hamilton

"What is it, Jasper?" the duke asked.

Tears blinded him as he said, "We haven't heard from Jude because he was killed in battle. At Nivelle, November last."

His father began sobbing uncontrollably. Jasper comforted the old man as best he could. Only as he wiped at his own tears did he see his mother.

The Duchess of Edgehaven sat dry-eyed, the news of the death of her second son not moving her in the slightest.

He had known she could be selfish and even petty—but heartless?

Jasper had never loved his mother, merely endured being around her. Seeing her now with no sorrow on her face caused him to harden his heart toward her. He might preach to his congregation of loving others.

But Jasper would never love the woman who gave birth to him.

CHAPTER TWO

JASPER TOLD HIS mother to ring for Bowen and then swept his weeping father into his arms, carrying him to his ducal bedchamber. Watson, the valet, was already present and turned back the bedclothes as Jasper set his father onto the mattress. As the two men undressed the duke, Bowen appeared, and Jasper asked for a physician to be summoned immediately.

"I want a doctor here within a half-hour, Bowen," he instructed.

"Of course, my lord."

"Also send a rider to my brother's estate. I think Lord Sutton should be here."

Left unsaid was that Jarrod might become the new Duke of Edgehaven within a few days.

Once his father was in bed and pillows lumped behind him, Jasper took a seat at the bedside and gathered the old man's hand in his. He nodded to Watson, and the valet slipped from the room.

"Father, what do you think is wrong with you?"

The duke shrugged.

"You have always been blessed with good health. It seems as if everything came on suddenly."

"I am just getting old, Jasper. That is what Dr. Davies has told me."

If he were being frank, Jasper didn't trust the diagnosis given by the Edgewood physician. Dr. Davies was in his seventies and though he had the duke's trust, Jasper couldn't help but think that Davies had missed something. His father had lost too much weight in too short a time. He had become weak and infirm within a few short months.

"Dr. Davies has told me the same thing, and yet I disagree, Father. I think there is more to it than old age."

"You think I have something growing inside me, such as a tumor?" his father asked, fear in his eyes. "Or a weak heart, perhaps?"

"It is just that you have been dizzy and confused in recent months. Your coloring has altered. You complain of stomach pains. You have lost a tremendous amount of weight. Yet Dr. Davies can seem to find nothing wrong with you."

His father smiled ruefully. "I am five and sixty, Jasper. I won't live forever, you know. Besides, these last few months have been difficult ones. Frankly, death would come as a relief."

He squeezed his father's fingers. "Don't say that. We still need you with us for many years to come. *I* still need you."

"Ah, you are a grown man, Jasper Lincoln. You thrive as a vicar. I have never heard another clergyman give a sermon the way you can. You draw in your parishioners and weave a story for them to listen to. It always has a moral, and you simplify things into terms easy to understand. I have no doubt you will rise high in the church, my boy."

"I have no such ambitions, Father. If I served out my entire career at Edgewood, I would be happy."

The duke's gaze bored into him. "Are you happy, Jasper? Truly?"

"I have done some soul-searching in recent days. If you are speaking of a wife and children, yes, I do believe I am ready for both. That my happiness would grow if I had a family of my own."

The duke winced, drawing in a sharp breath. His grip on

Jasper's hand tightened.

"Then my best advice to you, my son, is to marry for love. That was not something I was allowed to do."

Jasper studied his father a moment, reeling at the revelations revealed to him by both parents in so short a time. "Were you ever in love, Father? Before you married Mama?"

His fathered sighed. "I was, indeed. Very deeply in love. In fact, she was the daughter of one of your predecessors. The man who held the living at Edgewood two times removed before you. When I told my father of my intentions to offer for her, he merely laughed in my face. He told me there was no such thing as love, at least not for high-ranking members of Polite Society. That if I thought so much of the chit, I should make her my mistress. He forbade me to wed her and two days later, he summoned me to his study. His solicitor and another one were present, and I witnessed the marriage settlements being drawn up and signed."

"For you and Mama?"

How ironic that both his parents had loved others—and yet were forced to wed one another. No wonder their marriage had been such a miserable one. Jasper had not known this for thirty years, and yet it gave him insight into his parents and their relationship.

"Mama told me at tea today that she had once loved another man. Did you know of this?"

The duke pulled his hand from Jasper's and pressed both palms to his belly, moaning low.

"The pain is bad?" he asked, feeling helpless as he watched his father struggle.

His father's eyes fluttered a few times and closed. He fell into a restless sleep, not having answered his son's question. It wouldn't surprise Jasper if his mother had immediately informed her new husband that she loved another. Perhaps Father had done the same—and that had been the root of their animosity all these years. His father had understood the role he was born to play, heir to a dukedom, and had wed the woman his parents selected for him.

Mama, on the other hand, was strong in spirit. She would have never given in to such a pretense, possibly gloating that she had a sweetheart, one who would forever hold her heart.

That thought troubled him. Instead of a sweetheart, what if the man Mama loved had been her lover? Or continued to be one after her marriage? Both he and Jarrod favored Mama in looks, while Jude was his father made over. Jasper had always thought that the reason Mama was so short with Jude was because he looked exactly like the duke.

Could Jarrod—and possibly Jasper himself—be the sons of another man?

The thought chilled him. He could barely think it, much less confront his mother about it. Besides, what good would it do now, so many years after the fact?

The physician arrived and examined the duke, Jasper insisting he remain in the room. The doctor gave his patient some laudanum and soon, the Duke of Edgehaven was asleep, though he whimpered.

"Tell me what it is," he demanded. "What is wrong with him?"

"I haven't a clue, my lord. His Grace has been a bit dizzy and confused when I have been called to see him on two other occasions this past week. He has complained of a racing heart and his belly aching. It could be some kind of tumor growing inside him, eating away at him. I fear His Grace does not have long to live. At this point, it is best to keep him sedated and the pain at bay."

The physician explained how much of the laudanum was to be given to the duke and when to administer it.

"If I were you, I would summon your family. It is time for you to say your goodbyes."

"I have already done so," he replied, sadness washing over him.

The doctor left, promising to call again tomorrow, and Jasper kept a vigil at his father's side for several hours. It surprised him when his mother entered the room late that evening. Something told him she had never set foot in these rooms before. She was followed by a maid who carried a tray.

"You've had nothing to eat this evening, Jasper. I have brought something for you. And broth for your father."

The duchess motioned for the servant to set down the tray, and then the girl left the room.

"Father is sleeping, thanks to the laudanum the doctor administered. He should not wake until tomorrow morning."

"Then you need to eat and get some rest yourself. He will not miss you. Watson can sit with him so that he will not be left alone."

Jasper was reluctant to leave his father's side, but knew he would be of no use unless he got some sleep.

His mother rang for Watson, and the valet arrived a few minutes later, his worry obvious.

"Sit with His Grace through the night," Mama commanded. "If he awakens, get some broth down him. He needs the nourishment."

She moved to the tray and removed the bowl of broth from it and then lifted the tray, handing it to her son.

"Go to your room, my boy. Get some rest."

As they left the room together, he said, "I have sent for Jarrod and my nieces."

She looked startled. "Why did you do so?"

"The doctor told me to," he said bluntly. "He does not believe Father has long to live."

For a moment, her mouth trembled, and Jasper thought perhaps she was human, after all. She may not have liked her husband very much, but she had spent over three and a half decades by his side.

"I see," she said quietly, still looking troubled. "It is good you did so. I will inform Mrs. Bowen so that rooms are readied for them."

He had assumed Bowen would have done so once the messenger was dispatched to Jarrod's country estate, but he let it go. Let her think she was doing something helpful for once.

He took the tray to his room and dined on cold chicken, cheese, and fruit before stripping off his clothes and putting on a nightshirt, someone having unpacked his trunk for him. Jasper laid awake for a long while, trying to prepare himself for the loss of his beloved father.

Awakening early, he washed and dressed, hurrying to the duke's bedchamber. Watson still sat at his employer's side, his eyes red from crying and weariness blanketing him.

"I am here to relieve you, Watson. Go and get some rest."

"Ring for me if you have need of me, my lord." The servant's voice broke on the last word.

"I will do so," Jasper promised.

He sat in the chair next to the bed, looking at how his father had wasted away in the past few months since his return from the Season. The duke had come home having lost some weight and continued to do so throughout the autumn and winter. Jasper supposed the London physician was right. Most likely there was something inside the duke, eating away at him, causing the pain and weight loss and general malaise and confusion.

Jasper still couldn't imagine a world without the Duke of Edgehaven in it.

Bowen arrived, bearing a tray. "I have brought something for you and His Grace, my lord," the butler said.

"Thank you, Bowen. Please let me know the minute my brother arrives."

He hoped Jarrod would bring the girls as Jasper had requested so they could say a final goodbye to their grandfather. His father had been delighted to become a grandparent, not caring that Jarrod's wife sired two girls in a row. The duke had confessed to Jasper once that he didn't think Jarrod would make for a good duke because his temperament and disposition were too much like his mother's. His father had expressed his hopes that Jude succeed him as duke.

Now, Jude was gone—and there were only the two sons left.

Jasper knew his brother was obsessed with producing an heir, which is why he had pushed to get one off his countess for so many years. Lady Sutton had been a small, fragile woman, and it surprised Jasper that she had produced two healthy girls in a row. Yet the toll of those births must have cost her, for she never regained her health after their births and never delivered a living child after Fanny. He knew of several miscarriages and a few stillborn children, including the one that had killed her only a few months ago.

He secretly agreed with his father in thinking Jarrod would not make for a good duke. His brother was rash and lost his temper quickly. He was more interested in fashion than farming. Still, Jarrod had hired a competent steward to manage his country estate. Of course, Edgehill had Muir as its steward, and the property thrived under the man's hands.

He consumed the breakfast Bowen brought to him, and then remained at his father's side until noon, when Jarrod arrived.

His brother burst into the room. "How is he?"

"See for yourself," Jasper said, rising from his chair and going to stand at the foot of the bed.

Jarrod took the seat Jasper had vacated, his jaw falling as he studied his ill father.

"He looks terrible," Jarrod declared. "I last saw him at the beginning of June. We only stayed for the early part of the Season and retreated to the country because . . ." His brother's voice trailed off.

"You did everything you could, Jarrod," he reassured his brother.

Jarrod gazed at their father and then back at him. "How long does he have?"

"Not long, according to the doctor who called last night. Did you bring the girls?"

His brother nodded. "They are with their governess now."

"I don't believe he will get any better. The laudanum will keep him sleepy, if not asleep, the rest of the time he has. His pain has been great. His belly has bothered him. The doctor suspects a tumor or some type of growth is within him. Father won't look any better than he does now. Call Sylvia and Fanny in to say their goodbyes."

Jarrod left the ducal bedchamber, and Jasper resumed his bedside vigil.

A quarter-hour later, his nieces appeared with their father, and he rose to greet them. He had always liked both of them. Sylvia, as the older, was more outgoing and solicitous of her younger sister. Fanny could be quite shy but had a streak of mischief within her. He knelt and embraced each girl, kissing their cheeks.

"Grandfather is very sick," Sylvia said. "That's what Papa said."

"He is very ill, Sylvia. You need to say goodbye to him."

Jasper reached out his hands, and the girls each took one. He led them toward the bed, where his father still slept. As confused as the duke had grown, Jasper thought it best his nieces see their grandfather while he was asleep, in case he did not recognize them.

"He is so still," Fanny said softly. "Is he dead?"

"Fanny!" barked Jarrod.

Squeezing her hand, Jasper said, "No, it is all right to say that. Your grandfather has grown very ill since the last time you saw him. He will be going to heaven soon."

"I'll miss him," Sylvia said, her mouth trembling as she spoke. "He always gave us peppermints."

"That sounds like him. He used to do the same for the three of us when we were young."

That reminded Jasper that he would need to share the news of Jude's death with his brother.

"Kiss his cheek and be done with it," Jarrod ordered brusquely.

Fanny looked up at Jasper, and he nodded encouragingly. Both girls released his hands, and they did as their father requested.

"Go back to your governess," Jarrod said. "She is waiting for you in the corridor."

Fanny looked ready to burst into tears. Sylvia already had some streaming down her cheeks. It irritated him that Jarrod did not comfort his daughters. He had never seen his brother spend any time with his children while their mother was alive. His gut told him that pattern had not changed with the countess' death.

Kneeling again, Jasper hugged each girl and said, "We will talk later. I promise. We will go for a walk and spend time with the horses, and I will read to you. Now, dry your tears."

His nieces left the room, and he said, "I am the bearer of more bad news, I'm afraid. We received word yesterday that Jude is gone."

"Gone? Where?" Jarrod asked quizzically. "You mean . . . he is *dead?*"

"Yes, Jude was killed at the Battle of Nivelle. In November. I suppose it has been difficult to get post across the English Channel with the war at such a critical juncture now."

His brother collapsed into the chair, his head falling into his hands. Jarrod had always been much closer to Jude than he had been to Jasper. He knew the news of this loss would greatly affect his remaining brother. Coupled with his father's imminent demise, Jarrod was dealing with a world of grief.

"Can it get any worse? First, I wed a woman who only gives me useless girls. Then Father decides now is a good time to die. And I have lost Jude."

Jasper couldn't muster any sympathy for his brother. Jarrod had always been focused on himself, but it was never more obvious than in this moment.

"I will leave you to your grief," he said curtly. "You may spend some time sitting with Father."

"No, I hate being around death, especially after so many

stillborn babes were born in my household. I will go for a ride."

Riding had always been the favorite activity of all three Lincoln boys. Jarrod did so when he wished to think or escape things. Jude loved the outdoors and the exercise. Jasper had enjoyed being around horses and feeling at one with them as he raced his brothers across the meadow.

"It is rather cold today," he noted, having had to place several logs on the fire while he had sat with his father.

"The cold never bothered me. You know that." Jarrod shook his head. "Poor Jude. He was the one of all of us who enjoyed summers the most. Fishing. Swimming. Remember how Lord Darrow would spend time with us? I swear that man could dip a pole into water, and fish would leap onto his hook."

"We should see if he is here in London and if so, have him come see Father before he is gone."

"Why wouldn't he be here? He and his countess always return in January, if only to keep Father and Mama company before the social swirl begins."

"You may not have known, having stayed at your country estate for so many months. Lady Darrow passed in mid-October. You know how the Darrows often came to Edgehill for Christmas. Lord Darrow stayed home this year and mourned."

"I had no idea," his brother said. "Mama did not write and tell me of it."

"Go for your ride," Jasper urged. "I will write to Lord Darrow and see if he is in town yet."

Once Jarrod left, Jasper rang for a footman and asked for writing materials to be brought to him. A small writing desk stood in the corner, and he used it to send word to Lord Darrow, informing him of his closest friend's illness. When he completed it, he rang for a footman and asked the servant to deliver the missive.

"If Lord Darrow is not in residence, ask his butler if he knows when the earl might return to town."

"Yes, my lord."

Another two hours passed. His father awoke, very groggy, just as the doctor came to call. After another examination, he gave the duke more laudanum, and they waited as the duke drifted away.

"Now that His Grace is asleep, my lord, I will be frank with you. I do not see His Grace surviving the night. Did Lord Sutton arrive?"

"He did and saw His Grace earlier."

But worry filled Jasper. Jarrod should have been back from his ride long ago. Perhaps he had arrived home and couldn't face sitting at Father's side again, seeing his father slip away. It seems Jarrod had had little sympathy for his wife and her illnesses, caused by her numerous quickenings. He might feel the same about their father's illness.

"I will take my leave, my lord. Please summon me if His Grace grows worse."

The doctor left, and Jasper perched on the bed, dipping a cloth in water and wringing some from it, placing it on his father's feverish brow. The duke mumbled in his sleep, restless, agitated. Jasper kept bathing his face, talking in soothing tones to the man who had been everything to him.

Bowen brought a tray of food, which remained untouched. Watson appeared, but Jasper sent the valet away.

For hours, he continued talking to his father, of things they had done over the years, recalling sweet memories and the good times the Lincoln brothers had experienced in their father's company.

Finally, dawn came. He had not closed the curtains and watched as the blackness in the room turned to gray and then light poured in.

Then the Duke of Edgehaven stilled. No movement came. No sound. No breath was taken. He was simply gone. Jasper gave a prayer of thanks, grateful his father had not suffered more than he had. It meant the world to him to be in his father's company when he passed from this world into the next. Already, phrases began forming in his mind, the things he would say at the duke's funeral service. Jasper would insist upon being the observant at it.

Standing, he gathered his thoughts. He needed to find Mama and Jarrod and share the news with them. Before he could leave the bedchamber, though, his mother entered, her eyes red and swollen, as if she had been crying. She still wore her night rail, a dressing gown tossed over it. Her long hair, streaked with gray now, hung in a long braid down her back.

He wondered if she had sensed the passing of her husband of many years, and that was why she turned up now.

"I must tell you that Father just passed, Mama."

She sucked in a quick breath. "What?"

"He is gone, Mama. His soul freed from his ailing body."

She began laughing hysterically, the hysteria rising. Jasper went and put his hands on her shoulder, shaking her.

"Mama. Please. Control yourself."

She shook her head, tears welling in her eyes. "You don't understand. Oh, Jasper. This is unthinkable."

"We knew Father did not have much time."

She jerked away from him. "Not Edgehaven. It is *Jarrod*." Fat tears rolled down her cheeks. "Your brother is dead, Jasper. *You* are now the Duke of Edgehaven."

CHAPTER THREE

SHELBY AWOKE, LUXURIATING in her own bed. She had not slept in it for close to a month. Instead, she had been playing the role of a housemaid in the household of Lord and Lady Perth. That case had come to its conclusion yesterday, and so she had been able to return home.

Home . . .

As she lay in bed, she thought of just how much this place had been a home to her for the last fifteen years. It was hard to recall the street urchin she had been. Boyd Franklin's invitation for her to accompany him to his residence for a hot meal and to sleep in a warm bed for a single night had been the turning point in a young Shelby Slade's life. Mrs. F, as she fondly called the lady of the house, had taken Shelby in and treated her as if she were her own. The woman cleaned up Shelby and got her a proper wardrobe for a twelve-year-old girl. Mrs. F smoothed Shelby's rough edges, saying she didn't want Shelby to lose them, merely learn how to keep them hidden until they were needed.

That was the beginning of her education in so many ways. Mrs. F must have known Shelby would not do well in the confines of a schoolroom with others and taught her new ward herself. Shelby had always envied those who could read and write, and soaked up the knowledge presented to her. Soon, she was reading the newspapers and novels, discussing their contents with both Mr. and Mrs. F. They had never asked her to call them by any particular name, and she had been the one who hit upon an address that was a mixture of the formal and informal.

Mrs. F introduced her not only to reading and writing but other subjects. The woman was a wizard when it came to maths, and Shelby learned she, too, had an affinity for numbers. She had drunk in the history Mrs. F shared with her, as well. For such a kind, goodhearted woman, Mrs. F was fascinated with the more bloodthirsty aspects of history. War, in particular. Shelby had studied wars from those in Carthage to today's current conflict with Bonaparte.

Both the Franklins had taken her to various museums and outings throughout the city, saying they wanted her to be comfortable in any kind of situation. At that point, Shelby had no idea what she would be doing to earn her living in the coming years, but the Franklins wanted her to be able to move in any world she chose.

In the end, it wasn't really a choice at all. She had gravitated toward the stories Mr. F told when he came home, and they sat at the table together, partaking in their nightly meal. Mr. F had been a Bow Street Runner, a group of select and highly trained men who solved crimes others were afraid to investigate or turned a blind eye to. She had been fascinated by his stories of everything from petty theft to murder, and so it had not surprised the couple when she asked to join him at the agency.

Mr. F had risen through the ranks over the years and was the second-in-command by the time Shelby turned eight and ten. While other girls her age did everything to make their come-outs into Polite Society, or to begin working in factories, mills, and shops, Shelby Slade was named as the first female Bow Street Runner.

And she had never looked back.

Each day brought new challenges, some large and some quite simple. No two cases were ever alike, and she thrived on that variety. What she quickly learned was that she had a talent for taking seemingly unrelated details of a case and putting these puzzle pieces together, making connections her colleagues missed. She saw patterns where no other investigator did—and she solved cases at a greater rate than even the most experienced agents.

Shelby would take on any kind of case, but her favorite ones involved missing persons. Sometimes, a person went missing for diabolical reasons. They might be held for ransom or worse—be taken and killed so another might benefit from the death. Other people went missing for reasons of their own. A large part of those cases involved those trying to escape the life and mess they had gotten themselves into. Some ran from gambling debts. Others from unhappy marriages. In the end, she almost always found the person she was hired to find, be they dead or alive.

Rising, she made her bed as was her habit and then washed and dressed today as an average, middle-class woman. That wasn't always the case. Oftentimes, she dressed as a man, wearing the coat, shirt, and trousers of various classes of men. She also used spirit gum to attach a mustache above her lip and even used a few wigs every now and then to aid in her disguise. She had completed her current case as of yesterday and presented the high points to Mr. F. Of course, while she was at Bow Street headquarters, he was Mr. Franklin to her. No one had guessed at the close relationship between the pair when she started as a runner, though now it was common knowledge that she had a close relationship with the Franklins.

At first, Shelby had not wanted others to know that she lived with the Franklins. It was already controversial enough that Mr. F had brought a woman onboard to serve as a runner. She didn't want the others to feel there had been favoritism on his part. Shelby had proved her worth to her fellow agents early on, and there were several who clamored to work with her now. She preferred to complete her assignments on her own, mostly because others paid very little attention and gave no credence to her when she dressed as a woman. When dressed as a young man, she had become skilled at fading into the background, where she could overhear things that were not meant for public knowledge. Very few would suspect why she was placed in a household or why she asked certain questions, allowing her to be quite successful.

Leaving her bedchamber, Shelby went downstairs, finding Mrs. F lingering over a cup of tea.

Smiling warmly, Mrs. F said, "Mr. Franklin told me that you wrapped up your latest case. Tell me about it. I'll have Cook get you some breakfast while you do so."

"Keep your seat, Mrs. F. I will speak with Cook."

She went to the kitchens and asked Cook for a cup of tea, a poached egg, and some toast.

"Coming right up, Miss Slade," the woman. "And it's good to have you back where you belong."

Cook was their only servant. Mrs. F was quite particular and actually did almost all the cleaning herself. Once a month, she did have in a few workers to do some of the heavier cleaning, such as taking rugs outside to be beaten. They also had a laundress who did their wash for them. Other than that, Mrs. F preferred to keep her own house, and Shelby admired that.

She returned and took a seat at the table, Mrs. F's eyes bright now with curiosity.

"I do want to say how much I have missed you, Shelby. I hate when you have assignments that take you away from us for so long."

She chuckled. "I will say that I was quite happy to return to my own bed last night. That is why I slept so late this morning. It is the first good night of sleep I have had in weeks."

Shelby's sleep was often disrupted or lacking because a lot of her work happened at night, especially if she had been placed inside a household to solve a crime, as had been the case with this most recent one. While the occupants of a house slept, she was busy roaming the place, looking for clues. It had been her sleuthing into the wee hours which had helped break open this last case.

"It was an investigation of jewelry theft," she began. "Or should I say replacement. It all started when Lady Perth lost a diamond from a brooch she was particularly fond of. When she took it to the jeweler who had sold her husband the brooch, she found out the entire piece was paste."

"Paste! An entire diamond brooch? So, someone had replaced the brooch with a cheap imitation."

"Actually, it was quite a clever copy, but yes, that was the case. Lord and Lady Perth had no one to suspect, the servants in their house being particularly loyal. Many of them have worked in their household for a good number for years."

Mrs. F thought a moment. "I would think it would have to be someone within the household, Shelby. Who else would have access to such a valuable piece without evidence of a break-in? Hmm."

She allowed Mrs. F to ponder the situation a moment. Over the years, it had become a game, with Mrs. F asking questions and making guesses, trying to ascertain the guilty party in a theft case.

"Let me ask this—where was the brooch kept?"

"Ah, now you are thinking like a runner," she praised. "Lady Perth had several valuable pieces, all belonging to Viscount Perth. They were as much a part of his inheritance as the title he held and the estate he laid claim to. The viscount told me all the jewels his wife wore were family jewels and would be passed down to their only son, who would become the new Lord Perth upon his father's death. The only exception was the diamond brooch, which had been a wedding gift from the viscount to his bride many years ago."

"But *where* were these pieces kept?" Mrs. F insisted. "You are skirting the question now."

"In Lady Perth's bedchamber. I have learned that while a few ladies of the *ton* lock up their jewels in a safe—almost always located in their husband's study—the majority of them keep them in a dressing table in various boxes for convenience. At least they do so during the Season. Lord and Lady Perth remain in town almost year-round, however, and so she leaves her jewels in her bedchamber."

Mrs. F nodded sagely. "I suppose you know this because you found them."

"I did," Shelby confirmed. "If a mere housemaid could find them, who else could? That was the question. As I said, most of the servants were trusted because of their long years of service with the family. Lord Perth brought me on as a maid to solve the crime, not even telling his wife who I was so that she would not accidentally reveal my status. Once I saw how easily the viscountess' jewels could be accessed, I told Lord Perth to have all his wife's jewelry appraised."

Mrs. F's eyes lit with interest. "Don't tell me. They were all imitations, weren't they?"

She nodded. "You guessed correctly. All in all, a dozen necklaces, eight bracelets, six pairs of earrings, and the diamond brooch were nothing but fakes. Convincing fakes—but worth a fraction of the original pieces' worth." She paused. "All except one, however."

When she paused, Mrs. F encouraged, "Go on. Do not leave me hanging, Shelby."

"One necklace, composed of sapphires, was the only one whose stones had not been secretly replaced. After I knew that, I focused on two things. First, who had access to the house—and the viscountess' bedchamber. And two, once I knew this, I decided whoever was the thief would have access to someone talented enough to copy the jewels so closely that Lady Perth would not know the difference."

She took a sip of her tea. "I began investigating the most likely candidate, Lord Perth's heir. I discovered the son had a nasty gambling habit and owed several of the gaming hells large sums of money. He did not live with his parents but rather rented rooms, which he shared with a friend. He did come and go freely at his parents' house, though. I watched him carefully when he came for two visits. The third time, he excused himself from tea to go look for a book in the library."

Mrs. F's eyes glowed. "But he didn't go there, did he?"

"Not at first. Instead, he went to his mother's bedchamber. The household staff always gathered for tea of their own while the family took theirs, so every staff member was in the kitchens at that time. I followed him and watched as he entered his mother's bedchamber, hiding in a nearby alcove. He was inside for less than a minute, knowing exactly where the jewels were stored and which was the only necklace that held any value."

"That could have been dangerous if he had seen you, Shelby," Mrs. F fretted. "I do worry about you."

"You shouldn't. I learned years ago how to fight on the streets and my Bow Street training only enhanced that knowledge. I know how to take care of myself, Mrs. F," she assured the older woman.

"Well, get on with it. Do not leave me hanging."

"He stopped at the library and then returned to tea. By then, I had followed him back and quietly entered the drawing room as he was telling how he wished to share the book he'd retrieved with a friend. I stepped up and asked him if he also had permission to share his mother's sapphire necklace with anyone. You should have seen his face."

Mrs. F laughed aloud. "An impertinent maid—and a clever one, at that. How was it resolved?"

"Oh, he hemmed and hawed a bit, sputtering about this and that. When his father demanded that he empty his pockets, though, he became quite the blubbering bloke. Lord Perth was shocked that his only son would have betrayed his parents in such a manner."

"Of course, there was no calling in the authorities and pressing charges, I assume," Mrs. F said.

"You assume correctly. I confronted him with the fact that all the Perth pieces were clever imitations, and he admitted having replaced them, giving some outlandish explanation by saying he had found a wonderful land deal and was buying it up because of the minerals below. I shook my head and produced a few of his markers from the gaming hells I had visited and told him his shameful lying needed to stop.

"By then, he was crying so hard, no one could understand a word he said. So was his mother. Lord Perth took me aside and said it was a family matter now. He asked me if he could reimburse me regarding the markers, and I told him to see Mr. Franklin at Bow Street. The viscount promised to do so and thanked me for my work, asking for my discretion and for me not to share anything with the staff as I left. I packed my bag and went to tell Mr. F the highlights of the case and of Lord Perth's upcoming visit. I will write up my complete, detailed report this morning once I arrive at Bow Street."

Finishing the last bite of toast, Shelby blotted her lips with her napkin and rose. "I'm off to work."

"Will you be assigned a new case today once you finish writing and presenting your case?"

She shrugged. "Only if one is available. Mr. F will be the one to let me know."

Walking around the table, she went and put an arm about Mrs. F. Kissing the older woman's cheek, she said, "I hope you have a lovely day."

Shelby left the house, no reticule necessary. All her gowns were made up to contain deep pockets. She walked to headquarters and as she rounded the corner, spied a grand carriage.

"Oh, I hope it is a duke's vehicle," she said under her breath.

She had worked several cases for dukes the past two years, finding them not to be as stuffy as she'd once thought they were. Of course, these dukes had all married unusual women—and Shelby had become friendly with a few of them. Occasionally, she would take tea with some of them, enlightening them as she talked of some of her cases, always leaving out names and details which would identify those she investigated.

As she drew nearer, a footman opened the door, and a man descended from the carriage. He was dressed soberly, as a clergyman.

But he was the most handsome vicar Shelby had ever laid eyes upon.

He was just over six feet, with an athletic frame and an air of confidence. His hair was russet and must have appeared dark brown when indoors. Out in this morning's sunshine, however, it gleamed with red highlights. As she reached him and he turned to look at her, his deep, blue eyes drew her in. She had worked with and been around many men over the years, a woman moving through a man's world. In all that time, none had affected her the way this man did. It was as much a physical as emotional reaction. A feeling of connection with a total stranger.

No one else had climbed from the carriage, and she wondered if he could possibly be a solicitor. In some cases, gentlemen of the *ton* did not want to directly come to Bow Street themselves, instead sending a representative in their places. Still, this was a ducal carriage. By now, she was close enough to see the crest on the door and knew exactly which duke it belonged to.

The Duke of Edgehaven.

Edgehaven had a decent reputation among those in Polite Society, much better than many of his peers. He attended sessions of Parliament regularly and was not easily swayed when it came to his vote.

So why would Edgehaven send a clergyman to Bow Street?

She wanted the case. Whatever it was. She would go inside and head straight to Mr. F's office and ask if she might be considered for whatever the Duke of Edgehaven needed accomplished.

Because of that, she picked up her pace, nodding politely to the handsome vicar and quickly moving to her left to go into headquarters.

Then he called out, "Miss? Miss?"

Turning, Shelby waited as he approached her. She wasn't

wary. Merely curious.

"Yes?" she asked, her brows arched.

The stranger might have been a man of the cloth, but up close, he exuded power. Charm. Confidence. Things she didn't associate with a vicar. Yet she was good at reading people after all her time on the streets and as a runner, and instinct told her something was troubling him.

"Are you going inside there?" He indicated headquarters. "To where the Bow Street Runners are housed?"

"I am," she said, not giving anything else away. Wanting to see what he asked next.

"Are you seeking to hire a runner?"

She studied him a moment and then said, "No. I *am* a Bow Street Runner."

CHAPTER FOUR

JASPER FINALLY ROSE from the bed, where he had tossed and turned most of the night. He should ring for Watson, the valet he had inherited, but didn't want anyone around him now. He had come to value his privacy, living alone at the vicarage. To once again be living in an immense household with a plethora of servants was quite an adjustment.

He felt his life was in a shambles with the sudden deaths of his father and brother a week ago, not to mention receiving the news of Jude's death at that time, as well. The three deaths weighed heavily on his heart.

They had made the trek to Edgehill, where they had buried the best man Jasper had known and a beloved brother. He was now the Duke of Edgehaven, turning his life upside down. He had delivered the eulogies for his father and brothers and laid two of the three of them to rest in the nearby Edgewood cemetery. One day he hoped to journey to France and see where Jude had been buried.

His flock had been accepting of the fact that he was now the new Duke of Edgehaven. Many had expressed their sympathies to him for the losses he'd experienced and yet blessed him for the different role he would now play in their community. Jasper had notified his bishop and said he would continue to serve his parish as long as it took to find his replacement. The bishop himself had come to Edgehill to assure Jasper that would not be necessary. Until a new clergyman was appointed to the Edgewood living, his sexton, Mr. Orr, would serve in his stead.

Of course, the bishop had told Jasper that he himself could fill the living, being the Duke of Edgehaven. He had no candidates in mind, though, and said he would be happy with whomever the bishop named as his replacement.

Lord Darrow had been quite helpful during the process. The earl, acting as a surrogate father, had come immediately when summoned by Jasper. They'd had several long talks together, the kind, older man reassuring him that life would go on. Not as it had before, of course, but it would go on all the same. Lord Darrow had emphasized to Jasper that he still was in a position of authority and that Jasper's new parishioners were simply the tenants and staff at his many estates. He had inherited five other properties beyond Edgehill and had never been to a single one of them. He wrote to the stewards, butlers, and housekeepers at all five of these estates, informing them of the Duke of Edgehaven's death, as well as that of his heir apparent, promising he would come to visit as soon as he could.

Not only was he now in charge of so much land and so many people, Jasper also would serve as the guardian to his nieces. While Sylvia cried at the drop of a hat these days, Fanny had gone mute. The girl had not spoken a single word since her father's death.

It was Fanny who had been discovered next to Jarrod's body. He had fallen down a flight of stairs and broken his neck in that fall. Finding her father's body must have traumatized the little girl to the point of rendering her speechless. Dr. Barton had been summoned, and he told Jasper that it might be some time before Fanny spoke—if she ever did.

He was not going to accept that. He would do whatever it took to help bring his niece back to this world, from the one she was locked away in.

As expected, his mother had been dry-eyed throughout the

events of the past week. While he had circulated among the mourners who returned to Edgehill after the burial had been completed, he had heard others speak of how stoic the duchess was. Jasper wanted to laugh aloud. His mother wasn't stoic. She was relieved of the ball and chain which had been secured to her ankle for decades. Though she dressed as she was in mourning, he believed she would abandon it early and fully participate in the upcoming Season.

He washed and dressed, shaving himself, not used to having tasks such as this done for him. He still wore his clergyman's clothes, though his mother had urged him to go to a tailor and begin dressing for his new station in society. In a fit of rebellion, Jasper had not done so yet, although he knew he would need to sometime soon.

Details about the deaths of his father and oldest brother still troubled him, however. That was why he had decided to go somewhere for help.

To Bow Street.

He had heard of the Bow Street Runners and how they helped those in need. He was searching for answers he didn't think anyone might find, but Jasper was determined to go to Bow Street, all the same.

He went first to the schoolroom, where Sylvia and Fanny were having breakfast with their governess.

Sylvia sprang to her feet and ran to him, her arms fastening about his waist in a tight hug. Jasper smoothed the girl's hair and asked how she fared before telling her to have a seat again. Sylvia did as asked, and he went to Fanny, also brushing his hand over her hair. Fanny did not respond to the gesture, merely spooning more porridge into her mouth without speaking.

He looked to Miss Hall. "What is on the schedule today, Miss Hall?"

"We will be working on addition and subtraction, Your Grace. Also spelling. Lady Sylvia has become quite adept at spelling and loves a challenge when it comes to learning new words." The governess paused. "Lady Fanny is trying her best," she added, smiling brightly at her younger charge.

"Be certain that the girls get some fresh air, Miss Hall. In fact, I may take them to walk in the park myself."

"They would like that, Your Grace," the governess responded.

Jasper bid them farewell and went to his own breakfast room, glancing through the papers as he dined.

He called for his carriage to be readied and when the butler asked where he might be off to in order to tell the coachman, Jasper replied, "I have several errands. I will decide upon their order of importance later."

Bowen left the breakfast room and returned a quarter-hour later while Jasper still perused the newspapers, telling his employer that the carriage was waiting out front.

Leaving the breakfast table, he found Watson in the foyer, holding Jasper's coat and hat. The valet had also urged him to be fitted for a new wardrobe, and so Japer said, "Go to my father's tailor. Tell him I will be there later today to be fitted for all I need."

A pleased smile appeared upon the valet's face. "I will do so now, Your Grace."

Jasper left the house and went to his carriage, calling up to his coachman, "Do you know of the Bow Street Runners?"

"I do, Your Grace. Is that our stop?"

He hesitated for a moment and then committed to the action. "Yes, it is."

Climbing into the carriage, Jasper hoped he was making the right decision. If nothing came of an investigation, he would accept the findings, but in his heart of hearts he suspected wrongdoing. His father's sudden illness after a lifetime of excellent health didn't sit well with him. And while Jarrod did drink a bit, it had never been to excess, certainly not to the point where he would be so drunk that he couldn't make his way down a staircase. If answers to his questions could be found, perhaps it would restore Fanny's speech and bring Jasper closure regarding these deaths.

London traffic was heavy this morning, and they finally arrived at their destination. He climbed from the carriage and paused, looking at the building and wondering exactly what he was going to say. He glanced about him, trying to gather his thoughts, and saw a woman who walked with purpose coming toward him. She was taller than most women of the day and more attractive than almost any of them. It was odd how women at Edgewood had flung themselves into his path, and he hadn't felt a thing for a single one of them, yet a stranger on the streets had grabbed his attention.

As she reached him, she gave a brisk nod and turned, as if to enter the same building he stood in front of. That was when he called out to her.

"Miss? Miss?"

She faced him again, and he took a few steps until he was in front of her. From a distance, she had been quite attractive. Up close, however, she was breathtaking.

"Yes?" she asked, her brows shooting up in question.

The woman was tall and slender, her breasts small. Her brown hair was a medium shade and shone in the sunlight. But it was her unusual eyes which drew him in, golden eyes rimmed with brown. Ones that seemed to see—and understand— everything about her, even secrets others held close.

Pointing to the building, Jasper inquired, "Are you going inside there? To where the Bow Street Runners are housed?"

She seemed almost bored by his question as she told him, "I am."

"Are you seeking to hire a runner?" It was the first thing he could think of to say.

She paused, seeming amused by his question, before answering him. "No. I *am* a Bow Street Runner."

Her words took him aback, but he recovered quickly. "I did not realize any of the runners were females, Miss . . ."

"Slade," she provided. "Miss Shelby Slade."

He had never heard the name Shelby before, but it suited her. She possessed a competent, confident air, which few did, be they man or woman. Jasper decided in that moment that he wanted Miss Slade to take on his case.

"Might you take me inside and introduce me to who is in charge?"

"I would be happy to oblige you." She eyed him inquiringly, and he quickly provided, "Mr. Lincoln," knowing she searched for a name. "Mr. Lincoln. No, no. That is no more." Swallowing, he met her inquisitive gaze. "It's Edgehaven. I am now the Duke of Edgehaven."

She remained poised, only her eyes widening slightly. She did not curtsy to him, however, which filled him with relief.

"If you will accompany me, Your Grace, we will see you set up with Mr. Franklin. He is in charge of all matters at Bow Street. He was once a runner himself, and one of the best we ever had. Now, he assigns cases and dispenses advice, to both clients and runners alike."

"I assume this Mr. Franklin is discreet?"

"Mr. Franklin is most diplomatic."

Miss Slade flashed a smile, and Jasper's heart skipped several beats, startling him because it had never done so before. Something shifted inside him. He didn't know what his future held.

He only knew he wanted this woman in it.

Clearing his throat, surprise rippled through him at such an absurd thought. It was downright outlandish. He knew nothing about Miss Shelby Slade, other than she was a Bow Street Runner. He must consider his future. His family's future. He would require a woman from the highest echelons of Polite Society to become the Duchess of Edgehaven. He owed it to his father to continue the line of Lincolns for generations to come. He wanted, more than anything, to make his father proud of him and the choices he made. Even if the duke were no longer an earthly presence, Jasper believed him to be a heavenly one, looking down upon his son. At thirty years of age, more than ever, Jasper still wanted—no, needed—his father's approval.

"Please take me to this Mr. Franklin," he said, his voice firm.

"If you will come this way, Your Grace," the woman said, leading him inside the building.

They stopped at a reception desk, and she said, "This is His Grace, the Duke of Edgehaven, here to speak with Mr. Franklin."

The clerk manning the desk glanced to Jasper. "It is good to have you here, Your Grace. Mr. Franklin is engaged with a client at present. Miss Slade can show you to a reception room while you wait. Might I bring you tea or coffee?"

"Neither, thank you," he replied.

"This way, Your Grace," Miss Slade said, leading him up a staircase and down a corridor.

She opened the door to a room filled with windows. It held a large table with eight chairs placed at it, and she indicated for him to take the one on the end. He did so as Miss Slade closed the door, remaining with him.

"If you are hesitating about having come to Bow Street, let me assure you that whether you decide for us to open a case or not, you have done the right thing. If your instincts are telling you something is wrong or there is something troubling you, we are here to help."

He liked the sound of her voice, low and comforting. Nerves filled him, however, leaving him with no conversation. Certainly, he couldn't ask her anything personal, and so he said, "Tell me about Bow Street. Its beginnings. And how you might have come to serve here."

"Are we merely killing time, Your Grace, while we wait for Mr. Franklin—or are you truly interested in our origins?"

Jasper was taken aback, both by her astuteness and bold question.

"I am interested, Miss Slade, in the organization I may be hiring. If I know a bit about the place, it may help me to decide whether or not I wish to hire you."

"Very well, Your Grace. I am happy to tell you about how Bow Street began. Henry Fielding, a magistrate, founded the group in 1749. It included six men, who were to serve as a sort of police force for London. These officers had the nickname *runners* bestowed upon them by the public. We are known as Bow Street Runners to this day though many of the current force prefers the name agent to runner."

She paused, and he nodded for her to continue.

"Judge Fielding wished to regulate the process since there were men in London who would solve minor crimes for a fee. Fielding made certain his six agents were attached to the Bow Street Magistrate's Office and were paid for their case work with funds from the government. At the beginning, runners served writs and arrested criminal offenders throughout England, apprehending them on the authority of the magistrates."

Jasper could have listened to Miss Slade all day. He enjoyed the sound of her voice, becoming mesmerized by it.

"When Fielding passed, his brother, Sir John Fielding, became the new head. Sir John is the man who started the famed foot patrols in London. Over the years, our agents have become the investigative arm for prosecutors throughout England. We still do, however, take on some private cases."

"What might those involve?" he asked.

"A wide range of criminal activity, Your Grace. Everything from stolen goods to extortion to even murder. We remain under the control of the Home Secretary."

The agent paused, assessing him. "You seem to have come into your dukedom rather recently. Obviously, you do not dress as a duke. Where did you hold the living, Your Grace?"

"At the village near my father's country seat of Edgehill. The village is called Edgewood. It is in Hertfordshire. Before I assumed the living at Edgewood, I first began my career in the church in Kent."

Miss Slade nodded. "Ah, I have worked a few cases in both

Hertfordshire and Kent."

Her words piqued his curiosity. "What kind of cases have you been involved with, Miss Slade? You never mentioned to me how you came to be a Bow Street Runner."

She pursed her lips in thought, and Jasper couldn't take his eyes from them. They were plump and called out to be kissed. He pushed the thought aside, horrified that he even had it. No, he must banish all kinds of thoughts such as these regarding this woman. Despite her beauty and articulate manner, she did not have the pedigree he needed in choosing his duchess. If he knew one thing about the class he now joined, it was the high expectations they placed on a duke and the woman he selected as his bride.

"I have always enjoyed learning and am likely the most curious person you might ever meet," she said, laughing. "I am detail-oriented. Thorough. Methodical. If you decide to hire us, Mr. Franklin will be the one who selects the agent for your case, but I do have quite a bit of experience working with dukes and would like to be considered to run the investigation."

Her words interested him. "You say there are other dukes you have provided services for?"

Miss Slade nodded. "While I cannot supply the names of our clients—since we guard those for privacy's sake—I will tell you that I worked two cases for dukes two years ago and another two cases where dukes were our clients this past year."

"Can you at least tell me what those cases involved?" he persisted.

"In general terms. One regarded a dowry being kept from a young woman. We saw the dowry restored to her. Another involved a duke's mother being reunited with her childhood sweetheart upon his deathbed. A third involved tracking down a steward who had absconded with estate monies. For that same client, I located a missing person, as well. My final case involving a duke involved a secret society who had wronged a woman the duke loved. I found its leader, and the duke insisted the man apologize to the woman."

"I assume he had strong feelings for this woman," Jasper noted.

"He wed her—and they are very happy. I have remained friendly with the duchess," Miss Slade said, pride obvious in her voice. "So you see, Your Grace, I have experience in a variety of areas, as do all our agents. Mr. Franklin is the best judge of our abilities and matches them to each investigation accordingly."

If these alone were the only cases the agent had worked successfully, Jasper would hire her on the spot. She went on to tell him that she had served as a Bow Street Runner for nine years. The cases she mentioned were only the proverbial tip of the iceberg.

At that moment, an older man with an air of authority entered the room, and both he and Miss Slade rose.

"Mr. Franklin, I would like to introduce you to His Grace, the Duke of Edgehaven."

As Jasper took the older man's hand, she concluded with, "And this is Mr. Franklin, in charge of all cases at Bow Street."

He liked the looks of this man and the way he shook hands.

"I have yet to share the particulars of my case, Mr. Franklin, but would like to do so with you now. And Miss Slade. You see, I have decided that Miss Slade would be the ideal agent for my case."

CHAPTER FIVE

S HELBY WOULD NEVER have admitted it to anyone, least of all Mr. F, but she was smitten with the Duke of Edgehaven. She had never in her life been so suddenly affected by a man. It was as if a bolt of lightning had struck her, leaving behind strong feelings of attraction to this tall, lean man. But she prided herself on being a professional. If Mr. F assigned her to the Duke of Edgehaven's case, she would only look upon him as a client.

Even if he did have the most sensual lips she had ever seen. Especially for a former clergyman.

She had kissed a few men over the years more to assuage her curiosity than anything else. Nothing serious had developed, of course, because she was dedicated to her job. She was wary now of the strong attraction she felt to this man, duke or not, and knew only disaster would strike if she thought to pursue a relationship with him. Not that a duke would have anything to do with the likes of her. She was a working woman, one who earned her living in a man's world, the last type of woman a duke might ever consider.

Besides, she was not one to have an affair even if this man did indicate he was interested in her. She had watched men come and go in her own mother's life. She would never place herself in such a position. Never allow a man to have control over her. Shelby had worked hard to win her place at Bow Street and had gained a level of success few experienced. She would never give up the respect she had won from her fellow agents. She neither needed nor wanted a man or the traditional trappings of marriage.

Then Edgehaven said something which surprised her. He wanted *her* to be the agent of record on his case. Shelby tamped down her excitement, keeping her face a mask, knowing exactly what would be said next.

"It is all well and good that Miss Slade has made a favorable impression upon you, Your Grace," her employer said smoothly. "However, I am in charge of making the assignments at Bow Street. I match the skills and experience of my agents to the cases brought to us. If I believe Miss Slade to be the ideal candidate to investigate your issue, then by all means, she will be named the agent of record in the investigation. Not having heard any facts or details regarding what you wish us to look into, however, I reserve the right to make that judgment at a later date."

He paused, looking straight at the duke, as Shelby would have expected. "Do I make myself clear, Your Grace? I know dukes seem to have a way of getting what they wish, but in this case, I am the expert regarding my staff."

Without hesitation, Edgehaven said, "I do believe Miss Slade will be your choice in the end after you have heard what I have to say, Mr. Franklin. I will, however, bow to your judgment. I just ask that you keep an open mind."

"I am known for doing that very thing, Your Grace. Shall we adjourn to my office?"

Mr. F left the room, and Shelby and the duke followed. Her heart beat quickly, not only wanting to hear about the problem the duke had, but if Mr. F would believe she would be the best investigator for His Grace's case.

The door closed, they all settled themselves, Mr. F behind his desk and she and Edgehaven in the two chairs sitting in front of it. Mr. F and Shelby mirrored one another now as they both took up pencils and parchment, waiting for Edgehaven to speak.

"Go ahead, Your Grace," Mr. F encouraged.

The duke sat a moment, a contemplative look on his face. Finally, he began.

"I have two matters I wish for you to look into, both regarding recent deaths of relatives of mine. It may be mere coincidence—but the two occurring so closely together concerns me."

Shelby met Mr. F's gaze. He had taught her never to believe in coincidence. And if a civilian such as the Duke of Edgehaven believed such a coincidence had occurred, then they were doubly certain it had not.

"Until recently, I was the third son of a duke, holding the living at Edgewood, the village closest to my father's ducal seat in Hertfordshire. Mind you, I know my father was a man of five and sixty, and I acknowledge that men do not live forever. That being said, Father left to go to last Season, his usual picture of health. By the time he returned in August to Edgehill, he had lost weight. A good deal of weight. Father was the most jovial man I ever knew, and he had turned solemn. Even melancholy. I watched throughout the autumn as the weight continued to fall from him. His coloring changed. He grew listless."

When he paused, Shelby asked, "Did he see a doctor? If so, what diagnosis was determined?"

"Dr. Davies is the local physician for Edgewood's residents. While I would not call him doddering, I would say he is in his mid to late-seventies and not as sharp as he once was. He, from all indications, said it was old age finally catching up to Father. Since my father had known Davies for decades, he did not challenge the man's opinion."

The duke cleared his throat, and Shelby did not interrupt again, understanding that it must be painful for him to recount the circumstances regarding the death of the previous duke. She could read people well and without being told, she knew the two men had been extremely close.

"My parents always spent the autumn at Edgehill but returned to town immediately after Christmas each year. I am always granted two weeks by the church after the new year has come. I come to town to spend that time with my father each year."

She made a note to ask him more about his mother. A wife of many years would notice changes in her husband's physical and mental state, and the duchess could give insight into His Grace's situation.

"Much to my surprise, my father's health had taken a rapid turn for the worse in the week I had not seen him. While he had been thin and weak on Christmas Day, I now saw he was emaciated at this point, barely able to stand, needing the help of his valet to shuffle about. Frankly, his decline was frightening to me."

The valet was certainly another person she would wish to speak to if awarded this case. Servants knew everything happening in a household, whether their employers realized that or not, in particular a valet or lady's maid, who were especially close to the family members. Shelby had learned many a revealing—even damning—fact from upper servants.

"The afternoon I arrived in town, so did bad news."

She observed the shadow crossing his face and wished she could reach out a hand to comfort him. It struck her as odd because Shelby had never felt this way toward any client. Yes, she had experienced empathy for their positions but never became personally involved. She knew she danced a fine line now and almost thought it might be better if another agent were assigned to Edgehaven's case. Still, she wanted to hear all that he had to say and knew Mr. F would make the proper decision when time came to assign an agent. That is, if he even deemed it necessary to take the case. Shelby, at this point, merely saw a grieving son not yet coming to terms with the fact his elderly father had been quite ill.

"Things grew quickly worse when we received a letter informing us of Jude's death. My older brother served under Wellington and had been killed in France during the Battle of

Nivelle. It had taken weeks for us to receive word of his death. The news broke Father. He collapsed and only lived a short while after."

Mr. F spoke up. "I assume you called in a London physician at this point, Your Grace. What was his diagnosis of your father's condition?"

"Dr. Barton had seen Father twice already since my parents' return to town a week earlier. He believed the swift decline in my father's health must be due to some type of tumor growing within him. Dr. Barton did his best to make Father comfortable at his end."

"Meaning he was given heavy doses of laudanum?" Shelby asked.

"That is correct, Miss Slade. Father died, and we buried him at the Edgewood cemetery."

"Do you wish us to question these doctors about what they diagnosed?" she asked. "I know it is difficult when a loved one passes. Hard to accept they are now gone and even harder in your case, Your Grace, because you assumed your father's title. It must be quite difficult to go from being a man of the cloth to a duke overnight."

Then it struck her that he was a third son. Third sons oftentimes dedicated themselves to the church, just as second sons usually sought a career in the army, their families purchasing their officer's commission for them.

But that left the first son, Edgehaven's heir apparent. Where was he in all this?

She assumed he must have died at an earlier time in order for this man sitting next to her to claim the title. Yet if that were the case, why hadn't the new heir returned home? War was a dangerous game, and many lost their lives. Being an officer did not protect a man, as witnessed by the death of Edgehaven's second son during battle. She held her tongue, though, hoping to discover the answer to her questions as she listened to the duke. If he did not reveal those answers, she was determined to get them from him.

"I would like for at least Dr. Barton to be interviewed. To see if anything has come to him in the meantime as to what might have caused my father's sudden illness. Dr. Davies, I am afraid, would not have much to contribute. There is more to my story than that, Miss Slade. As you have said, I was obliviously a third son who went into the church. The other piece of the puzzle which I am having difficulty with is what happened next to my oldest brother, the Earl of Sutton."

The duke paused. "You see, Sutton came to town at my urging. Dr. Barton had told me the end was near for Father and Sutton had not seen Father in several months. My brother had lost his own wife in childbirth November last and had stayed home during the Christmas holidays to mourn with his two daughters."

Edgehaven took a deep breath and continued. "Sutton, naturally, would have become the next Duke of Edgehaven upon Father's death. He died, though, mere hours before our father did."

Mr. F sat up, his gaze meeting Shelby's. This was where the coincidence had occurred, and she knew Mr. F suspected foul play in the matter. Yet the only one who would have benefitted from the heir apparent's death would be the man seated next to her. If he had caused the death of his older brother, then why would he wish for Bow Street to look into the matter?

"Sutton had the occasional drink but never drank to excess," Edgehaven explained. "Yes, he was having trouble accepting the idea that Father would soon be gone. The last I knew, my brother had gone out for a ride. Riding comforted him. It had since we were boys. When my mother came to the ducal bedchamber and I informed her Father had just passed, she was the one who broke the news to me. That Sutton had been deep in his cups and somehow had tripped and fallen down the stairs, breaking his neck in the fall."

Shelby was now thoroughly intrigued. Yes, grief might have

caused Lord Sutton to drink too much—but to drink to excess—so much that he died from his drunkenness? It did not sit well with her.

She glanced to Mr. F and saw he felt the same.

Edgehaven took a deep breath and slowly expelled it. "Perhaps you see my dilemma now. Two deaths from natural causes, hours within one another. It could have happened that way. Most likely, it did occur this way."

He looked to her, and she said, "But you have doubts, Your Grace. Doubts weighing upon you so heavily that you have come to Bow Street for answers. It is for Mr. Franklin to decide whether or not we take your case."

Shelby turned her attention to her mentor and saw he was contemplating things. She glanced back to the duke and saw Edgehaven looking eagerly at the man who would make the decision on whether or not to investigate the suspicions held by the duke.

Finally, Mr. F said, "We do not believe in coincidence here at Bow Street, Your Grace. For that alone, I will recommend that we move forward and investigate these two deaths. Individually seen, they seem logical. It is the timing of them, however, which troubles me so."

Edgehaven nodded. "Yes, Mr. Franklin, I agree with what you are saying. That is why I have come to you for help in this matter. I am glad you feel strongly enough to open an investigation."

"Not only do I wish to open the matter, Your Grace, I agree with you in regard to the agent I will assign to the case. Miss Slade has a wealth of experience and would be ideal to look into these matters for you. I have a delicate question to ask at this point, though. Do you believe anyone in your household might be responsible for these deaths?"

The question took Edgehaven aback. "I . . . I don't know, Mr. Franklin. I truly have no idea."

"Sometimes, we insert a runner into a household during an investigation. Miss Slade here recently spent a month as a housemaid as she investigated a robbery which had occurred within an earl's house. Would you be opposed to Miss Slade taking up a position with your staff?"

The duke pondered the question and said, "I believe a housemaid would be too limiting, Mr. Franklin, but I do have an idea that I hope Miss Slade might find acceptable. It would grant her not only greater access throughout the house but give her greater ability to come and go without being questioned."

Edgehaven turned to Shelby. "I propose that you become my new secretary."

"That is a brilliant—and bold—idea, Your Grace," she told him, smiling approvingly at him. "I do believe it would work, however. I could be in your household and ask the questions I usually do and yet also be able to leave when I wish, claiming I am on business for you as I investigate avenues outside the household."

She looked to Mr. F. "Do you find this plan suitable, Mr. Franklin?'

"I think posing as His Grace's secretary would grant you a great deal of freedom, Miss Slade. While it would be highly unusual for a woman to hold such a position, I'll daresay it is not entirely unheard of." He looked to Edgehaven. "Are you known to be a progressive, Your Grace?"

Their client smiled, melting Shelby's heart. She imagined all the women in his parish had been half in love with him, studying him at leisure when he rose to give his sermons each Sunday.

"I was a man of the church, Mr. Franklin. We are known to think a bit differently from the rest of society."

Mr. F nodded. "What of your current secretary, though? How will you explain away his absence and offer Miss Slade as his replacement?"

The duke said, "The previous secretary retired. My father had not yet replaced him since he was dealing with illness."

"Then it is settled, Your Grace. Miss Slade will be assigned to work both angles of the investigation. She may, at some point, decide to use another runner. Possibly for background information or for one arm of the investigation. Would that be agreeable to you?'

"As long as Miss Slade heads the investigation, I have no qualms with her bringing in anyone else to assist her," Edgehaven stated.

"Then I will leave things to the two of you to write the fiction necessary for Miss Slade to enter your household."

They left Mr. F's office, and she said, "We need some private time together before I show up at your door, Your Grace."

"My carriage is waiting outside, Miss Slade. I could have my coachman drive us about while we discuss whatever is necessary. Then I would be happy to drop you at your home so that you might pack and come to my residence."

Shelby did not want him to see where she lived. It might cause too many questions. She also did not want his coachman to know where she resided. Privacy was foremost in her mind.

"In case you haven't learned, servants gossip ferociously. They will have a field day with you naming a woman as your new secretary. It wouldn't do for us to drive about for an hour or more at this point." She thought a moment. "Have your driver take you to this address. It is for an employment agency. Tell the man in charge you wish to interview two candidates for the position of your secretary. That way when I arrive, your servants will already know you are interviewing for the post."

She scribbled the address on the page in her hand and tore off the information, handing it to the duke.

"I will take a hansom cab to Hyde Park while you do so." Shelby told him the gate to enter and where to find her along the Serpentine. "I think better when I walk, and we have much to discuss."

He grinned boyishly. "I do the same. I wrote almost all my sermons in my head as I walked the countryside. Or weeded."

"Weeded?"

"Yes. I maintained a lovely vegetable and flower garden at the vicarage. There is nothing quite as satisfying as pulling weeds."

Shelby chuckled. "Having been raised in London and never having pulled a weed, I will take your word for that, Your Grace. Once you have left the employment agency, have your driver drop you nearby where I will be and then ask to be picked up in an hour's time. We should be able to discuss all we need during that time together."

"I will do as you ask, Miss Slade. Thank you for taking on my case."

"Your thanks should be directed to Mr. Franklin."

"I knew you would be the one who could help me."

She studied him a long moment. "I hope I can, Your Grace. For your sake, I wish that I find no foul play and that your father and brother met with innocent deaths. Whatever I find, I hope it will bring you peace of mind."

"With things in your capable hands, Miss Slade, I know that will be the case. I will see you in an hour's time."

The duke nodded to her and turned and left. Shelby watched him go and told herself this was only business. A new, interesting case to investigate. The sooner she did her job, the sooner she could move on. It would already be difficult to be in this man's company with the odd, new feelings running through her. She would see the case to its end and obviously never see Edgehaven again.

The thought brought an ache to her, which she quickly brushed aside. She told herself she was not a typical, foolish woman. That she was a Bow Street Runner and would be her usual dog with a bone until she resolved the matter at hand.

Raising her chin a notch, she left headquarters and hailed a hansom cab, her destination Hyde Park.

And a rendezvous with a duke.

CHAPTER SIX

JASPER LEFT THE employment agency, which Miss Slade had recommended he go to. He had appointments with two different gentlemen, both scheduled for tomorrow morning. He hated being deceitful and if either candidate proved to be a good one, he promised himself he would try to help find them a post with someone else. Perhaps, even himself. His father had lost his own secretary during the middle of last Season. The man had a mild heart attack and had decided to retire from service, moving to Bath, where he had a daughter he would live with. Although Jasper didn't think he had need of a secretary, he assumed it was a post dukes always seemed to fill since they had heavy calendars and many obligations to fulfill. He realized he would also need to take his seat in the House of Lords. That would be something else a secretary might keep up with, the various times for sessions and meetings he would need to attend.

He told his coachman to take him to Hyde Park, mentioning the specific gate to enter before boarding his vehicle. Already, he looked forward to the conversation he and Miss Slade would have. She was a most unusual woman, starting with those golden eyes rimmed in a warm brown. She would make for a formidable duchess.

He shook his head. He couldn't believe he was even dreaming about such a thing with a woman he had only met a single time. She was nothing what Polite Society would think the Duchess of Edgehaven should be. But thoughts of a conventional marriage with a woman of his own class suddenly held no appeal to him. Not after his encounter with Miss Shelby Slade.

It was hard to imagine that he had decided a week ago that it was time for him to wed and start a family. Children—and companionship—were always something he had longed for. To think, however, that a Bow Street Runner would make for his duchess would turn the *ton* on their ear. He—and Miss Slade— would need to prepare themselves for being the talk of all Polite Society once their engagement was announced.

That is, *if* she would be amenable to such a union.

Jasper had always been a steady, confident, reliable person. Becoming the Duke of Edgehaven had allowed his confidence to brim.

So much that he would offer marriage to an unsuitable woman?

That was exactly what he intended to do.

He was taken with Miss Slade, not so much her beauty, but her intelligence and spirit. Something told him he would have his work cut out for him in convincing her to wed him. She seemed most dedicated to her profession and probably had an unfavorable impression of members of the *ton* because of the many cases she had worked for them. She had seen the underbelly of Polite Society, in a way many others had not.

Jasper wondered what she might uncover in her own investigation into his household. A part of him believed she would find absolutely nothing. That his father had merely been old and ill and passed merely because it was his appointed time to do so. That Jarrod did wind up drinking to excess, frightened by the new role he would take on and the many responsibilities which he was totally unsuited to handle. Not to mention having to raise two young daughters on his own—or finding a new bride who would do the raising for him.

Then again, it hadn't sat well with Jasper, these two back-to-back deaths. He knew they, coupled with Jude's death, had made him a most unlikely duke. If anyone profited from those three deaths, it was Jasper himself. He wondered if anyone might have had a grudge against his father or brother which had led to their deaths.

As the carriage rumbled on, he wondered if he would be stirring up some kind of hornet's nest or if it would be a fool's errand he was sending Miss Slade upon. He did believe in Fate, however, and that might be, in the long run, the reason he had been compelled to come to Bow Street. Else how could his path have crossed with Miss Shelby Slade's? If he'd never ventured to the famed headquarters, he doubted he ever would have come across Miss Slade.

He would let her investigation run its course. They would come to know one another better during this time together. Serving as his secretary would give them much time alone, beyond her sleuthing. He believed by the time her investigation concluded, they would not only be comfortable in one another's company but that she would be willing to leap from her world into his.

That thought should unnerve him, but it didn't. Jasper had never been a rash man, rather a most methodical one. It had served him well as a clergyman, and he still believed taking his time and studying things before acting would do him well as a duke. It was only in regard to Miss Slade and marriage that he seemed to be acting rashly. He knew, though, that Miss Slade was a decent person. Dedicated to her clients. Keenly intelligent. He would learn more about her in the weeks to come and hoped she would like what she discovered of him.

He watched out the window as they entered the park and reaching the point where he needed to disembark, Jasper rapped upon the roof. Instantly, the carriage slowed and glided to a halt. He flung the door open, leaping to the ground before his footman could place stairs down for him.

Looking up to the driver, he said, "I am not used to being

cooped up for so long. I would like to walk for a bit. I will return in an hour or so. Wait here."

"Yes, Your Grace," the coachman said, lowering the reins, his posture relaxing.

Jasper strode off in the direction of the Serpentine, amazed at how no one, least of all his servants, questioned the actions of a duke. He reached the water, not having seen another soul on this chilly day, and continued along the path. Glancing up ahead, he spied a woman rising from a bench and recognized Miss Slade's trim figure. She did not move toward him, rather let him come to her. Once again, he liked how she didn't fuss and fret over him simply because he was a duke. It felt good to be treated normally.

Joining her, he said, "Everything went well at the employment agency you sent me to, Miss Slade. In fact, I have appointments at ten and eleven tomorrow morning to interview candidates for the post of secretary to the Duke of Edgehaven."

"Walk with me," she said, taking off at a brisk pace. Not so fast that they couldn't converse, but not the leisurely stroll of a *ton* couple out for a day in the park. Because of that, he touched her sleeve.

"Though I have seen no one here since I arrived, do not bring unwanted attention to us. You are in the presence of a duke, so walk more slowly."

"Good advice, Your Grace."

"About that," Jasper began. "I do not mind you addressing me thus when others are about. It would be expected. We are to have a different kind of relationship, however, Miss Slade. I would prefer you address me as Jasper in private."

It was his first move on the imaginary chessboard where winning the game would mean winning her.

She cocked one eyebrow. "Is that so, *Jasper*? I have never addressed any client by his Christian name, be he duke or shopkeeper. Why would I begin to do so now?"

He knew he was asking her to break all social conventions, but felt it important for this to occur. To bring them closer together. He was also not above using his cham. Most of all, though, he wanted to be honest with her. Now and always.

"I know it is most unusual, but everything about my life is unusual at this point. It was but a little over a week ago when I gave what would come to be my final sermon in front of my congregation. In that short amount of time, I have lost the livelihood that I not only prepared for, but enjoyed immensely. I also lost a beloved father and two brothers and have had the mantle of a dukedom thrust upon my shoulders. Other than God, Miss Slade, I have no true friends and not a clue as to what I am doing. I could use a friend. Since we are to spend a great deal of time with one another, I am asking for you to be a friend to me. I know it is not quite what you signed up to do, but I would appreciate your friendship, all the same."

A slow smile graced her lovely face, becoming a brilliant one. In that moment, Jasper lost his heart to this woman.

"Then this will be an odd sort of friendship. No, let us say unusual. I will take you up on it, Jasper. Only you must call me Shelby."

He felt he had climbed a mountain in making such progress with her and returned her smile. "All right, Shelby. Let us walk and talk about my case as we do so."

As they set out at a more leisurely pace, he said, "I will tell you I feel terrible about these interviews tomorrow. If either candidate is a strong one and I have wasted his time, I will need to find a position for him. Or them."

"You do realize you could hire one or both of them and merely have them start a month or so from now."

"Is that how long you envision the investigation to be?"

She shrugged. "They can last anywhere from two days to two months. Sometimes, they run even longer. I gather that you are quite well off, Jasper, now that you are a duke. It would be easy for you to put a man on salary and simply tell him you did not wish for him to start for a couple of months. Say, until the Season began. When your social calendar would need attending because it is so full."

"Why would that be the case?" he asked. "I have lost touch with most of the boys I went to school with, as well as the men I attended university with. They have moved on to other lives beyond being my friend and fellow student. Some have assumed titles of their own. Others have gone into the military or the church. I have no one to invite me to social affairs, at least until I visit White's and assume my membership there. Perhaps I will make a few friends that way and then be invited to a ball or card party here or there."

She laughed, a warm, rich sound which caused him to tingle all over.

"You are a bit naive, Jasper," she told him. "Do you not realize you will receive an invitation to absolutely every event held this Season? Like it or not, you are the Duke of Edgehaven. Not only is a duke invited to all social affairs on the chance he might attend, but you are that rare jewel."

"I beg your pardon?"

Once more, Shelby laughed, drawing him in. "You are a naïve little clergyman, aren't you?"

She brought them to a halt and placed a hand on his sleeve. Even through the thick fabric of his coat, her touch caused him to tremble.

"You, my new friend, are that rarest of birds. A single, quite eligible duke. By the time most dukes assume their lofty titles, they have long been wed and sired children, knowing of the path that lay before them and their obligation to provide an heir and a spare. Jasper, whether you understand this or not, the ladies will flock to you. In fact, they will smother you with attention. You better prepare yourself for quite a busy Season."

Her words shocked him. "This is a new world to me, Shelby. Yes, I was brought up as a duke's son, but I was a third son. I had all the privileges associated with my birth and father's rank, including never having to worry about a roof over my head or food on my table. I even attended a few balls held by my parents during my university years, but to be frank? No one gives a third son—not even a duke's third son—more than a passing glance. I saw, even then, the attention my oldest brother drew as the heir apparent. In fact, by the time I took my orders, Sutton had already wed and sired a daughter. Jude had also left by then, Father having purchased Jude's military commission."

A wave of sadness struck him anew, and she squeezed his forearm. "Did you ever see him again?"

"No," he said softly. "Jude was the bridge between Sutton and me. I loved both my brothers dearly, but Sutton and I were much different people. He also was five years my senior and had his own group of friends. Jude made an effort to be close to the both of us. Once he left for war, I had a feeling I might never see him again."

He began walking again, causing her arm to drop from his, leaving him bereft. Though he longed to take her hand and slip it through the crook of his arm, they were in a public place. Especially since she was to be an employee to him at this time, he would not make such a gesture, despite the fact the park was empty at this hour. Though he might not see anyone about, it was possible they were there and could see Shelby and him.

"You have suffered numerous blows. Emotional blows," she added. "You seemed to have been extremely close to your father. Losing a beloved parent is never easy. You have lost brothers who were friends to you, a part of your childhood which also cannot be replaced. On top of all that, you have lost your livelihood. Your very identity. The man you had matured into. But you have great things ahead of you, Jasper. You can make as much or little of being the Duke of Edgehaven as you wish. Already knowing you the little I do, I believe you will take a strong interest in the tenants on your many estates. You will help tend to your family's fortune. You will seek a bride, possibly even this Season, and settle into your new role as duke. True, it was not the one you envisioned for yourself, but you can be a good duke, perhaps even a better one than your father."

"It would take much effort on my part to live up to that standard," he said fervently. "Father was an extremely good man and a friend to all. If I could be a tenth the man he was, I would be happy."

He stopped and faced her. "Shelby, that is why I am on this mission, be it one from God or of my own making. I wish to know if any foul play resulted in the deaths of my father or brother. I don't know if I can be the duke I am meant to be until I have those answers."

"That is what I am here to accomplish, Jasper," she said, her eyes kind even as they glowed at him. "I hope you don't mind if I pepper you with questions now. If I am to investigate, I prefer to begin now, since you will be my greatest resource."

She asked him many questions, saying she wished to gather a picture in her mind of what the previous duke had been like. He talked of his father's likes and dislikes and told her several stories illustrating the good, kind man he was.

Shelby asked specifically when his father's health began to decline.

"It was sometime during last summer when they attended the Season. My parents always returned to town immediately after Christmas. Unusual, I know, but Mama is one who is quite unhappy in the country. You will meet her, of course, and will understand that you do not want to displease her in any fashion. It was merely easier for my father to return to town with her each year before many couples of the *ton* did so."

"It is unusual," she noted. "Most of Polite Society do not return until March or even April, when the Season starts. What did they do upon their return? I am seeking a clear picture of their lives before and after His Grace's illness struck."

"Father rode daily in Rotten Row. Even at his age, he enjoyed a bit of sparring at Gentleman Jackson's. He was a great lover of books and haunted many of London's bookstores. Of course, he spent hours at his club with Lord Darrow."

"Tell me about Lord Darrow and their relationship," she

urged.

"The earl was my father's closest friend over the years. Frankly, I cannot tell you how or when they met, now that I think about it. He was, along with Lady Darrow, a constant in our lives."

Jasper explained how the earl had taught the Lincoln boys to swim and fish and how they often were in one another's company.

"I will wish to meet Lord and Lady Darrow," she said. "Merely to get a better idea of your father."

"Lord Darrow will make himself available to you if I request him to do so. Or you can meet him during one of the many times he comes to call. However, Lady Darrow passed in October. She was ill for a few months before that. In fact, I think they even left last Season early because of her health. Mama would have taken offense to that, of course. She would have found it inconvenient."

"You don't like your mother much, do you?"

"While I held a great affection for my father, my mother is another matter. She favored me above her other two sons, blatantly, making my life awkward at times. As an adult, I have as little to do with her as possible. Mama is everything I despise in a woman. Vain. Selfish. Self-centered. I honor her merely because the Bible instructs me to do so."

"I will also be speaking with her to get a clearer picture of her relationship with your father. Don't worry. I am quite subtle and have a talent for drawing information from others without them even realizing it."

"I learned shortly before Father's death that he and Mama were forced to wed by their parents."

Briefly, Jasper recounted what he had learned from both his parents.

"You do know this is not unusual," Shelby said. "From my understanding, many couples in the *ton* are encouraged to wed a certain individual selected by their parents."

"Mama revealed that she was in love with a viscount, though.

That his eventual rank as an earl wasn't high enough to please her father, which is why he arranged the match with my father, who was already a duke. They were always cordial but distant whenever we were in their presence. Mama told me, though, that she had harsh feelings toward my father. I think she must have always loved her earl. Father, too, was in love. With a clergyman's daughter. He said his own father was appalled hearing that and that he suggested making the girl a mistress, not a wife. Within a few days, my parents were betrothed and then wed."

"And unhappy all these years," she said, sadness in her voice. "I am sorry, Jasper, but at least they had their children. It seems your father took great joy from having three sons."

"And two granddaughters," he added. "I have two nieces now, the children of my brother, whom I am now the guardian of." He sighed. "I think that is the biggest reason I came to Bow Street, Shelby. You see, little Fanny, who is six years of age, is the one who discovered her father's body. She sat by it, holding his hand tightly, and had to be pulled away from him. Fanny has yet to say a single word since that time."

Jasper turned to her. "I want to learn whatever I can about Sutton's death, as well as Father's. I owe it to Fanny. If there is anything to tell her, to bring her comfort or explain the circumstances, I must do so. If it truly were an accident, I wish for her to know this. I fear with her discovering his body, she might blame herself in some way. And if foul play did occur? I must know that, too."

"I will do my best to bring closure for you and your family, Jasper. I will need to speak with Fanny, but rest assured, I am quite good with children and will be gentle with her."

He could picture her with a babe in her arms.

His babe . . .

"You are the agent. The professional. You have done this for many years. I will bow to whatever suggestions you make."

She asked if he thought Dr. Barton would be willing to talk to her, and he thought there would be no problem in doing so.

"I will leave you now and call upon Dr. Barton. I have several questions to ask him," Shelby said. "And I will arrive for my interview at noon tomorrow, saying the agency sent me."

"Then I will let my butler know I expect three individuals to arrive for interviews tomorrow." He paused. "Thank you for taking my case, Shelby."

"That was all Mr. Franklin's doing," she said quickly. "But I will say I am grateful to have been assigned to it. I won't let you down, Jasper."

"I put my faith in you, Shelby. And God, of course," he added, causing them both to chuckle.

"Might I make one suggestion before we part?" she asked. "Especially since it is the advice of one friend to another?"

"Of course."

She grinned. "You simply must get yourself to a tailor and stop dressing as a serious, earnest man of the cloth."

With that, she left him, laughing.

Jasper watched her until she was gone from his sight. One thing was certain.

He would never become bored with Miss Shelby Slade.

CHAPTER SEVEN

BEFORE SHE DID anything else, Shelby wanted to visit with Dr. Barton. The physician might have answers which she sought—and not even know he held them. She had obtained his name from Jasper and had an idea where the physician might be found. After checking with one of her sources, she arrived at the doctor's residence. Physicians who catered to the *ton* rarely saw patients in an office setting, instead attending to their patients in their own homes. Because of that, she doubted she could knock on his door and pretend to be a patient with symptoms and ask to be seen by the man.

Instead, she would invoke the duke's name to have doors opened to her. It was unfortunate that she had no calling card from Edgehaven to use but hadn't bothered to inquire for one from him. If the man still dressed as a clergyman over a week after he had inherited his title, then Shelby doubted he'd taken time to have engraved calling cards made up.

She rapped upon the door and a dour-looking woman answered. Before the servant could inquire as to why she was at the threshold, Shelby said with conviction, "I am here at the request of the Duke of Edgehaven. I must speak with Dr. Barton at once."

Boldly, she pushed past the startled woman, who turned and faced Shelby but did close the door.

"Dr. Barton just returned from being out on a call, Miss."

Spying a chair in the foyer, she said, "Then I will wait for him here," and seated herself, her voice and ramrod posture giving the servant no chance to shoo her out the door.

Resigned, the servant sighed and disappeared, hopefully to inform her employer of his visitor. Shelby had deliberately not given her name or referenced Bow Street in any manner. Sometimes doing so came in handy, and she wasn't opposed to throwing her weight as an agent about. At other times, however, she played her cards close to her chest, not wanting to give rise to undue gossip. In this case, she would do what she could to protect Jasper and his mother from any unnecessary speculation.

The woman appeared again, looking unfavorably upon Shelby, and said, "Dr. Barton will see you in his study."

Rising, she followed the servant and entered a room where Dr. Barton sat behind a desk.

"Thank you," he said dismissively, the servant closing the door to give them privacy. Looking to Shelby, he said, "My servant had no name provided to her. She did say, however, that you were here on behalf of His Grace, the Duke of Edgehaven. Please, have a seat."

She did so and removed parchment and pencil from her reticule in order to take notes, although she had an excellent memory and rarely needed to refer to them.

"Yes, His Grace did send me. I am Miss Slade. He has asked me to make discreet—very discreet—inquiries into the deaths of his father and brother."

The physician steepled his fingers. "I see. And you are from Bow Street, I assume?"

"Yes. I am an agent representing His Grace."

The man looked at her with interest. "I had no idea they employed women."

She did not share that she was their only female employee, merely saying, "Sometimes, there are places and circumstances where it is easier to send in a woman to find the necessary information."

"Exactly what type of information do you seek, Miss Slade?" Dr. Barton inquired.

"I wish to know everything about the condition of the previous Duke of Edgehaven. When did you first call upon him when he exhibited problems? And what were his symptoms and your diagnosis?"

The physician sat back in his chair, thinking a moment. "I have seen mostly to Her Grace while Their Graces spend time in London. Her Grace suffers from megrims, you see. His Grace, on the other hand, was always the picture of health. I had never treated him for any illness at all, despite his advanced years."

He paused, and she was experienced enough in interviewing witnesses that she knew to allow him time to think.

"It was last summer when I first saw His Grace as a patient. Late July or early August, if I recall correctly. I could check my records if that would be helpful to you. Their Graces had been at a ball the previous evening and His Grace had awoken feeling nauseated and complaining of stomach cramps. When neither subsided, the butler summoned me to their residence at Her Grace's insistence, since His Grace said he wanted nothing to do with a doctor."

"What was your verdict?"

"At that point, with the symptoms he exhibited, I believed His Grace might have suffered a mild form of food poisoning at the ball he had attended. He admitted to a healthy appetite, having sampled a good portion of the buffet. Her Grace was more helpful in recalling what was on her husband's plate. When she mentioned the salmon cakes, I thought that they might be the cause of his problems. Her Grace said she had taken but a single bite of one of them, finding it slightly off in taste. His Grace recalled eating two of them, however. I chalked up his problems to food poisoning, the fish having sat out too long and gone bad. I told His Grace to drink fluids and get plenty of rest. I even advised him to skip that night's social affair if he could do so.

"I was next called in two weeks later. His Grace was complaining again of stomach pains and experiencing vomiting and a bit of dizziness. His complexion was ruddier than it had been since my previous visit. It appeared he had lost a bit of weight. I gave him a thorough examination and found he had an abnormal heart rate. At that point, I inquired of his age and told him he was experiencing mild heart symptoms, which led to his color changing and the nausea and dizziness."

"Heart problems can cause stomach pains?"

"We did not address those at that time, Miss Slade. His Grace wished to push aside what I told him. He was one of those men blessed with excellent health his entire life and did not want to know if anything were truly wrong with him." He shrugged. "I believe at that point the duke thought if he pretended nothing was wrong, the signs of illness would simply vanish simply because he willed them to do so. He was quite a force of nature. Strong-willed and determined."

"Did you see him any other times before he returned to Hertfordshire?"

"I did, at least one more time. Wait. Let me consult my diary. I can be more precise if I do so."

Dr. Barton flipped open a bound ledger on his desk and perused it a few minutes, telling Shelby exactly when he had first seen Edgehaven and the dates of his subsequent visits. She noted these dates in her notes. He mentioned the last time he had seen the duke before he and the duchess left to return to their country estate.

"What was your final advice to His Grace?"

"His Grace exhibited all the previous symptoms I had observed on my last visit. Ones I have spoken of. His face also appeared swollen, in addition to being red. By this point, I suspected—especially with his weight loss—that besides his heart growing weak, a malignant tumor might have taken hold of his insides."

"Did you share this conclusion with His Grace?"

Dr. Barton nodded. "I did so, Miss Slade."

"How did His Grace take the news?"

"With melancholy. He begged me not to mention anything to Her Grace and said they would soon be returning to the country. I thought the country air might do him some good and also prescribed a lighter diet for him, things I believed his belly might tolerate more easily than the rich, heavy food which was his normal fare. I did not see His Grace again until his recent return to London, shortly before the new year rang in. Frankly, I was shocked by the decline in his health and how fragile he had become in just a few short months. I suspected several things ailed him by that point, things beyond my cure. Those, coupled with old age, simply could not be beaten back."

Suspicions began to form in Shelby's mind. Every fourth Saturday of the month, all runners who were in town and not currently working gathered at headquarters, where unusual cases were presented. She had led some of these discussions herself, based upon her caseload, and she had learned a great deal from other agents' presentations, as well.

One case, four or five years ago, involved arsenic poisoning. The symptoms the runner described were very much in line with what the dead duke had experienced. Small doses of arsenic were odorless and tasteless in nature, easily confused with flour or sugar and readily available. It was used mostly as a rat poison and could have been purchased without arousing any suspicion. In fact, after the presentation, Mr. F had contributed to the discussion, saying arsenic had been used for years in the Medieval and Renaissance eras and had gained the nickname "inheritance powder" because of its use by impatient heirs utilizing it to hasten the death of one who held a title.

She would need to ask this man about the possibility of arsenic being the cause of Edgehaven's death.

"By this point, there was nothing I could truly do for His Grace. He was so weak and fragile, he could not even walk on his own without assistance. The pain inside him had grown exponentially, confirming my previous diagnosis of a tumor within him, its growth spreading. By the time I last called upon His Grace, Lord Jasper had arrived in town for what I gather was his usual sojourn spent with his parents, leave granted by the church. I explained to him at this point all we could do was keep his father comfortable. I also mentioned if he had other relatives, they should come to say their goodbyes to His Grace. Lord Jasper sent for his brother and nieces so they might bid His Grace farewell."

"His Grace told me you gave his father laudanum."

"Yes, in quite heavy doses, I might add. His Grace was in severe pain by this point. It was merely a matter of time before he passed. When he did so, it surprised me that the duke had lasted as long as he did, most likely due to the good health he experienced before his illness."

"Are you familiar with arsenic, Dr. Barton?" Shelby asked.

The physician frowned. "I am, Miss Slade." He hesitated, and she saw him thinking. Then his eyes widened, making the connection. "Good God! You don't believe His Grace was poisoned, do you? By arsenic?"

Shelby knew she danced a fine line now. Dr. Barton was a respected physician and would be loath to go to the lengths she needed to confirm her suspicions. Experience told her that she needed to pursue this possibility, though.

And it was up to her to convince Dr. Barton to do so.

"I am concerned enough that I believe this avenue must be explored, Doctor," she said gravely. "After all, we are speaking of a duke, a pillar of British society. While I understand your reluctance and realize what I am asking of you is quite unorthodox, I believe it is imperative to find the true cause of His Grace's death. That means we must check for any sign of the poison."

Worry now filled Dr. Barton's face. "The symptoms you have described *are* all ones similar to someone exposed to arsenic over a long period of time."

"From what I gather, it builds inside the body, creating a myriad of problems over time."

"But . . . that would mean someone in His Grace's household had . . . murdered him."

"Yes, I believe that to be a distinct possibility."

Confusion filled the physician's face. "Why would someone do such a horrible thing? His Grace suffered quite a bit, especially at the end."

"If I can answer the why, Dr. Barton, I might be able to answer who was behind this atrocious act. First, I must learn if it truly were arsenic positioning or not. His Grace is buried in Hertfordshire at the local church near his ducal seat. How do you suggest I go about having the body disinterred?"

Shock filled his face. "That simply isn't done, Miss Slade. Not by reliable members of the community, such as the local magistrate." His face darkened. "Are you familiar with the term grave robbing? It used to be associated with unscrupulous men unearthing graves and stealing items buried with a corpse, ones of archaeological significance. In more recent years, a black market has sprouted so that these men remove bodies from their graves and sell them. There are men who wish to study the human anatomy and are willing to pay a pretty price for the ability to do so."

Shelby nodded solemnly. "I knew that the cadavers of men condemned to death can be sold for the purposes of medical research."

"Yes, but those cadavers are few and far between. It is why a market for them has been created. They call it body snatching. The men who steal these bodies from their graves are known as resurrectionists."

Dr. Barton shook his head. "As to your question, Miss Slade? At this time, we have no reliable test to inform us whether His Grace was poisoned by arsenic. Because of that, there is no reliable way for you to ascertain whether or not His Grace was poisoned."

Shelby hid her frustration. "I understand and am disappointed to learn this. At least I am armed with the symptoms that the duke experienced under your care."

"I suggest you also speak with his country doctor. He might be able to add more information regarding His Grace's health during his months away from London."

"I may," she said. "The only problem is that I have learned that Dr. Davies, who is at Edgewood and did minister to the duke during this past autumn, is quite elderly. I doubt he will know as much of this as you do, Dr. Barton. I also am loath to leave such information in the hands of a man who might prove to be unreliable. Above all, His Grace wishes for this matter to remain private."

She produced a card from her reticule and said, "I am writing His Grace's Mayfair address on the back of my card. If you can think of any information to add, please contact His Grace here, and he will pass along the information to me."

Shelby handed over the card and rose. "I thank you for your time and once more must ask for your utmost discretion in this matter, Doctor. His Grace does not wish for any news of this to get out, especially if there is a killer on the loose. We would not want him to be warned by our investigation into His Grace's death."

"I regret not having thought of poisoning sooner, Miss Slade."

"There was no reason to expect foul play, Dr. Barton, and there still may be none present. You considered the age of your patient and took in his symptoms. Many of them mirrored heart problems, as well as the growth of a tumor. Murder by slow poisoning would not have occurred to you."

"If you do determine that poisoning occurred, might you inform me?" the physician asked.

"That would not be a problem in the least, sir. You are a professional, and His Grace would trust in your discretion. If it does turn out that our suspicions are correct, I will return again to interview you for my final report and can even see that you receive a copy of it."

"I would be most grateful, Miss Slade."

Shelby said her goodbyes and returned to Bow Street head-quarters. She had time to write up the report she had planned to do regarding her last case and spent two hours completing it. When she finished, she spoke to Mr. F's secretary, and he found a place in the schedule to slide her in.

She arrived and was all business, filing her report with her mentor and leaving the single copy on his desk, where the secretary would record a copy of it for their files.

"Excellent work, as always, my dear," Mr. F praised. "Now, what do you think of Edgehaven? I knew you were eager to be assigned to his case."

"I find His Grace to be quite sincere. I do believe the suspicions he has may be justified. Do you have time for me to share with you?"

"Of course. I am most curious to see what you have already uncovered in such a short amount of time."

Quickly, Shelby outlined the additional information she had, especially her lengthy conversation with Dr. Barton and how she suspected the previous duke might have been the victim of arsenic poisoning.

"It sounds as if you have hit on something, Shelby," he said. "If you are correct, that means someone in the duke's household had it out for him."

"Usually in a case such as this, it is either for gain or revenge. The one man who stands to gain the most from Edgehaven's death would be his heir apparent. We know Lord Sutton died near the same time his father expired. That is why I am ready to rule out gain. The second son was in France fighting, and I cannot see him hatching some scheme to make his older brother the duke from so far away, much less committing the plot into writing, especially after years abroad at war. I cannot suspect the third son at all for this crime Mr. F. You have met His Grace. I'm certain you do not see him as a killer."

"I know he was, until recently, a clergyman." He paused. "But I have taught you to suspect everyone, Shelby. Unless you have irrefutable proof, the new Duke of Edgehaven should remain a suspect in this case."

"This man is above suspicion, Mr. F. I feel if he could give back the title, he would do so. Or let it pass to another relative. He is in mourning, not simply because he lost a loving father, but for having lost the living at Edgewood. I gather he was quite good in his position and had found a true calling. He expressed honest remorse for not being able to tend to his parish anymore."

"He did live nearby," Mr. F reminded her. "The new duke would have the means—if not the loyalty—of some of the servants in his father's household. I would not rule him out entirely."

"I have to disagree, Mr. F. I can tell when someone is lying. This man is not. He truly misses being a clergyman and serving the church and God, along with his flock. It is no act on his part. Besides, why would he come to Bow Street and ask for us to open an investigation if he were the culprit? At this point, no one *but* the duke believes the two deaths were suspicious and might be connected. One was the death of an elderly, ill man. The other ruled an unfortunate accident."

"I suppose you are right, as always. I have taught you to trust your instincts and yours are honed as sharp as any agent's I have seen, including my own. Keep me apprised when you can, Shelby."

"I will do so, Mr. F," she promised.

"As his secretary, will you live in the duke's household?"

"I will determine that soon. I do not believe it is custom, so most likely, you will see me some at home."

She rose and went to him, bending to brush her lips against his cheek. "I hope to see you at dinner this evening. Then I will be off to visit the gaming hells."

He frowned. "Another case?"

"No, the same one. I wish to seek information regarding the playing habits of the previous Duke of Edgehaven and his heir apparent. If either had any outstanding debts. I doubt it, but you know I choose to be thorough."

He caught her hand and squeezed it. "That's my girl."

Shelby left his office, happy to put her last case behind her and ready to concentrate solely on this new one. She would dress in one of her numerous disguises as she visited the gaming hells of London tonight, hoping to discover all she could about the previous Duke of Edgehaven and his son, Lord Sutton.

With a spring in her step, she left headquarters and returned home, curious to see where her investigation would lead.

And eager to spend more time in the Duke of Edgehaven's company.

CHAPTER EIGHT

S HELBY ENJOYED A quiet dinner with Mr. and Mrs. F and then spent an hour reading, catching up on the newspapers Mrs. F had saved from the last month while Shelby had been working as a housemaid. She read of the war news and then focused on two things that always interested her.

The gossip columns and the obituaries.

She didn't have much to read in the gossip columns. With it still being January, very few of the *ton* had returned to London. They would come in droves during March and April. Still, she liked to keep up with them since the majority of their clients came from members of Polite Society. She thought of the columns as an epic, such as Homer's classics, *The Iliad* and *The Odyssey*, with a huge cast of characters, many of whom were related to one another. Her fascination with titles and who inherited them and who wed whom proved quite entertaining.

She thought about what she knew of the Duke and Duchess of Edgehaven. Before his death, the duke had appeared only infrequently in the newspapers, usually in relation to some grand contribution he made to some widows' or orphans' homes. He had also loaned a few pieces of artwork to various museums. Never had scandal tainted his—or his duchess'—name.

The Duchess of Edgehaven was known for her keen sense of fashion and the fact she did not tolerate fools. Some of her most cutting remarks which had been overheard by others made their ways into the gossip columns of the more than one dozen London newspapers of the time. Shelby was a bit wary about meeting the duchess, especially knowing that Jasper did not have a good relationship with his mother. How ironic that her favoritism, which the duchess probably had thought would bring her closer to her son, actually had the reverse effect and had driven a wedge between the pair.

She was curious about the woman, though, and would make certain she spoke to her at some point early in the investigation. After all, the duchess had been wife to the duke for well over three decades and might have some insight to pass along to Shelby. Still, she would play her role as secretary to the new Duke of Edgehaven, and no one in the household—not even the duchess—would know of her true identity.

The one person she wished to interview whom she thought would not need to be kept in the dark would be the Earl of Darrow. From the relationship Jasper had with the man, he was as a second father to the previous duke's children, as well as the man's closest friend. She would check with Jasper, of course, but thought he would give her permission to tell Darrow of her role in the investigation into the deaths of the duke and his heir apparent.

Once she had skimmed the newspapers, she placed them in the bin and returned to her room.

It was time to become Mr. Andrews tonight.

Mr. Andrews was one of her longstanding creations. The wig she used was close to her natural color, as was the heavy mustache she attached just above her upper lip. Shelby sat at her dressing table, braiding and pinning her hair to her head before placing the wig atop it. She attached the mustache and slipped on the spectacles which helped hide her unusual eye color, wishing she had a way to disguise it. So far, no one haunting the gaming hells had associated a Bow Street Runner with Mr. Andrews. The glasses helped, as did the hat whose brim she wore low on her brow.

She changed from her clothing into Mr. Andrews' typical garb. He wore muted grays and dark blues, clothes of good but not excellent quality. He also gambled some, small amounts here and there, in order to justify his presence in the gaming establishments. Mostly, though, Mr. Andrews was a gossip who faded in and out of the woodwork. He listened and learned and upon occasion offered sums of money to workers at the gaming hells. He had regulars he paid to bring him tidbits of gossip concerning a variety of people and areas. Most thought Mr. Andrews quite harmless.

Shelby counted on that as she subtly pumped others for information as Mr. Andrews. She also made certain to slip a guinea to each person who spoke with her, no matter how big or small the gossip they shared. Because of Mr. Andrews' generosity, she had found those sources were more willing to help out and share things that most likely they would have kept to themselves. She counted on that willingness and generosity of spirit as she hit the first gaming hell.

Mrs. Martin's was located in St. James, one of the most fashionable neighborhoods in London. Yet even in such an exclusive area, gaming hells could be found. It was owned and run by Stephen Martin. Shelby assumed at one point there had been a Mrs. Martin, possibly the current manager's mother, but it was hard picturing Stephen Martin as a child who had a mother. Martin was ruggedly handsome, though his good looks had been marred by the knife which had been slashed across his cheek at some point, leaving a brutal scar from the top of his cheekbone to the corner of his sensual mouth. Shelby had seen no woman named Mrs. Martin ever grace the gaming establishment. She thought Martin must have simply named his place the plain, innocent name to help hide what the establishment truly was.

Entering now, she made her way into the heart of the gaming hell, away from the men who were here more for a tumble with a doxy and only played a few of the games of chance before partnering with a woman for a few hours' romp. Within the heart of Mrs. Martin's could be found the hard gamers, frequently called greeks when they won and pigeons when they lost. Mrs. Martin's and other gaming hells made their money from these so-called pigeons, who like the birds they were named after, felt the need to come back to the place of their losses again and again to try and win back what they forfeited earlier.

As Mr. Andrews, Shelby strolled the room, keeping to its edges as she watched gameplay and listened to gossip. Some of her regular sources came to say hello, gliding by and offering a word or smile. Eventually, they would make their way to her as the evening progressed if they had something of importance to share with her.

She joined those at the faro table for a bit, winning a little more than she lost, and then moved on to dice, where she lost her previous winnings and then some. Making her way around the room once more, she was joined as she went by four sources, all at different times. Discreetly, she handed over a guinea even before they began to talk, showing the faith she placed in them and their information.

What she learned was worth every coin spent.

By the time she left around three o'clock the next morning, Shelby was armed with quite a bit of interesting information and did not feel the need to spend any more of her time in the gaming hells. She doubted she would discover anything else—and wondered how Jasper would react to the news she brought to him.

Returning outside, she signaled a hack and took it home, slipping through the front door quietly so as not to disturb Mr. or Mrs. F. She doffed her Mr. Andrews' clothes, folding them neatly and placing them on a chair, knowing the heavy scent of tobacco clung to them. They would also need to be laundered because one drunken patron had crashed into Mr. Andrews, spilling his drink down what she wore. Even now, hours later, she caught the scent of brandy.

She washed her face and used her tooth powder before unpinning her hair, leaving it in the braids. Slipping into a night rail, she pulled back the bedclothes and climbed into bed, weary after such a long day. At least she would be able to sleep later than usual since she did not have to be at Jasper's until her noon interview.

Closing her eyes, Shelby fell asleep with the Duke of Edgehaven's image teasing her.

JASPER LISTENED WITH only half an ear to the man he was supposedly interviewing. He wouldn't even consider it an interview, though. The first candidate sent by the employment agency showed true promise. Jasper was able to ask the man numerous questions and received numerous satisfactory answers. This second prospect, however, droned on and on, rarely coming up for a breath, delivering more an eternal soliloquy. Jasper had tried to interrupt Mr. Smythe several times, but the man kept speaking. Therefore, he simply would let him talk himself out.

He wondered if Shelby might already have arrived for her supposed interview and couldn't believe how much he was looking forward to seeing her again. He wondered if she had drawn out anything new from Dr. Barton.

A knock at the study's door sounded, and he raised his hand and frowned severely, indicating for the prospective employee to cease speaking. Jasper almost breathed a sigh of relief with the silence that occurred.

"Come," he called, grateful when his butler entered the room.

"Your Grace, your next appointment has arrived."

"Thank you, Bowen. You may escort Mr. Smythe out." Turning to the man seated before him, Jasper added, "Thank you for your time, sir."

"If you have any questions of me, Your Grace, please feel free to contact me. Do you know when you might have a decision regarding the position?"

"I will let the agency know soon," he assured the loquacious man, hoping they would never run across one another again.

Rising, Mr. Smythe did the same and gave a curt bow. "It was wonderful meeting you, Your Grace. I hope we will have the opportunity to work together."

The job candidate crossed the room, and Bowen stepped aside to allow him to leave. Then the butler turned back to Jasper. "A Miss Slade, Your Grace."

"Show her in, Bowen."

His heart began beating more swiftly, anticipating seeing Shelby again. When she entered the room, his mouth grew dry, making it difficult for him to swallow. He felt like a schoolboy, wet behind the ears. Pulling himself together, especially since Bowen was still present, Jasper said, "Come in, Miss Slade. You come highly recommended by your employment agency."

"Thank you, Your Grace," she said as Bowen slipped from the room, closing the door behind him.

She gave a brusque nod and waited for him to seat himself. He was used to waiting until a lady sat and supposed this was part of his new protocol, outranking everyone in the room and seating himself before others did so.

"How have the interviews gone?" she asked. "You look a bit harried."

He indicated for her to take a seat in front of the desk, and he joined her at the chair sitting next to it, forgoing sitting behind the desk and putting distance between them.

"You read me quite well, Shelby. The first applicant the agency sent will make for a fine secretary. He is knowledgeable, both in the job he would do for me and regarding his knowledge of the *ton*. He would be an excellent reference for me. I believe I could learn quite a bit from him. He most recently worked for an earl who passed two weeks ago, one who had no heirs, else I assumed he would have remained in his position. I plan to offer him the post. As you suggested I will simply put him on a retainer, having him report when we wrap things up."

"Remember, Jasper, there is no timetable for that. This investigation could possibly take months. And what of the second candidate?" she asked, biting back a smile.

"I have never heard a man talk so much and say so little in an hour's time. If you had not shown up when you did, he would still be talking until teatime."

She laughed, the sound that brought him sheer joy.

"Well, we cannot have your teatime interrupted, can we? Be sure that you write to the agency and indicate which man you have selected for the position. If I were you, I would have your choice report directly to you tomorrow morning. At that time, you could tell him that he will not be needed until shortly before the Season begins, say the first of April. Let him know you will place him on salary now so that he has something to live on until then."

"I will take your advice. In fact, I took some of it yesterday and made my way to a tailor after I took my nieces for a long walk. The tailor was the one my father and brother used. Very soon, I should have several items of clothing to wear so that you will not chastise me for continuing to look and dress as a clergyman."

"They do say clothes make the man. It will be easier for you to make your transition into Polite Society if you are appropriately garbed. Have you been to White's yet?"

"No. I suppose that is something else I should add to my growing list."

She grinned unabashedly. "It is on *my* list, Your Grace," she teased. "As your secretary, I will suggest things for you to do and keep your calendar. Once we have concluded our interview today, you will need to inform your staff of your decision to hire me. I do have one question, however. Did your father's previous secretary live in?"

"Not to my knowledge. No, now that I think about it, I do remember seeing him come and go a few times. Would you prefer to live here?"

The thought of having her under his roof almost undid him. It would be the greatest temptation he had ever faced.

"No, I expect to work long hours, but I would prefer the freedom to come and go as I choose. Some of my sleuthing might come late at night and into the wee hours of the morning, as it did yesterday."

"You were out late? You look no worse for the wear. In fact, you appear fresh as flowers blooming on a spring day."

Her cheeks flooded with color, and Jasper realized she might not be immune to his charms. He knew how to use them and had done so at times when he needed things from his congregation, such as donations for repairs at his church.

"I spent several hours last night at Mrs. Martin's."

He looked blankly at her. "I have no idea who Mrs. Martin might be. Is she somehow related to your investigation?"

She chuckled. "It is one of the more popular gaming hells in St. James. But first I want to address with you my visit with Dr. Barton. I spent a good hour with him yesterday afternoon."

"An hour? What did you have to talk about for so long? Did he recall something I should know about?"

"We will never know for certain since no tests exist to bring us confirmation, but I believe your father was poisoned, Jasper."

A chill shot through him. "Poisoned? You think Father was *poisoned?*"

"There was a case presented in one of our staff meetings. We gather monthly at headquarters to discuss unique cases so that all agents might learn from other agents' investigations. I remembered this one from a few years ago. It involved arsenic."

"Arsenic," he echoed, growing thoughtful. "It is very common. Easy to purchase. I even had some at the vicarage."

"Exactly. So many people use it to keep rats or mice away. It is also used for a variety of purposes beyond that. Arsenic has also been employed throughout history to eliminate people. It is odorless and so would not be smelled. If someone had placed it in your father's food or drink, it is also tasteless. He would never know of its presence."

"That would mean someone in this household doctoring his food. Or at Edgehill."

"Or even a servant who moves between both residences, such as his valet," she suggested.

"Father's valet—now mine—a man called Watson. He is mild-mannered and always eager to please. Loyal to a fault. I cannot fathom why Watson might have a motive to kill his own employer."

"That is for me to ascertain. I will either rule Watson out as a suspect or if I find something, I will push him. Subtly, at first, and then harder if I have to. You must remember, Jasper, if it turns out to be this Watson, he may not have a grudge at all against your father."

"Then why on earth would he—or anyone—do such a terrible thing?" Jasper demanded, clearly unnerved by the thought of the man who now shaved him being his father's murderer.

"Sometimes, people rack up gambling debts. If this Watson did so, he might have wanted to find a way to pay them off. If he is a good and loyal servant, as you seem to believe, then he might have known of a legacy bequeathed to him by your father."

"It is true that in the will there were small amounts of monies bequeathed to longtime servants, Watson among them. Not so great an amount, however, that might cause him to murder poor Father."

"I am merely giving you an example of one person who might be a suspect and a reason why he might be motivated to end your father's life. Gambling debts can be accumulated by anyone rather quickly, be they members of the *ton* or its servants. Some gaming hells hire ruffians to threaten those who have lost large amounts at the tables. Even the kindest of people, when threatened with loss of their lives or their loved ones being hurt, will lash out and do whatever it takes to protect themselves. I would not mind seeing a copy of His Grace's will and what amounts were bequeathed to which servants."

"I have a copy of it here."

He rose and opened a drawer of the desk, removing his father's will. Returning to Shelby, he handed it to her, saying, "It was read after the funeral when we were at Edgehill. A few of the servants from town came down for the service and burial, Watson among them."

Shelby skimmed the contents of the will and asked, "Were Mr. and Mrs. Bowen also present?"

"Yes, they are the butler and housekeeper here in town and have been employed for a good number of years. As was Cook, though she did not travel to Hertfordshire. She told me her place was here, keeping the kitchens running, just as His Grace would have wanted."

"I see." Shelby finished examining the will and returned it to Jasper. "Let me share a little of what Dr. Barton and I spoke of yesterday."

He returned the will to the drawer and took his seat beside her again.

"First, I do not want you to blame Dr. Barton in any way," she cautioned. "The symptoms your father displayed mimicked heart trouble and possibly something malignant growing inside him. I doubt any physician would have leaped to the conclusion that His Grace was slowly being poisoned."

Shelby walked Jasper through various symptoms associated with arsenic poisoning, and he realized his father had every single one of them.

"So many of these would be laid at the doorstep of heart trouble alone," she told him. "It seems as though your father first had these symptoms last summer while he was in town for the Season, and they gradually worsened throughout the autumn. When Their Graces returned to London after Christmas, Dr. Barton said that your father was remarkably worse. He believed this was caused not only by your father's age but things worsening within him. Since these symptoms grew gradually worse over several months, it would not have caused any questions.

"Unfortunately, as I mentioned previously, no test has been developed to ascertain if His Grace was poisoned with arsenic, but if that is the case, we are now armed with that knowledge. Knowledge which his murderer does not know we possess at this point. I could go to Hertfordshire and also speak with his physician there to confirm what Dr. Barton told me. From what you have said, though, I don't think it necessary to interview Dr. Davies. Dr. Barton saw His Grace at the beginning of his illness and at its end. He is most reliable at recalling the details. Because the illness came on gradually, it means if your father were poisoned, his poisoner knew he could take his time. Having the luxury of time on his side—if there truly is a murderer behind His Grace's death—allowed for this slow death, one in which no one suspected what might be happening under their very noses."

Her gaze met his. "A patient killer such as this is also a clever one, Jasper. You will need to be extremely careful in your dealings with everyone in your household."

"You believe that I, too, might be at risk?"

"Not at first. But any kind of symptoms—any feeling odd or different—and you must see Dr. Barton at once. Frankly, I believe whoever acted in your father's murder will lay low. He may not have any reason to move against you. This could merely have been a grudge he held against His Grace."

"I don't see how that would be possible, Shelby. My father was well-loved by everyone he met."

"And yet you yourself told me that you only recently learned some remarkable revelations about both your parents. How each had been in love with someone else and yet been forced by their parents to wed one another. Your father could have held secrets you had no idea existed. Because of that, I will tread lightly—but I will get to the bottom of this, Jasper. I promise you that."

"I have faith in you, Shelby. I know if Father was taken from

me that you will find whoever is responsible for his early death."
Jasper sighed. "I had just come to the conclusion as this new year
began that I wished to wed. I wanted to have children so that
they could know their grandfather."

She placed her hand atop his, causing a rush of feelings to run
through him. "You are a man of faith, Jasper. Simply because you
no longer preach the word of God to your congregation does not
mean that your faith has abandoned you. You will wed someday
and have those children—and His Grace will be looking down in
approval."

Tears stung his eyes as she withdrew her hand. He longed to
take it again and hold it, never letting go. For comfort.

For more than comfort . . .

"Now that I have spoken to you of my conversation with Dr.
Barton, we must talk about something else quite serious in
nature. It is in regard to Lord Sutton."

"What? You have found something out about my brother and
his death?"

"Not about his death—but about something he left behind.
Actually, someone."

Shelby cleared her throat and held his gaze as she said, "Lord
Sutton kept a mistress here in London. And she is with child. His
child."

CHAPTER NINE

"WHAT?" JASPER SHOUTED, outrage and disbelief pouring through him.

"Keep your voice down," Shelby cautioned. "Else we'll have your butler and half your staff rushing to your aid—and wondering about our relationship."

He sprang to his feet and began pacing the room, his thoughts swirling.

Jarrod. With a mistress. No, one who was increasing. A babe who would never know their father.

Halting, he said, "Tell me everything you know."

"Take a seat, and I will. And no interrupting me."

Reluctantly, he returned to sit, itching to ask questions—and afraid of the answers he might receive.

"Her name is Adele Simmons. She is the half-sister of one of the card dealers at Mrs. Martin's. She was serving as one of the hostesses of the gaming hell." Shelby paused a moment. "She was not a bit o' muslin."

He frowned, unfamiliar with the term, knowing the very straight and narrow path he had walked as a clergyman before coming into his title left him at a bit of a disadvantage. "A what?"

"A light-skirt. A woman of easy virtue," Shelby explained. "Mrs. Martin's is not only a gaming hell. It also caters to gentlemen who, shall I say, wish to have certain favors bestowed upon them."

Her cheeks pinkened, and he felt his own face flame at discussing such a topic.

"Miss Simmons served more as a woman who moved men through the gaming establishment. Signaled for them to have drinks or food brought to them. Helped manage their evening by sending them to certain tables to play or reserving an agreed-upon woman to entertain them when they had finished playing their games of chance."

"You are saying this Miss Simmons did not earn her living on her back," he said flatly.

"No. Not until Lord Sutton came along," she revealed.

Jasper winced. "Go on."

"Apparently, they met when Lord Sutton visited Mrs. Martin's two years ago. From everyone I spoke to at this gaming hell, your brother was a casual gambler. He did not make terribly large wagers and owed no gambling debts at Mrs. Martin's at the time of his death. I will certainly visit other gaming hells to see if they are owed anything, but I can tell you if he did, someone from that establishment would have likely contacted you by now. Still, I will be thorough."

She took a deep breath. "From speaking to several sources— including Miss Simmons' half-brother—by all accounts, Lord Sutton cared for Miss Simmons and had planned to provide for her and the babe after the birth."

"That will fall to me now," he said.

"If you choose to do so, Jasper. I do believe it would be the honorable course of action, taking care of this woman and her unborn child. She is living at a boardinghouse. Lord Sutton paid the rent through August."

He took in Shelby's words, wondering what kind of woman had tempted his brother beyond his marriage vows. Then again, Jarrod had always been something of a ladies' man. Jasper had heard him bragging enough about his conquests. After he began his career in the church, though, his brother never mentioned his affairs to Jasper. He had assumed Jarrod had settled into his marriage and was faithful to Mary. Apparently, that had not been the case. Or Jarrod did as many of the men of the *ton* did, and kept a mistress while allowing his wife to run his household and give birth to his legitimate children.

"Have you seen this Miss Simmons? Met her?" he asked.

"No, but Mr. Simmons, her half-brother, provided the address of the boardinghouse to me. Actually, he lives there with his sister."

"Take me to her, Shelby. Now."

"First, tell me what you are going to say to her, Jasper."

He raked his fingers through his hair. "I haven't the slightest idea," he said irritably.

"Then decide before we leave this house," she said firmly. "I won't have you berating Miss Simmons. You need to have a clear plan of action. No making decisions on the spot. What is most important is the babe."

Anger simmered within him at her telling him what to do. He took a calming breath, tamping it down. "You are right. I am frustrated with Jarrod. There is no need for me take out any of that frustration on Miss Simmons, especially in her delicate condition. What do you suggest?"

"I would make arrangements with your solicitor to see that regular payments are sent to Miss Simmons and the child. Enough to keep a roof over her head and food on her table. It would be generous of you to provide not only those things but also help to educate the child."

"I agree. Let me meet Miss Simmons, and then I will make an appointment with my solicitor to draw up papers to that effect." He hesitated. "Can we go now?"

"Yes, Jasper. I do have one more thing to share. Mr. Simmons did not know that Lord Sutton had died until I informed him of the earl's death. In fact, he and his sister had last seen his lordship when he came to London at your request. Lord Sutton may have told you that he wished to go riding, Jasper, but he went to see

Miss Simmons instead."

His gut twisted. "So, she doesn't know of Jarrod's death?"

"She will by now. Mr. Simmons was going to inform her of it. You will not have to break the news to her."

He rang for his butler. "Then we must go and offer what comfort we can to her."

Bowen appeared, and Jasper ordered that his carriage be readied. He also introduced the butler to Shelby, sharing that she was his new secretary. To Bowen's credit, he disguised his surprise at a woman being awarded the post rather well.

"Will your butler tell the household of the decision you have made in hiring a woman to serve as your secretary?"

"I haven't a clue," he admitted. "Bowen—and Mrs. Bowen, who serves as my housekeeper—are extremely efficient. I don't know them well enough to know if either is a gossip or not."

The butler returned and announced that the carriage was ready and waiting out front. They went to the foyer, where Mrs. Bowen lingered, so Jasper introduced Shelby to the housekeeper.

"It is good to meet you, Miss Slade," Mrs. Bowen said. "Will you be living with us? I can have a room prepared for you and arrange for your things to be moved here. Just say the word."

"No, I prefer to keep my own rooms where I currently live," she told the housekeeper.

"But Miss Slade will breakfast with me each morning," Jasper added, wanting to start his day with her.

"Very good, Your Grace," Mrs. Bowen said. "I will let Cook know."

They went to the carriage, and Shelby provided the address to the coachman before Jasper handed her up. He sat opposite her in the carriage, wishing he could be seated beside her but happy to look upon her all the same.

"Do you have any other earthshattering announcements?" he asked her.

"Other than suspecting your father was poisoned and your brother's mistress will give birth to his child soon? No, not a thing, Your Grace," she teased. Then her expression grew serious. "Thank you for wanting to care financially for Miss Simmons and your nephew."

"Of course, I will do so. It is the Christian thing to do."

"Not all so-called Christians act according to the tenets they espouse. I suppose I have a strong sense of right and wrong. I have always wanted to set the world right since mine was turned upside down so many years ago. Many in the world are downtrodden, such as Miss Simmons, and need a champion to show them compassion and perhaps even get them justice. It is one of the reasons I committed to working as an agent at Bow Street. I want to not only solve cases but mete out justice for those in need."

"What was so difficult in your world, Shelby?"

She shook her head. "Nothing worth repeating. Speaking of issues from long ago will not change the facts. Let me say that I will never quit as I try to right things for others. I feel if I am not part of the solution, I am part of the problem—and I never want to be a burden to others. I have worked hard to make my body strong and my mind even stronger as I fight for others in this world."

"You mean physically, as well as verbally, I suppose," Jasper said.

She grinned. "I can fight dirty with the best of them. I grew up on the streets of London and learned numerous tricks which would get me thrown out of Gentleman Jackson's if I were fighting a bout there. Everything—and I mean everything—is fair game."

"Remind me never to tangle with you," he said lightly, desperate to ask her about her childhood and how she wound up a child of the streets, as well as how she was taken off them and made into who she was today.

They arrived at their destination and knocked upon the door of the boardinghouse. A woman with graying hair answered, looking at the pair of them and then over their shoulders at the ducal carriage sitting in front of the building.

"We have come to visit with Miss Simmons," Shelby said. "I spoke to Mr. Simmons about visiting with his half-sister last evening. He assured me that would be acceptable. I am Miss Slade. This is His Grace, the Duke of Edgehaven."

"Oh!" the woman exclaimed, clearly startled by having a duke at her door. "Won't you come in, please?" She stepped aside and allowed them entrance into the boardinghouse. "Usually, guests visit in the parlor." She indicated the room behind them. "I hope this will be adequate, Your Grace."

"More than adequate, Madam," Jasper responded. "Might we close the doors for a bit of privacy?"

"Whatever you wish, Your Grace. Let me go fetch Miss Simmons. It might take her a bit to make her way downstairs in her condition."

The woman, whom he assumed ran this establishment, hurried up the stairs. He motioned to Shelby, and they went to the parlor. It was shabby, with the carpet so bare it might as well not have been laid upon the floor. The furniture looked as if someone had already thrown it out once.

Shelby sneezed. "It's the dust. This room is filthy, Jasper. I worry if it is in this condition, what must the Simmons' room—or rooms—be like?"

"This is no place for an increasing woman," he agreed. "We must convince Miss Simmons to come with us."

"And go where?" she asked, a smile tugging at the corners of her mouth.

"Anywhere but here," he said, not ready to commit to having his brother's mistress take up residence with him and his two nieces. "What of the place you stay? Do they have rooms available?"

"No, not at this time. I suppose that can be my first task—looking for a new place for Miss Simmons to live. I am assuming Miss Simmons will not wish to be parted from her half-brother."

The woman, who had yet to give them her name, appeared

again. "Miss Simmons doesn't feel like coming downstairs," she said apologetically. "Even for a duke."

"Then we will go to her," he said firmly. "Take us to her, please."

The woman hesitated a moment. "All right."

They followed her up the staircase and to the first room on the right. The woman knocked.

"Miss Simmons? His Grace wishes to visit with you in your room."

"No," said a small, stubborn voice.

Jasper said, "Step aside."

The woman did as asked, and he said loudly, "Miss Simmons. I know you know who I am. It is imperative that we speak. You will either open this door—or I will knock it down. The choice is yours."

The woman behind him gasped. Shelby merely chuckled.

The sound of a lock being thrown clicked, and the door opened a foot. He saw a short woman with blond hair and blue eyes peering up at him, her face red and swollen from crying.

"May we come in?" he asked gently. "I have come with Miss Slade, my secretary. We will not take much of your time."

Adele Simmons leaned to her left, and Jasper stepped back so the woman could see Shelby.

"We would appreciate speaking with you, Miss Simmons," Shelby said, stepping up, smiling gently at the woman. "It is in regard to your future and that of your babe's."

Hope sprang in the woman's eyes. "All right."

The door opened wider, and Shelby stepped through first, followed by Jasper. Miss Simmons closed the door and turned to face them. Not only was her face bloated, but her body also was swollen, heavy with child.

"Come and sit, Miss Simmons," Shelby said, going and taking the woman's elbow and guiding her to one of two chairs in the room.

Once seated, Miss Simmons let out a loud sob. He allowed

Shelby to minister to the woman, feeling helpless. While he had comforted parishioners when one of their loved ones had died, he had no experience in helping mistresses get over the loss of their paramours. Shelby smoothed Miss Simmons' hair and wiped the tears from her cheeks, holding her hand and smiling encouragingly.

"His Grace wishes to talk with you about Lord Sutton and your child," Shelby said.

Jasper stepped closer. "I assume your half-brother told you of Sutton's death," he began.

"Yes," Miss Simmons said, a fresh flood of tears leaking from her eyes and down her cheeks. "I had no idea. Jarrod came to see me when he arrived in London. Oh, he was so upset about his father being ill. He was very worried about becoming the new duke. He said he felt totally unprepared to do so. That he would do a terrible job."

He took a seat next to her and reached for her hand, so small in his. "I am sorry for your loss, Miss Simmons."

"Jarrod told me he might not be able to visit me again for a few weeks. That he would need to bury his father and get things settled at Edgehill. Then he would send for me." She rubbed her belly. "I told him by then I would have already had the babe, most likely. He worried about me since I'm so small. Said his wife had died giving birth to one." More tears cascaded down her cheeks. "I knew it was wrong to be with a married man, but Jarrod was so kind to me. So patient. And he didn't run when he learned a babe was on the way. Most men of the *ton* would have done so. Not Jarrod. Oh, I knew I could never wed him, but he promised to look after me and our babe."

"I will do the same. I am his brother, the youngest of the three of us. Did he tell you our middle brother was killed in action?"

Miss Simmons nodded. "He did. Jarrod was more upset about Jude's death than his father's impending one. He loved his brother very much and hated that they hadn't seen one another in many years. He did love his father, though. He told me all kinds of wonderful stories about growing up and things the duke taught him."

Jasper made an instant decision. "Might you be willing to leave London, Miss Simmons? I could see that you are given a cottage at Edgehill. You could raise your babe there."

She shook her head sadly. "No, Your Grace. There would always be whispers. My boy—or girl—would have to live with those whispers. Of hearing how he or she was a bastard and having to use their fists to defend themselves and me. Don't get me wrong. It is a kind offer, and I do appreciate it. But I've never been to the country. I'm a London girl. Took my first breath here, and I'll take my last here, as well."

"Then I would like to move you and your half-brother to something more . . . private. This boardinghouse must have quite a few people living in it. I would see that you and Mr. Simmons have a quiet place in which to raise the babe. I also want to see to the child's education."

His words brought a fresh flood of tears. "Oh, Your Grace, that would be wonderful. Jarrod always talked of how kind and understanding you were. He said you would make for a better duke than he could be. Thank you."

She took his hands and pressed her lips to them, hot tears spilling from her eyes over them.

Then she let out a guttural cry, and a loud swoosh sounded. He glanced down and saw her skirts wet, water spreading on the floor. Confusion filled him.

"When is your babe due?" Shelby asked, taking Miss Simmons' hand.

"Not for another month," the woman wailed. "Oh, no." She winced in pain.

"It is too late to move her," Shelby quietly said to him. "We must send for a midwife. The babe no doubt comes early because of the shock she received at hearing of Lord Sutton's death." She looked to Miss Simmons. "Adele, have you seen a midwife?"

"Yes. Jarrod insisted that I do so." She gasped again, more water rushing from her. This time, though, blood was mixed with it, staining the wooden floor.

"Quickly, give me her name, and I will see her brought here at once," Jasper said, despair filling him.

Miss Simmons managed to get out the name, and Shelby said, "Go. I will stay and make her comfortable."

He fled the room, racing down the stairs, finding the boardinghouse owner lingering in the foyer.

"I need the midwife summoned at once!" he barked. "Miss Simmons' time to deliver has arrived early."

"I will see to it myself, Your Grace," the woman said, rushing out the door.

Jasper returned upstairs and saw Shelby had drawn back the covers and gotten Miss Simmons into the bed. She was removing her shoes and stockings as the woman wailed miserably.

"Wait downstairs," Shelby said to him.

He nodded and turned, escaping the room and returning to the parlor downstairs, where he began pacing the length of it over and over.

The midwife arrived and hurried upstairs. The boardinghouse owner offered to bring Jasper tea, which he declined.

Seven hours later, a disheveled Shelby appeared in the doorway. He sprang to his feet.

"A boy—or a girl?" he asked. "And how is Miss Simmons?"

"A girl," she said wearily. "Miss Simmons . . . did not survive the birth."

The news was as a punch to his gut. Still, the babe lived. A part of Jarrod and Miss Simmons would live through their child.

"I will see to the burial arrangements," he said.

"No, that is not something a duke would do for his brother's mistress. I will do so. Your involvement would only bring about questions better left unasked. I will consult with Mr. Simmons and see that she is buried here in London."

The door to the boardinghouse was flung open. A man entered, anger rolling off him in waves.

Immediately, Shelby went to him and took his arm, bringing him into the parlor. "Mr. Simmons, come and take a seat. I am the one who sent for you."

"Who're you?" he asked.

"I am Mr. Andrews' sister. Remember, my brother asked if I could call upon Miss Simmons last night."

He nodded and then turned to Jasper. A belligerent look filled his face. "You must be *his* brother. The earl's. You've got a look about you that reminds me of him. Well, just leave us in peace. Your brother got my half-sister with child, and now he's dead and gone. It's not your problem. It's ours."

"No, Mr. Simmons," Jasper said. "It is all of ours." He hesitated and then said, "Miss Simmons did not survive the birth—but her babe did."

Loud curses fell from Mr. Simmons' lips and he took a wild swing at Jasper. Before he could react, Shelby blocked the man's arm and latched on to his wrist, spinning Simmons about and twisting his arm behind him.

"Ouch!" he proclaimed loudly.

"Be still, Mr. Simmons. His Grace has done nothing wrong. He did not start up an affair with your half-sister. He did not cause her death. But His Grace is willing to pay for Miss Simmons' burial costs."

She waited a moment, and Jasper saw the fight had gone out of the man. Shelby released him, and he stumbled a few steps before catching his balance. Warily, he looked from her to Jasper, pain now etched into his face, the realization of losing his half-sister now a reality.

"What am I to do with a babe? I work long hours at Mrs. Martin's, dealing cards. I know of no one who can care for it."

"For her," Jasper corrected.

Mr. Simmons snorted in disgust. "I sure don't have use for a female child." His expression soured. "Take her to a foundling home."

"You don't want her?" he asked, anger mixing with shock. "She is your blood relative."

"Not much of one. Adele was only my half-sister. She was pretty but didn't have much sense. I got her a job at Mrs. Martin's, and we shared a room because neither of us could afford one on our own. Now that she's dead, I don't owe her—or her brat—anything."

"I will see that an undertaker comes to claim the body," Jasper said stiffly. "I will send word of when the burial service will occur."

"No need," the man said. "Adele is dead. I wash my hands of her and her child."

He looked to Shelby. "Go and bring the babe. Now."

She left the room. Not a word was spoken during her absence. When she returned with a small, wrapped bundle, Shelby said, "The midwife has agreed to wait with the body until the undertaker can fetch Miss Simmons. She is also going to pack up her things."

"She ain't got anything," Mr. Simmons said belligerently. "Just a few clothes—and she won't be needing them now. Leave them. I can sell them."

"Then do that," Jasper said, stepping to the man, their noses almost touching. "Take what you will. I know the room is paid for until the end of summer. Stay in it if you choose. But never contact me for anything, Mr. Simmons. Is that understood?"

Simmons nodded. "I'll wait here until Adele is gone."

He turned and took Shelby's elbow, guiding her from the building. On the pavement, Jasper came to halt, looking down at the tiny face as the babe slept.

"The midwife gave me the name and address of a wet nurse you can hire," Shelby told him. "We should stop there now and see if the woman can come with us because soon this little one will awaken and be starving."

"Very well."

He asked her the address and passed it along to his coachman.

The footman kept silent, his eyes wide, though, as he set the stairs down for them. Inside the carriage, Jasper sat next to Shelby, looking down at his niece.

"She is a Lincoln," he said softly. "Perhaps we should name her Adele, after her mother."

"That's a lovely idea." Shelby thought a moment. "What about calling her Della?"

He tried it out. "Della. I like the sound of that."

They arrived home another two hours later, having found the wet nurse and convincing her to pack up and accompany them back to Mayfair, as well as stopping at an undertaker's and arranging for him to claim Adele's body. The nursery had not been used in many years, and Mrs. Bowen and two maids attacked the room with gusto as Shelby walked the length of the drawing room numerous times, the babe in her arms.

She came to a halt before him. "You are doing a truly kind thing, Jasper."

"I could not leave her. She is my niece, as much as Sylvia and Fanny are. Blast! How am I going to tell them about Della? About their father's infidelity?"

"At this point, you do not need to do so," she assured him. "Della is simply a cousin of theirs, one who has come to live with them. With you. They will accept her. You can share as little or as much with them as you see fit. You have time to think it over, Jasper. No decision need occur tonight. The servants can be told the same thing. They will accept it because it is His Grace who has proclaimed it so."

Mrs. Bowen appeared. "The nursery is ready, Your Grace."

"Thank you, Mrs. Bowen. Come and meet Lady Della. She is a cousin to my nieces and will be raised alongside them."

The housekeeper smiled down at the infant. "Ah, she is a beauty, Your Grace. It will be nice to have a babe in the house again. Shall I take her to the wet nurse now?"

Shelby handed Della over to Mrs. Bowen. "A nursemaid for Lady Della should be hired tomorrow morning. I will first go to the employment agency before coming to work, Your Grace, and handle it."

"Very good, Miss Slade," Jasper said formally. "Thank you for your assistance in this matter."

He watched the two women leave the drawing room and plopped upon the nearest seat once they were gone, running his hands through his hair, exhausted by the day's happenings. Now he had three little girls who would depend upon him—and he had yet to start a family of his own.

Still, seeing Shelby hold Della in her arms had given Jasper a sense of peace. Shelby had looked at ease holding the babe, and he knew she would make for a good mother. Before being a mother, however, she needed to become a wife. He wanted her investigation over as soon as possible.

Only then would he broach Shelby Slade about sharing a future with him.

CHAPTER TEN

J ASPER ROSE AND rang for Watson. He decided he needed to get more into a routine and did not want the valet to feel neglected. Watson shaved him and then helped Jasper to dress, and he decided to go to the schoolroom first. He liked starting his day by seeing Sylvia and Fanny and wanted them to be the first to know about Della's arrival.

He found the girls and Miss Hall eating their breakfast. Sylvia greeted him with a hug, while Fanny flicked her eyes to him and then returned her gaze to her porridge. He desperately wanted to unlock the door Fanny had hidden herself behind.

Taking a seat at the table across from the girls, Sylvia told him what they were both working on with Miss Hall. Knowing that Shelby wanted to interview both girls, he decided the best way would be in a casual setting, and so he said to Miss Hall, "I will be taking the girls for a walk this morning. After my own breakfast. It will give you time to yourself for an hour or two."

"I would be happy to accompany you, Your Grace," the governess said.

"No, that will not be necessary, Miss Hall. In fact, I think I will walk with the girls every day though the time we leave will be dictated by my schedule."

Looking back at his nieces, he smiled. "Today, though, is a special day."

"Why, Uncle Jasper?" Sylvia asked.

"You are going to meet one of your cousins. She arrived in the world only yesterday and has come to live with us."

Fanny's jaw fell and then she quickly spooned a bite of porridge into it.

Sylvia, on the other hand, was full of questions. "A cousin, Uncle? A babe? What is her name? Can I meet her now?"

"Her name is Adele, but she is to be called Della," he revealed. "And you may visit her when I do. After you have eaten a good breakfast. I will return when I finish my own and you may meet Della, then we can go for our walk."

Jasper excused himself and went downstairs, where he found Shelby already seated in the breakfast room. It surprised him because he knew she was to visit the employment agency this morning.

She rose and bowed her head slightly. "Your Grace."

"Good morning, Miss Slade. I see you already have your cup of tea. Is your breakfast on its way, as well?"

"I was waiting for you before ordering it, Your Grace," she demurred.

He signaled Bowen as a footman poured coffee for him. "Have Cook send two breakfasts at once," he instructed.

He was glad to start his day with Shelby and decided it had been a good suggestion on her part for them to meet this way in front of others. There were two footmen, along with Bowen, who were always on duty at this morning meal. Talking over business with her in front of them would solidify her position as his secretary in his household and allow them to talk of more private issues behind closed doors.

"I visited the employment agency before I came here, Your Grace. They will be sending over a few applicants to be interviewed for the position of nursemaid to Lady Della. I also informed them that you wished to see the first of the two gentlemen you interviewed yesterday. They said they will send Mr. Roberts here at eleven o'clock this morning, as he had another interview scheduled for nine.”

Jasper hoped the prospective employer would not snap up Mr. Roberts, having been impressed with the applicant.

“You have already had a busy morning, Miss Slade.”

They dined and then he asked her to accompany him upstairs to the schoolroom. On their way, he said, “I have already talked to my nieces this morning and let them know of Della’s arrival. They are eager to meet their new cousin. I also told their governess that once they had visited the babe, I would take them for a walk this morning. I thought being outside the house would be the ideal circumstance in order for you to speak with them, no prying ears around.”

“Ah,” she said with a smile. “You already have the makings to become a Bow Street Runner yourself.”

“I will accept that as a compliment though I do not believe I could do the work you have done in the past. You mentioned in your last case that you became a housemaid?”

“I can lay a fire with the best of servants. And my dusting skills are a sight to behold,” she teased. “Working in a household, especially as a maid, you see and hear things that others do not. The *ton* has no idea how much their servants truly know about their lives. In this case, I was able to catch a jewel thief.”

“You will have to tell me more about this case someday,” he said as they arrived at the schoolroom.

He noted the dishes had already been cleared, and Sylvia and Fanny had slates before them. Sylvia put hers aside and looked at Shelby in curiosity. Fanny kept her chalk in hand and marked upon the slate, ignoring their arrival.

“Girls, I would like for you to meet my new secretary. This is Lady Sylvia, who is nine years of age, and Lady Fanny. She is six,” Jasper said, pride in his voice. “My secretary, Miss Slade.”

“But . . . you’re a girl,” Sylvia said, awe in her voice. “I didn’t know girls could be secretaries.”

Shelby smiled warmly at the girl. “I believe girls can be anything they choose to be, my lady.”

Jasper noted how Fanny watched Shelby from the corner of her eye.

"How long have you been a secretary?" Sylvia asked.

"To His Grace?" Shelby laughed. "I started the position yesterday so it is too soon to judge whether I will continue to work for His Grace or not."

Sylvia's eyes grew round. "You think Uncle might dismiss you?"

"Not at all," Shelby said, brimming with confidence. "If anything, *I* would leave here first, that being *my* choice. So far, I like working for His Grace and look forward to getting to know you and your sister better, my lady. I hear we are to go on a walk this morning after you meet your new cousin."

Sylvia grinned. "It's a babe! Born just yesterday." Looking to him, she asked, "Can we go now and see her, Uncle Jasper?"

"That is why I am here," he told the girl. "Miss Hall will have your cloaks ready for our walk, but first we must head to the nursery."

Sylvia leaped to her feet, and Fanny actually set aside her slate and rose.

"I wanted to go across the hall and see Della, but Miss Hall said we must wait for you," Sylvia admitted.

"Listening to your governess is always the best thing to do," he said. "I had one myself before I went away to school."

"Will I go to school? Will Fanny?"

He could not imagine sending them away and said, "No, you will be able to receive your education with Miss Hall. Where I go, you always will, too. We will spend part of our year in town and part at Edgehill. Of course, I will soon need to visit some of my other estates. You will remain in London since I will be moving from place to place rather quickly."

"But I will miss you," Sylvia wailed, tears forming in her eyes.

He placed a hand on her head. "I will not be gone long. Miss Hall will keep you company."

Still, her tears began to fall so he said, "There is no need to cry, Sylvia. I will never be gone for very long. If I were to be absent an extended amount of time, then you and Fanny would accompany me."

"Oh, thank you," the girl exclaimed, wrapping her arms about him.

He wondered about her strong reaction. Was it because she had lost her father and was afraid she would lose him, too, and that was why she behaved in such a manner? Or had Jarrod left the girls and their mother at his country estate while making trips to visit his mistress? He might never know the answer.

"Let's go see little Della," he said brightly.

Sylvia slipped her hand into his, and Fanny stood. Shelby moved to the girl.

"I am always a bit nervous when I meet new people, Lady Fanny. I can be quite shy, in fact. Might I hold your hand so things don't seem so scary to me?"

Fanny nodded and offered her hand to Shelby. Jasper thought that small bit of progress was more than he had made with Fanny since Jarrod's death.

"Now, where is the nursery?" Shelby asked.

He held Sylvia back, giving her a silent warning not to speak.

Fanny began to move, pulling Shelby along with her, and they went into the corridor and down it. He followed with Sylvia and saw Fanny stopped in front of the door.

"Let's go in, but we must be quiet in case Lady Della is sleeping," Shelby said.

When they entered, he saw the wet nurse they had hired in a rocker, the babe in her arms.

Smiling, the servant said, "Lady Della has just eaten her fill and been burped."

He took the lead. "Might I have her?"

The wet nurse looked startled, and he realized dukes most likely did not come to nurseries and certainly did not ask to hold babes.

She rose and handed the infant to him, cautioning him to

support the babe's neck. He was glad to be told to do so because he hadn't known he should.

Jasper gazed down at little Della. A wave of love swept over him. She had no one. No, that wasn't right. She had him and her cousins. Whatever her beginnings, Della would always be loved. He sat in the rocker the wet nurse had occupied.

"Come. Meet Della."

Both Sylvia and Fanny came to him and gazed at the babe with smiles. Della looked at them in curiosity.

"This is Sylvia and Fanny. They are your cousins, Della."

"She's awfully tiny," Sylvia said. "Where is her mama?"

"Sometimes, giving birth to a babe is very difficult," he said gently. "Not every woman is strong enough to survive child-birth."

"Like our mama," Sylvia said, her mouth trembling. "She died when a new babe came. They both died."

"I know. You must be very sad about that. Your mama was a very sweet, loving woman."

Fanny nodded her head vigorously but kept silent.

"Your mama was strong enough, though, to give life to the two of you," he continued. "I am so grateful because I love you both very much." Tears stung his eyes.

Then Fanny reached out and cradled Della's cheek. Jasper saw the slow smile forming on her lips. Sylvia, too, touched the babe's head.

"When will she talk?" Sylvia wanted to know.

"I have no idea," Jasper responded. "I have never been around a babe, but she will need to learn her words from the two of you. You will spend much of your time playing with her and teaching Della all kinds of new things. I hope you will treat your cousin as a sister would."

Fanny nodded again. Once more, he believed progress was being made. If anyone could unlock Fanny's silence, it would be this infant.

"May I hold her?" Sylvia asked.

"That is a lovely idea," Shelby said. "It would be best for you to be seated when you do so. Trade places with your uncle."

Rising, Jasper allowed Sylvia to take his seat and then slowly lowered Della as Shelby explained, "Lady Della's neck is very weak, Lady Sylvia. It will take her a few months before she can hold it up on her own. Until then, you must always support it."

Sylvia smiled. "I am your cousin, Della. My name is Sylvia. This is Fanny. She is also your cousin. We are going to play together and have a wonderful time."

Fanny stroked the babe's cheek, and nothing was said for a few minutes, all of them staring at the babe. Della began to grow sleepy, yawning, her eyelids drooping.

Finally, he said, "It is time for our walk in the park. Miss Slade will accompany us. You girls go and fetch your cloaks now."

He leaned down and slipped Della from Sylvia's arms into his. Returning the babe to the wet nurse, he said, "A nursemaid will hopefully be hired by the end of the day."

"I haven't minded looking after Lady Della, Your Grace. I can do so as long as long as I'm needed to."

Jasper and Shelby left the nursery and went downstairs. He sent Watson for his coat, and Bowen brought Shelby her cloak. The girls came scampering down the stairs, and they left the townhouse, headed for Hyde Park, which was nearby. Sylvia prattled on until they reached their destination and then asked if they could walk along the Serpentine.

"I find walking by the water to be soothing," he said. "I think it an excellent idea."

The girls ran ahead, Sylvia claiming Fanny's hand, and he said to Shelby, "They accepted Della well, didn't they? I thought they would ask more about her parents and where she came from."

"Children are good about accepting what you tell them. When they are older, you can decide whether or not you wish to share with them Lady Della's origins. I did note that you have called her Lady Della."

"She is the daughter of an earl and my niece," he said firmly.

"I do not believe anyone will question the word of a duke. I will introduce her as Lady Della—and she will be accepted that way."

"I think I will join the girls now," Shelby said. "If you would, Jasper, hang back a bit. Let me get to know them without you hovering nearby. I know you are protective of them, but I want to see if they will open up to me. And see if I can get Fanny to say a word."

"I hope you can," he said fervently "She is a sweet child. She has always been a bit shy, while Sylvia has been outgoing. I hate that Fanny is locked into a world of her own making. If you can free her from it, Shelby, that will be a true blessing."

"I will do my best," she promised. "I think it will take more than one conversation, but I am hoping now to begin build trust between us."

Jasper watched her move toward his nieces and said a prayer, asking God to use Shelby as His instrument in bringing Fanny back to the world.

CHAPTER ELEVEN

SHELBY CAUGHT UP with Sylvia and Fanny, who walked hand in hand. As she approached, she heard Sylvia say, "I'm glad we have a cousin. You're going to have to teach her to draw, Fanny. I can't draw a bit."

"You like to draw, Lady Fanny?" she asked, making sure she moved to Sylvia's side in order to give Fanny some space.

The girl met Shelby's eyes and nodded. Ah, a first. Acknowledging a question. Not with words—but it was a start.

"I also like to draw," she said. "Now sing?" She laughed. "You would *not* want to hear me ever sing. You would cover your ears and run away."

Sylvia giggled—and so did Fanny. It was the first sound the girl had made.

"I think you are just saying that, Miss Slade," Sylvia said. "No one could sound that bad."

"You think not?"

Shelby cleared her throat and then began singing, loudly and terribly off-key. This time, both girls burst into giggles.

"Shall I go on, my lady? Or do you believe me now?"

"That's awful," Sylvia declared. "I can sing very well. Fanny, too, when she wants to."

"Oh, I would love to hear you both sing. I appreciate a good voice. I just don't have one."

By now, Sylvia had taken Shelby's hand as they walked along the path next to the Serpentine. The older girl began singing and after a verse and chorus of the song, which Shelby was unfamiliar with, Fanny joined in. Faint. But she sang. Sylvia continued the song, and Fanny's voice grew slightly in volume. A thrill shot through Shelby.

The song ended, and Sylvia did not acknowledge her sister had joined in. The older girl began talking about her favorite foods and why she liked spelling so much. While Shelby listened to the older girl, she kept a careful eye on Fanny.

"My favorite food is blancmange, but I like sweets of any kind. Tarts. Cakes. Do you like sweets?" she asked.

"Mama didn't let us eat sweets often," Sylvia said. "Cook did always make us a cake on our birthday, though. I like apple cake."

She let a few seconds pass and then asked, "What is your favorite sweet, Lady Fanny?"

"Tarts," the girl said with no hesitation. "Apple and peach."

Since Sylvia did not react to her sister's speaking, Shelby suspected Fanny was at least doing some talking, only not around any adults.

"I adore tarts myself," she said. "Strawberry and pear are my favorites. Perhaps we could ask Cook to make some tarts for us when we return."

They stopped to look at some ducks which had landed on the water, talking the entire time, and when they started up again, Fanny took one of Shelby's hands and Sylvia the other. She continued asking them questions, with Sylvia doing the majority of the talking but Fanny making a contribution to the conversation here and there, if only a word or so.

Finally, she glanced over her shoulder and nodded to Jasper, who picked up his pace and joined them.

"What have you ladies been discussing?" he asked.

"We've talked about food and which dolls are our favorites," Sylvia said. "And Miss Slade is going to take us to a bookstore soon. And tarts."

"Tarts?"

"We all like tarts," Shelby said. "The girls and I think we would like to ask Cook to make some tarts for our tea today. Perhaps you would like to join us, Your Grace."

He smiled. "Well, if tarts are a part of tea then I certainly am interested. We shall all have tea together in the schoolroom."

"Will Grandmama come?" Sylvia asked and Shelby noticed Fanny's nose wrinkled slightly at the idea.

"I doubt it," Jasper said. "Unless you want her to come."

"No," said Fanny emphatically, the one word ringing in the air.

"Then it will just be us. And Miss Hall if you'd like her to join us."

"Why don't we give Miss Hall a bit of time to herself?" Shelby suggested. "Even servants like to visit with their friends over tea. She can go to the kitchens while we stay in the schoolroom. For now, though, you have been away from your lessons too long. Your Grace, I suggest we return to the house. Sylvia is eager to learn more words today."

"I learned how to spell bamboozle and chatterbox yesterday, Uncle Jasper," Sylvia said proudly. "Miss Hall teaches me what the word means and then how to spell it. I love interesting words." She took her uncle's hand. "I wonder what new words Miss Hall will have for me today."

"I have one for you," he said. "Cornucopia. Ask Miss Hall what it is, and then you can spell it for us at tea today." He glanced to Fanny. "And Fanny will spell gibberish and let us know what it means."

In response, Fanny grinned shyly at her uncle.

They left the park and returned to Mayfair. As the girls were admitted by Bowen, Jasper turned to Shelby.

"Let us go to my study, Miss Slade," Jasper said formally. "And Bowen, I am expecting Mr. Roberts to return again today, as well as a few applicants to be interviewed for the position of nursemaid to Lady Della."

"Yes, Your Grace," the butler said. "I will let you know when they have arrived."

Shelby handed her cloak to Bowen, and Watson appeared to take Jasper's. She would need to talk to both these servants but could not be obvious about it. Perhaps tomorrow when the servants took their tea, Shelby could join them. For now, though, she was looking forward to their teatime with the girls later today.

She followed Jasper into his study, and he closed the door, beaming at her.

Placing his hands on her shoulders, he said, "You have worked a small miracle. I heard Fanny singing softly. Singing! And I couldn't hear her speak since I was so far behind you, but the way you and Sylvia reacted, I thought Fanny did say a few words. And then that loud *no* which came from her!"

His hands touching her brought a delicious sensation. It began rippling through her. Shelby swallowed, trying to formulate a response and think of Jasper as her client.

And not the man she longed to kiss . . .

"She did speak some. I think Fanny has been speaking to Sylvia all along because Sylvia did not seem surprised in the least when Fanny spoke. But we must take it slowly."

"Slowly," he repeated, his gaze suddenly burning as he looked at her.

Something shifted between them. The air seemed to crackle. Her insides churned. His fingers tightened.

"Shelby?" he murmured.

"Yes?" she said breathily.

"I . . . I . . ." His voice trailed off even as his fingers began kneading her.

"Jasper," she said unsteadily, her voice soft, her tone uncertain.

Then he lowered his head, and she closed her eyes. Hoping. Praying.

That he would kiss her.

His lips touched hers. It was as if fire burst from the contact. Desire drenched her. The heat of his moving fingers—and now his lips moving on hers—consumed her. While she had been kissed before, those kisses paled in comparison. This one was hard. Demanding. Possessive.

Her arms went about his waist, and he yanked her to him, her body colliding with the firm muscles of his chest. His hands slid from her shoulders to her face, cradling it, his thumbs moving sensually against her skin, spreading the fire.

Jasper eased her mouth open and caught her by surprise, his tongue slipping into her mouth, stroking hers. No man had ever kissed her in this manner.

Her gut told her no other man ever would.

Blinded by need, she answered his call. Her tongue began mating with his and soon warred with it. But there were no winners or losers in this battle. Only the delicious sensations that now rippled through her limbs, calling out for more. His hand cradled her nape and tugged, tilting her head, giving him better access. The kiss deepened as want—need—caused her to quiver.

Then a knock sounded, and they sprang apart so quickly, Shelby almost fell. She had lost her anchor, and she quickly twirled, gripping his desk in one hand and picking up a page with her other, pretending to study it as the door opened.

"Your Grace, Mr. Roberts is here, as well as one of the candidates from the employment agency.

"Send in Roberts first, Bowen. I would speak with him first."

"Yes, Your Grace."

She fought to keep her breathing even, not daring to look up, continuing to stare at the page before her.

Jasper touched her elbow, and she turned. His blue eyes burned with heat as he looked at her.

"Take a seat over next to the globe," he ordered.

Shelby set down the page and moved quickly to the chair, perching on its edge, her heart still hammering against her ribs. She licked her lips and heard a groan.

"And try not to do that," Jasper chastised.

She didn't know what she had done wrong. She still had no idea how the kiss began between them or why she had let it continue. The Duke of Edgehaven was a client. She could not jeopardize the agency losing him as one. Shelby decided she must ask Mr. F to replace her with another agent. It would be easy to do so. Plenty of good ones would do.

"Mr. Roberts, Your Grace," the butler said.

"Ah, Mr. Roberts," Jasper said. "Do come have a seat." He gestured to the group of chairs she sat in and did her best to collect herself.

Rising, Jasper introduced them, saying, "This is Miss Slade, my current secretary."

Shelby nodded to Mr. Roberts and Jasper took a seat, indicating for them to do the same.

"Miss Slade will be leaving in a couple of months' time, which is why I am now looking for her replacement. I would like that to be you, Mr. Roberts."

"I am flattered, Your Grace," said the man, who looked to be in his early thirties, with dark hair, brown eyes, and a pleasing manner. "But I am afraid I must—"

"Of course, I understand you might be seeking immediate employment. Since I believe you to be such a good candidate for this post, I am willing to pay you, starting immediately."

Confusion filled Mr. Roberts' eyes. "I beg pardon, Your Grace?"

"It is not right for me to have you wait about, not earning a pound, while you do so. I have not been Edgehaven long, you see. I was a clergyman until recently and know exactly what living hand to mouth entails. While I received compensation for my services, a country parish does not provide much. I even grew my own vegetables."

Jasper paused. "Because I am in a different position now, I am capable of placing you on salary, Mr. Roberts, and will do so immediately if you choose to take this position."

Flabbergasted, Mr. Roberts said, "But I cannot have you paying me for doing no work, Your Grace."

"Are you willing to come to work in my household?" Jasper pressed. "If so, I do have an assignment for you."

Shelby had been ready to volunteer that she was leaving earlier than His Grace had first thought. Now, though, she kept silent, curious as to what Jasper would offer this man.

"Since I am new to the dukedom, I need a thorough inventory of all my properties. I have six total, five of which I have never seen, the other being Edgehill, where I grew up. I would like to send you to these five estates I am unfamiliar with, Mr. Roberts. Have you meet with each steward, as well as the household's butler and housekeeper. Take meticulous, copious notes regarding everything you see. You would be my eyes and ears, Mr. Roberts, allowing me to learn all I could about each of these properties before I ever visit them."

Mr. Roberts nodded eagerly. "I would be most happy to do so, Your Grace. I could review the ledgers with the stewards and see how the crops and livestock are doing. Meet with the tenants and compose a list of them and their needs. Do the same with the household staff. I could tour the house and see if any improvements or changes are due to be made and even prioritize those for you."

"That sounds most thorough, Mr. Roberts," Jasper said, a pleased smile lighting his handsome face. "Could you venture a guess how long this might take?"

"Not knowing where your estates lie, I cannot estimate the travel at this point. I do believe I would need to be at each one at least a week at the minimum. Two weeks would be better."

"It is mid-January now. If you visit each estate for two weeks, including travel, that would take us to the end of March or beginning of April. At that time, the Season would be about to begin. I would need you here for it. Do you believe you could accomplish your task in that amount of time? Of course, I can have you come with me to Edgehill and do the same after the

Season concludes since I am already familiar with that property. I would still like to have those lists you mentioned regarding Edgehill, all the same."

"I would be honored to enter your employ, Your Grace," said Mr. Roberts, confidence in his voice. "I can leave as soon as you need me to. I have no family and therefore, no arrangements I would need to make regarding them during my absence."

"Then I will write the letters today which will introduce you to those who run each property. I think it best to rent a post chaise to the first destination. Miss Slade will compose a list of each property and its location. Return here tomorrow morning for it and the introductory letters. You can present those as you arrive each time. I think it wise not to give any forewarnings. That way, you will gain a true picture of how things operate when I am not present. Once you reach an estate and then finish your business there, you can be driven to the nearest village and take a mail coach to the next property."

Jasper then named a salary, causing Shelby to have a bit of envy. She didn't make nearly that much as a runner. What Mr. Roberts was doing was easily something she herself could have done. Then again, she doubted any nob would hire a woman to do a job usually assumed by a man, no matter how capable that female might be.

"What if I leave earlier than expected, Your Grace?" she tossed out.

He turned and smiled at her. "I can manage on my own for a bit, Miss Slade, if that were the case. I would like Mr. Roberts to complete this project for me and then return to London."

Jasper rose, the two of them following suit. He offered the new secretary his hand, and they shook.

"I cannot thank you enough, Your Grace," Roberts said.

"You quite impressed me yesterday, Mr. Roberts. I merely needed to sleep on the matter. I will see you tomorrow morning, say nine o'clock?"

"I will be here, Your Grace. Good day."

Needing to put some distance between her and Jasper and have time for thinking about what had occurred between them, she said, "I will accompany you as you leave, Mr. Roberts. I will need to rent your post chaise and might as well do so now since His Grace has another position he will be interviewing for today."

Jasper frowned at her. "I thought you might do that hiring, Miss Slade."

"No, it is your niece, Your Grace. You should be the one to hire the proper nursemaid. I will return in time for tea, however."

He frowned. "Join me when you do return, Miss Slade."

"I also have a few errands to run on your behalf, Your Grace," she said firmly. "I will see you at teatime—and not before." She turned and said, "Come along, Mr. Roberts. We have taken up enough of His Grace's time."

Shelby knew Jasper was angry at her, but she didn't care. She accompanied Mr. Roberts to the foyer, calling for her cloak, and said, "I will have the list of properties readied for you, sir, along with the names of the staff members you will be dealing with. Bring your bags with you when you come tomorrow morning for you will be leaving shortly thereafter."

"Yes, Miss Slade. Thank you so much. I am sorry to hear you are leaving His Grace's employ but feel I am most fortunate to be stepping into your shoes."

"You will do well, Mr. Roberts. His Grace is a good man to work for."

Bowen brought both her cloak and Mr. Roberts' coat. They shrugged into their winter wear and left the house together, with Shelby bidding the man good day. She went to the closest stables which rented post chaises and booked one for Mr. Roberts, informing the owner that it would need to be at the Duke of Edgehaven's residence by nine o'clock the following morning. The man did not question her request. Usually, a customer came to the post chaise—and not the vehicle to its riders. Dukes, however, made their own rules.

She then went to a street vendor and bought a meat pie,

taking it to a nearby bench and sitting. As she ate, she debated on how to tell Mr. F that another agent would be needed to replace her. She worried, though, that rumors might start if she abandoned the case. Bow Street Runners were trained to seek out information. She had learned they could also be ferocious gossips. With her being the sole female agent, she could not afford to be the object of that kind of gossip.

Determination filled her. She would see this case to its end.

And make certain she never kissed the Duke of Edgehaven again.

CHAPTER TWELVE

JASPER INTERVIEWED THREE prospective nursemaids in a row. They all seemed capable of caring for a child. He thanked each one of them, saying he would be in contact with the employment agency regarding his choice. By the time the third one had left, he couldn't have named a single one of the women.

Because he had been distracted the entire time he had talked to them.

Why in God's name had he kissed Shelby?

More importantly, why had he waited so long to do so?

It had been years since he had kissed a woman. He hadn't forgotten how to do it. What had surprised him was how different kissing Shelby was than any previous paramour. She tasted different. Felt different. Responded different.

And he knew now that he'd had a forbidden taste of her, his appetite could not be whetted until he had more of her.

Much more.

He blinked, startled by the strong feelings rushing through him. Dare he ask if they might indicate love?

No, it was impossible. Love didn't spring magically to life.

Or did it?

He shoved aside all thoughts of Shelby Slade and took out his writing supplies, dashing off the same, brief note to each steward and ones which mirrored it to all his various butlers and housekeepers. He knew enough about servants to know that if he only wrote to the butlers, the housekeepers would feel left out, even if oftentimes they were married to the butler. In each letter, he introduced Mr. Roberts as his new secretary and asked that the staff members cooperate and provide Roberts with whatever he asked for during his stay. He concluded with saying that the information gathered by his secretary would be carefully read in order to help him gain a clearer picture of the estates he had inherited and ended with a promise that he still would visit as soon as he could manage.

After it had been determined whether or not his father or brother had been murdered, of course. And once that information was ascertained and he spoke to Shelby of marriage between them, they might make a honeymoon of visiting the various properties to familiarize themselves with his holdings.

He was getting ahead of himself. First, Shelby needed to come home and allow him to apologize to her. One step at a time.

He sealed each of the letters and left them on his desk, along with a list of his estates and their locations. Shelby couldn't prepare such a list because she didn't know anything about their names or counties. He hoped Roberts never asked him about her work. He doubted the man would, suspecting Roberts to be a most proper sort and never one to question his employer, especially since that employer was a duke. Besides, if Jasper wed Shelby as he planned to do, Roberts would never entertain the thought of asking private questions about the new Duchess of Edgehaven.

Restless, he stood and paced about the room and was still doing so when Shelby knocked and entered. Relief filled him as she closed the door and came toward him.

"I have arranged for the post chaise to come here to pick up Mr. Roberts tomorrow morning." Her brows rose. "It is only because you are a duke that I was able to come to such an arrangement. Have you written the letters for—"

"Yes, I have done all that and interviewed three women who all seemed the same to me. Shelby, I am—"

"I think it would be best if we returned to a more formal arrangement, Your Grace," she said smoothly.

"You are angry with me."

"No. More upset with you and angry at myself," she admitted. "I should not have allowed you to kiss me, much less let it go on for so long."

"Perhaps you were enjoying it?" he ventured.

Her lips thinned. "Whether or not I did, it was highly inappropriate and will not be repeated, Your Grace. You are a client. I am the agent fielding your case. It is my reputation on the line. I will find the answers to the questions you seek and then leave. Have you a list of your properties and their locations?"

"I have already written that out for Roberts," he told her.

"It should be in my hand." She moved to the desk and picked up the single page. "Yes, I will copy it now."

She seated herself and did so. Jasper stood at the window and looked out, stealing surreptitious glances at her as she concentrated.

"There," she said, standing, taking what he assumed was his list and tearing it into pieces before placing it in a bin next to the desk. "This way, Mr. Roberts will not have any questions."

She reached for the stack of papers on the desk and thumbed through them, nodding to herself as she read. For a moment, she bit her bottom lip, lost in thought, and desire flooded him.

Setting aside all but one page, she brought it to him. "This is the nursemaid you should hire for Lady Della. Shall I write to the agency and send the message straightaway?"

"Yes, please," he said, eager to watch her at work again.

Once more, she sat at his desk and scribbled on a page before folding it. Using his sealing wax, she said, "Come here, Your Grace, and use your signet ring to emboss the seal."

He did as she asked as she rang for a footman.

"See this delivered at once to this address."

"Yes, Miss Slade."

The footman left, and Jasper said, "I haven't kissed anyone for a long time."

His words startled her, but she recovered quickly. "Is that so?"

"Yes. Since my university days. I knew I was to become a member of the clergy and so . . . well, I took advantage of my freedom while I had it. Sowed a few wild oats, so to speak. Once I began my training, however, I never touched another woman. Until today. I am sorry that—"

"Don't tell me you are sorry when I know you are not," she said, anger flashing in her eyes. "You aren't sorry regarding the kiss. Frankly, neither am I. It was a most pleasurable experience, but one we must put behind us. I am here to investigate suspicions you have. I will do that and give you my report."

He bit back a smile.

She had liked his kiss . . .

"In the meantime, it is time to go to the schoolroom for tea. I informed Bowen when I returned to the house that we would be taking it there with your nieces."

Jasper chuckled. "I never would have thought to do so. Thank you for thinking of it. You actually would make for a very good secretary, Shelby. You are efficient and organized."

"It will be the last time we do so, Your Grace," she said stiffly. "I need to draw firm lines between us. Yes, I will do my best to get what information I can out of your nieces, but it will not be while you are around."

He wouldn't apologize again because she didn't want to hear it. And he wouldn't mean it. Jasper had never liked an insincere apology and wouldn't start spouting them now.

"Then we should go up to the schoolroom," he said, moving toward the door.

They arrived as Miss Hall was finishing up a lesson. The governess said, "I will be back at five o'clock for us to do our reading together, my ladies."

She left the room as the tea trays arrived, carried by two maids, under Mrs. Bowen's supervision.

As the maids set down the trays, Sylvia said, "I can now spell cornucopia, Uncle Jasper. I also know what it is." Clearing her throat, she said, "I was amazed at the cornucopia of fruits, vegetables, and fish for sale when we arrived at the market." Smiling brightly, Sylvia asked, "How was that?"

"Excellent," he praised. "Would you pour out for us, Miss Slade?"

"Of course, Your Grace."

Shelby asked the girls if they wished for tea. Sylvia did, saying she liked plenty of sugar and milk in hers. Fanny merely shook her head.

"She drinks milk," Sylvia said of her sister. "When I was six, I still drank milk at tea. I am nine now. How old are you, Miss Slade?"

"That is not a polite question, Sylvia," Jasper chided.

"Why not? Adults are always asking me my age, Uncle. I was merely curious."

Shelby stirred the tea and handed the saucer to Sylvia. "I hope this is satisfactory, my lady. As for my age, I am seven and twenty."

"Oh. You are old like Uncle Jasper."

"I am only thirty years of age," he protested. "That doesn't seem old to me at all." Glancing to Shelby, he added, "Neither does seven and twenty."

"Well, I think it's terribly old," his niece said. "When I am that age, I will have been married for many years and have loads of children."

"Unless you are like Mama," Fanny said quietly before taking a sip of her milk.

His gaze met Shelby's, and she shook her head imperceptibly, telling him not to draw attention to the fact that his niece had just uttered her first sentence in front of him since the death of her father.

"Ah, I see we do have tarts," Shelby proclaimed. "Cook said she would bake apple and peach ones for us."

"Thank you for asking Cook, Miss Slade," Sylvia said. "I thought you would have forgotten."

"I have quite a decent memory, my lady." Shelby grinned. "And a taste for tarts myself."

The three females laughed and Jasper supposed it was due to something they had spoken of earlier.

They enjoyed a pleasant teatime. Shelby told the girls of some of the many museums in London, and Jasper was able to chime in and talk about exhibits he had seen at some of them, one of his favorite pastimes done with his father.

"Why don't we ever go to museums?" Sylvia complained.

"Well, it was something I did with my father, not my governess or tutor," he said. "Perhaps it is something you and Fanny might wish to do with me during our months spent in London each year."

He watched a smile turn up the corners of Fanny's mouth.

"Yes!" Sylvia cried. "And Miss Slade can go with us. She's ever so much fun."

"But I have work to do for His Grace," Shelby said lightly. "It will be a fun outing for the three of you."

Fanny began shaking her head vigorously.

"You have something to say, Fanny?" Shelby asked.

The girl looked up, her eyes pleading. Jasper couldn't stand it.

"You don't have so much work that you cannot accompany us to a museum every now and then, Miss Slade."

Her gaze met his. "Certainly, Your Grace. I would be happy to go on any outing with you and your nieces."

Fanny nodded, pleased at what she had heard. She picked up a tart and bit into it. "Mmm."

The fact she felt comfortable enough to make even that small sound gave him hope that she would speak as she once had. Shelby's presence made a difference. Fanny was more relaxed around the Bow Street Runner.

Bowen appeared at the schoolroom's door. "Your Grace, the nursemaid has arrived. I thought you should know. Mrs. Bowen had the woman's things brought up and placed in the room next to the nursery."

"Thank you, Bowen. I will come and see her and Lady Della at the same time."

"I want to go, too, Uncle Jasper," Sylvia said, blotting her lips with her napkin and coming to her feet.

When Fanny didn't move, Shelby said, "Lady Fanny and I will stay here and eat some more tarts. In fact, there may not be any left by the time you return," she said flippantly.

That caused Fanny to giggle.

"Come along, Sylvia."

They went down the hallway and into the nursery. Jasper recognized the woman now holding Della as the second of those who had come to the house this morning.

"Thank you for coming so swiftly, Nanny," he addressed her, not recalling her name and thinking he had never heard a nursemaid called by her name, just as Cook had always been known as Cook.

"I am so pleased to be here, Your Grace," the woman said. "I can tell Lady Della has an even temper and is a sweet babe."

"I got to hold her," Sylvia bragged.

"Did you now?"

"This is my oldest niece, Lady Sylvia. She and her sister, Lady Fanny, reside with me, as does Lady Della."

They stayed in the nursery a few minutes and then returned to the schoolroom.

Shelby and Fanny were nowhere in sight.

CHAPTER THIRTEEN

THE MINUTE JASPER and Sylvia had left the schoolroom, Fanny turned to Shelby and asked, "Do you want to see my dolls?"

Keeping her face relaxed, Shelby said, "I would be delighted to. I never had any dolls when I was your age."

"No dolls?" Fanny asked, her brow furrowed quizzically.

"No. I had no toys. We were very poor and had no money to spend on such things. It is nice you have them to play with, though. Let's go see them."

Shelby followed the six-year-old girl from the schoolroom, hoping she would open up more since the two of them were now alone. They went through a connecting door, and she saw it was a bedchamber with two beds, each the perfect size for a child. Fanny moved to the bed on the right, where two dolls were propped against the pillows. Picking up one, Fanny handed it to Shelby.

"Oh, she is very pretty. Does she have a name?"

The girl nodded but did not reveal what the doll was called. Instead, she picked up the other one and hugged it tightly to her.

"You are very fortunate to have two dolls to play with, my lady. Why, they could even have conversations with one another if you wanted to let them do so."

Shelby extended a hand, hoping Fanny would hand over the other doll, which she did. Holding one in each hand, she had the dolls face one another and begin a conversation between them.

"Hello, how are you?" she said in one voice.

Then pitching her voice slightly higher, she had the other doll reply. "I am well. How are you?"

"I am sad today. I had a dog. He was my friend. He died."

"Oh, I am sorry to hear you are sad about your dog. Can I make you feel better?"

Shelby had the doll nod to the other one. "I want to talk about my dog. His name was Brownie. He was my best friend and went everywhere with me. Now, I don't have a best friend anymore."

"I am not a dog—but I would like to be your friend."

Then Shelby brought the dolls together and let them hug one another. She then handed both dolls back to Fanny and said, "Your dolls can say whatever they are feeling to one another. Or you. *You* can also talk to your dolls and tell them how you are feeling. If you are mad. Glad. Sad." She paused. "Would you like to try?"

Fanny held the dolls to her and shook her head. Shelby did not want to press the child. Already, enough progress had been made today by Fanny speaking some in Shelby's presence.

"Why don't you stay here and play with your dolls until Miss Hall returns for your reading time?"

The girl nodded, and Shelby added, "I hope to see you again tomorrow, my lady. Perhaps we might go for a walk in the park again."

Fanny's face lit with a smile, and Shelby saw one day the girl would mature into a very beautiful woman.

She left the girls' bedchamber and returned to the schoolroom. Alone now, her thoughts turned to Jasper again.

And that kiss . . .

She hoped that she had made the boundaries between them clear, and yet at the same time, she wanted to dismantle the wall she had erected and kiss him again. Do more than kiss him, actually. The kisses she had shared with previous men had done nothing to stir her blood. Shelby knew she was playing with fire and yet wondered what it would be like to couple with Jasper. Perhaps he would be willing to do so after she had completed her investigation. Only once, though. She couldn't let him steal her heart.

Even though she knew she was lying to herself. Because Jasper already had. She hoped at least she could find the answers he sought and give him closure about the deaths of his father and brother. If something more personal occurred between them after the investigation concluded, then she told herself it would merely satisfy her curiosity about what happened between a man and a woman.

As she sipped the remainder of her tea, Miss Hall entered the schoolroom and asked, "Where is everyone?"

"The new nursemaid arrived and His Grace and Lady Sylvia went to meet her and introduce her to Lady Della. Lady Fanny is in her room, playing with her dolls."

A shadow crossed the governess' face. "I simply do not know how to reach Lady Fanny," Miss Hall admitted. "She has always been a reserved child but since being found next to her father's lifeless body, the girl has not said a word."

"She is talking some," Shelby revealed. "I heard her say a few words today to her sister. Lady Sylvia did not seem surprised by it so I gather that when the girls are alone, Lady Fanny does speak. At least sometimes."

Miss Hall brightened. "Well, that is wonderful news! I thought the shock of seeing her father in such a state had totally meant speech had fled her. Thank you for letting me know about this, Miss Slade. Perhaps as women, we might not be as threatening to Lady Fanny. Hopefully since she has opened up to her sister, we might be the next people she speaks to."

"I hope you are right, Miss Hall. Lady Fanny did take me to see her dolls, and I told her when she played with them, she could always talk about her feelings to them."

"A wise suggestion, Miss Slade. Again, I thank you. For now, though, I will fetch Lady Fanny and begin our daily reading."

When the governess and Fanny returned to the schoolroom, Jasper and Sylvia did, as well.

"It is time for our reading now," Miss Hall informed them.

Sylvia looked to her uncle. "Miss Hall likes to read to us, but sometimes we read to her. Would you stay a bit, Uncle Jasper? And listen to us read?"

"I would be happy to do so," he told Sylvia, his eyes flicking to Shelby.

"I believe we have concluded our business of the day, Your Grace," she told him. "I will see you tomorrow morning."

Leaving the schoolroom, Shelby was grateful not to spend any more time alone with the duke today. Jasper—no, His Grace—most likely would press her on the matter of their kiss. She needed to start thinking of him as a duke and not a man who had happened to kiss her. He was a client of Bow Street and one of the highest peers of the realm. She would treat him accordingly. Nothing personal could take place between them.

Because if it did, it would give her hope. Hope of a future together with a man she was totally unsuited to be with. Wouldn't the *ton* have a laugh at her expense if they knew for a second she had entertained a future with a duke?

She went down the staircases to the ground floor and heard a loud, sharp voice as she reached the foyer. Immediately, Shelby spied a woman who looked to be in her mid-fifties. She was still quite handsome and dressed elegantly in a gown of pale moss, jewels at her ears and wrist.

"Am I not informed of anything that occurs in this household any longer?" she berated Bowen.

The butler's expression was pained as he said, "What would you like to know about, Your Grace?"

His address—and the woman's biting tone—confirmed to Shelby that this was Jasper's mother. Shelby had often thought a person's true nature was revealed in the way they treated others, especially their servants. Her immediate impression of the

Duchess of Edgehaven was that of a woman of superior rank who never let anyone forget that fact.

"You know what I speak of, Bowen," the duchess said harshly. "Why should I have to learn that a child had been brought into this house—*my house*—by a parlor maid, of all people?" She sniffed. "This is most unacceptable. Who is this child? And why was she brought here without my knowledge, much less my consent?"

By now, Shelby was thoroughly irritated at the woman's behavior, duchess or not, and spoke up.

"I believe it is His Grace's residence, Your Grace, and therefore the duke may have whomever he wishes reside within its walls."

The older woman wheeled, looking Shelby up and down, judging her instantly.

"And who might *you* be?" she asked haughtily. "Another addition to my household?"

She closed the distance between them and with a slight nod indicated for Bowen to leave them. The butler slipped away, the duchess' attention focused totally on Shelby.

"I am Miss Slade, the new secretary to His Grace since the previous one retired due to his ill heath last year."

Shock filled the old woman's face, and then her eyes narrowed. "A *woman*?" she asked, her derision obvious. "I know of no women who serve as a duke's secretary. You must be some trollop my son has hired under the guise of secretary."

Anger flooded Shelby, and she knew her cheeks burned in humiliation. "I resent your accusation, Your Grace." She knew this woman wished for her to back down.

Something Shelby had never been willing to do.

"You are besmirching not only my reputation but that of your son's. His Grace is a good man, a former man of the cloth, and if you knew him better you would know he is not one to bring a light o' love into his household, much less even have one."

The duchess gasped loudly. "My, but aren't you a bold missy?" she declared. "Do you know anything of this babe who now resides under this roof?"

Shelby grinned to herself, the duchess having said *this* roof instead of *her* room.

"That is a family affair, and one in which I recommend you take up with His Grace."

"Oh, I will do so, Missy. I will tell him what an insufferable, rude woman you are. That you should be dismissed outright, given no references."

"You may say whatever you wish to His Grace, but I will remain in my current post until *I* choose to leave the position."

A garbled sound came from the duchess, one of outrage and disbelief.

"How dare you speak to me in such a brazen manner. You are a no one, while I am a *duchess*."

"Simply because you are a duchess does not mean you should treat anyone with disrespect, especially one your own son has retained. His Grace is an intelligent, kind gentleman. Still, he is not one to suffer fools readily. If I were not suited for the position, he would never have hired me."

"What is going on?" a deep voice asked.

Both women turned to see the duke moving down the stairs.

"I want this woman gone, Edgehaven! And an explanation for what child you have brought here to live without my permission."

"As far as Miss Slade goes, she is my secretary to hire—or fire, Mama. Miss Slade is most capable. I have no reason to dismiss her."

Disbelief flooded the duchess' face. "She has been extremely rude to me, Edgehaven. Such behavior surely must be punished."

"I have only know Miss Slade a short while, but I do not believe she has it in her to be rude to anyone. Firm? Yes, I can see that. If you were the one being rude to her, then I am certain she let you know that."

"I will not be spoken to like this in my own household, Edge-haven. By you or this . . . creature."

"I shouldn't have to point out that it is my house, Mama, and you live here simply because of my goodwill. If I choose to do so, I can send you to the country for your entire mourning period."

"And miss the Season? You wouldn't dare do that to me, Edgehaven."

"Then do not test me further, Mama. As for the babe who is in the nursery, come to my study, and we will discuss the matter in privacy." He looked to Shelby. "You, too, Miss Slade, are invited."

Reluctantly, she followed the pair to his study and closed the door behind her. Shelby hovered near it, not taking a seat, thinking it wise to merely be an observer of the upcoming conversation, which would no doubt grow heated.

The duke motioned for his mother to take a seat, and she did so. He took a place across from her.

"I have learned that Sutton was conducting an affair, Mama. During the last two years of his life, when he was still married to Mary. A child was conceived, and Sutton promised the mother that he would care for it. When Miss Slade and I went to visit this woman yesterday, her labor pains began."

He paused and then added, "The mother did not survive the birth."

The duchess sniffed. "Do not tell me. Another female, I'm certain, if Sutton was the sire."

Shelby thought it interesting how the duchess did not seem overly fond of her firstborn.

"Yes," the duke confirmed. "I named her Adele, after her mother, but have chosen to call her Della. *Lady* Della," he emphasized.

Horror filled the duchess' face. "No. You cannot bring her up next to Sylvia and Fanny. I won't have it, Edgehaven. It simply won't do."

"Della is my niece, as much as the other two are, Mama. She

will be called Lady Della, and I will be guardian to her as I am to Sylvia and Fanny. You have no say-so in this matter."

"Sutton was such a fool. He would have made for a terrible duke." She paused, her gaze burning into her son. "But you are not turning out to be much better," she complained. "I always thought you level-headed, thinking matters through before acting. This sudden decision to take in a bastard child and raise her alongside your legitimate nieces is unthinkable."

The old woman glanced to Shelby. "As is hiring a female to act as your secretary. Tongues will wag, Edgehaven. The gossip will be that you have hired some woman of easy virtue under the guise of your secretary and have her living under your roof."

The duke looked coolly at his mother. "For your information, Miss Slade has chosen not to move into my household. She will merely report for duty each morning. As for gossip, I cannot stop what others think or say about me. Of course, Mama *you* could try to quell any gossip that falls upon your ears. After all, am I not your favorite? Your only living son?"

The duchess' fingers flew to her temples, and she pressed against them. "I feel a megrim coming on. All this has been too much, Edgehaven, even for you. Send for Dr. Barton at once."

The duchess left the room, and Shelby said, "I will see that Bowen sends for the doctor. Good evening, Your Grace."

She left the study, now seeing what the duke had meant. His mother was a most foul-tempered woman, incredibly unpleasant to be around. The former duke had probably considered death a blessing, being able to escape from the woman he had called wife.

Bowen had returned to the foyer, and she told the butler, "It seems as if Her Grace is suffering from a megrim. She wishes for Dr. Barton to call and minister to her. I will be leaving for the evening."

"Shall I call for a hansom cab for you, Miss Slade? It is already dark."

"No, thank you, Bowen. I have been taking care of myself for a long time. Just send a footman for the doctor if you would."

The butler fetched her cloak and handed it to her. "Thank you for stepping in and distracting Her Grace, Miss Slade."

"You shouldn't have to suffer her tirades."

Bowen gasped.

"I will make certain that His Grace knows of the abysmal treatment and sees it corrected."

"Miss Slade!" the butler said.

"No, Bowen, Her Grace has gotten away with mistreating others for far too long. Perhaps her husband saw no reason to rein her in, but I will venture her son will have success in doing so. Goodnight."

With that, Shelby flung her cloak about her shoulders and sailed through the door the footman opened for her, leaving both servants dumbstruck.

CHAPTER FOURTEEN

Jasper sat as Watson tied the cravat. He had to admit that the valet did a much better job of taking care of Jasper than he ever had himself.

He had spent a restless night, sleep coming in fits. He still worried about being a duke and if would ever live up to his father's legacy. He fretted over having his mother about, living in the same household with her now. He wondered if Fanny would finally start speaking again and how his brother's death had affected his two children.

Most of all, Jasper was anxious about his relationship with Shelby and the fact he had kissed her too soon. The kiss itself told him that there was something raw and real between them, but he chastised himself for taking the opportunity to kiss her before she was ready. Jasper had intended to let them get to know one another more. Let her complete her interviews and investigation and hopefully set his mind at ease regarding the recent deaths in his family. Only then was he supposed to have broached the subject with her of a possible future together.

Now, thanks to his rash action, he had driven a wedge between them. The lighthearted friendship that had begun to bud between them was no more. In its place was nothing more than a business relationship.

And he feared once that business was complete, Shelby would

move on and never speak to him again.

"There you go, Your Grace," said Watson, a smile on his face. "You are ready to take on the day. There won't be a man at White's turned out as well as you."

He had shared with the valet that he was supposed to go to White's this morning with Lord Darrow, who had sent him a note late yesterday, asking if he could take Jasper to the club in order to help him set up in his membership. He had sent his own reply, asking the earl to breakfast with him before they made their way to London's most exclusive gentlemen's establishment, knowing that Shelby wished to speak with Lord Darrow to get a clearer picture of Jasper's father.

"Thank you, Watson. I have never been blessed with the skill to tie a proper cravat."

"Oh, it takes practice, Your Grace," Watson told him. "Might I ask when your next fitting at the tailor's is? Once you have your new wardrobe, you will be the envy of the gentlemen of the *ton*. You cut a fine figure already but in your ducal clothes, you will have no peer who comes near you."

Drat, he had no idea when he was supposed to return to the tailor. Jasper was usually so good with details. At least he had been when he was a mere clergyman. He knew the names of all his parishioners. Who was expecting babes. Who had purchased a new pig or if cat had its litter of kittens. As a duke, it seemed he had so much to learn and remember that everything fled his mind. He was unsure of himself in this new role. Unfortunately, far too much of his time had been devoted to thinking of Shelby. He needed to put her—and her delectable lips—out of his mind and concentrate on the matters at hand.

"I will have Miss Slade check on the next appointment, Watson. For now, I need to get to my breakfast table since I have invited Lord Darrow to the meal."

Relief filled him when he reached the breakfast room and saw that he was the first to arrive. He asked Bowen if Cook had been told that Lord Darrow was coming, and his butler told him a buffet was being prepared for breakfast.

By then, Shelby had arrived. She greeted Jasper and took her usual seat. He did the same as one footman poured coffee for him and tea for her.

"I have asked Lord Darrow to join us this morning," he informed her. "We are to go to White's this morning. Something about needing to transfer Father's membership to me. And I am unclear as to when my next fitting at the tailor's is."

"I will check on the appointment and place it on your calendar, Your Grace," she said, stirring sugar and milk into her tea and then sipping it.

"Lord Darrow," Bowen announced.

His father's old friend stepped through the doorway, bringing his usual good cheer into the room. Jasper made the introductions, and he noted the earl's ready smile for Shelby. Jasper had never thought of it, but Darrow was a most handsome man and had always had a way of putting both men and women at ease. He thought of the strain in his own parents' marriage and wondered if Darrow's had also been a marriage of convenience—and if the earl had sought out other women for extramarital affairs himself or knew if Jasper's father had done the same. It would be a delicate topic to broach but one which had him curious now, especially since he had only learned of his brother's recent affair with Adele Simmons.

"Breakfast is ready to be served, Your Grace," Bowen informed him, and the three of them went through the buffet, making up their plates and returning to the table.

They spoke in generalities. He was learning nothing of consequence was to be said at a meal, due to the numerous servants who remained in the room. It was only behind closed doors that truths could be expressed.

"Could we spend a few minutes in my study, my lord?" Jasper asked his guest. "I have a few instructions to give to Miss Slade before we make our way to White's."

"Certainly, Your Grace," Lord Darrow said.

As they adjourned, Bowen joined him and said, "A word, Your Grace?"

"Come."

They left the breakfast room, and Shelby looked over her shoulder. He motioned for her to continue and stopped to see what his butler needed.

"What is it, Bowen? You appear upset."

"I want to warn you about what Miss Slade might address with you this morning, Your Grace, and needed privacy to do so. You see . . . well . . . there was a bit of a . . . contretemps yesterday, Your Grace. With myself, Miss Slade, and . . . Her Grace."

He groaned inwardly, wondering what embarrassing situation had occurred. Mama had already berated him for hiring Shelby and confronted him for bringing Della into the household. Had she and Shelby had further words after they left his study? His mother had claimed a megrim coming on and asked for Dr. Barton to be sent for. Jasper had not bothered to make himself available to speak to the physician after he attended Mama.

"Tell me, Bowen. Quickly. I need to return to Lord Darrow."

The butler cleared his throat. "Miss Slade came upon Her Grace talking to me yesterday. Rather . . . pointedly, as is her way."

Jasper knew the butler was being circumspect. "You mean she was upbraiding you, most likely."

Bowen's cheeks colored. "Yes, Your Grace. Her Grace was upset that she had not been made aware of the arrival of Lady Della. She was in the middle of scolding me rather heatedly when Miss Slade interrupted the exchange. Since Her Grace had not known of Miss Slade's hiring, it further infuriated her. As did Miss Slade's . . . um . . . response to Her Grace's behavior."

"I see."

Oh, Jasper most certainly did. He could see Shelby coming across Mama verbally thrashing Bowen and stepping in. Shelby would have a strong sense of right and wrong, ignoring the class distinctions that separated a duchess and her servant.

Nervously, the butler said, "Miss Slade mentioned that she would be speaking to you today regarding the incident, Your Grace. I wished to warn you about the issue and make perfectly clear that I did not ask for Miss Slade to intervene, much less address the matter with you."

He supposed the butler worried about losing his position and said, "Thank you, Bowen. I will take care of things." He paused. "And might I ask if this is a habit of Her Grace's? To verbally abuse not only you but my other servants?"

The butler turned beet red. "It is not for me to say, Your Grace."

"Then let me say this. It will happen no more. Thank you alerting me to the situation."

"Miss Slade was so passionate, Your Grace. And she did speak most frankly to Her Grace. I hope that her confronting Her Grace will not cost Miss Slade her post."

"Rest assured, Bowen. The only villain in this happens to be my mother," he said bluntly.

The butler's jaw dropped, and Jasper strode toward his study, wondering just how much mischief Mama had caused over the years. Though it was looked upon as a privilege to serve in a duke's household, he knew servants regularly came and went—both here and at Edgehill—because Mama complained so much about how hard good help was to keep. Knowing now how she berated the staff, the high turnover did not surprise him.

He entered the study and found Lord Darrow and Shelby standing in front of a large, framed map which hung on one wall.

"Here is where my country estate lies," the earl said. "Devon is God's country, Miss Slade. You won't find a prettier county in all England."

"Then I must visit there someday, my lord. Perhaps my next case will take me there."

"Case?" Lord Darrow said, his brow furrowing.

"Have a seat, my lord," Jasper encouraged. "There is something I must tell you."

After they were seated, he said, "Miss Slade is only pretending to serve as my secretary. In truth, she is a Bow Street Runner."

The earl's jaw fell open. "What?"

"It is true, my lord," Shelby assured the earl. "His Grace hired me to look into a matter for him. Oftentimes, I pursue an investigation from within a household, posing as an employee."

Darrow shook his head. "What on earth could you possibly have to investigate *here*, Miss Slade?" He glanced to Jasper. "What situation has developed that could possibly call for a runner? They investigate crimes and disappearances."

"I was uneasy after the deaths of Father and Sutton," he explained.

"Uneasy?" asked the earl. "But . . . your father was ill. And had been for months." His lips thinned in disapproval. "As for Sutton? He was into his cups and fell. Yes, it was a tragedy, but I cannot for the life of me think why you would wish to have a Bow Street Runner investigate their deaths, Jasper."

For the first time since he'd inherited the dukedom, Lord Darrow used Jasper's Christian name.

"I am not certain anything genuinely is wrong, my lord," he responded. "I merely hired Miss Slade to ease my mind. It seemed such a coincidence that both deaths occurred on the same day, merely minutes from one another. Miss Slade is here to look into things for me."

"We aren't believers in coincidence at Bow Street, Lord Darrow," Shelby added. "Frankly, I doubt I will find anything questionable to report regarding either death, but I have pledged to look into them, all the same. As it is, my investigation led His Grace to Lord Sutton's mistress, who was heavy with child."

Lord Darrow's jaw dropped. "What?"

Jasper took up the tale. "Yes, her name was Adele Simmons. She worked at Mrs. Martin's."

The earl nodded thoughtfully. "Yes, I am actually familiar with Miss Simmons. Your father and I went to Mrs. Martin's upon occasion, Edgehaven. Miss Simmons always assisted us with our coats and saw that we got food and drink." He paused, the tips of his ears pinkening. "And arranged for us to have . . . company for a few hours."

"So, Father was unfaithful to Mama," he said.

Lord Darrow frowned. "See here, now. I don't think it your place to judge your parents, Your Grace. Either of them. They are—were—most unhappy together." He cleared his throat. "I know so because I was close with your father for many years."

"Then Mama, too, stepped away from her marriage vows?" he asked.

The earl shrugged, his face now turning red. "I suppose so. It *is* fairly common among the *ton*, you know. Or you will understand, now that you are a part of it." He paused. "And don't look at me with such consternation, Edgehaven. Polite Society's parents pull the strings and force unions upon couples each Season, whether they know and like one other or not. Your parents were told to wed by their fathers and did so. They were unhappy for the entirety of their marriage—but Her Grace did produce three healthy, outstanding young men." His face fell. "It is a pity you are the only one left."

A wave of sadness rushed through him. In that moment, Jasper felt very much alone, knowing Jude would never come home from war and that Jarrod would never live to see his daughters mature and marry.

"Were they truly that unhappy?" he asked, knowing if anyone knew the truth, it would be this man.

Lord Darrow shook his head. "I believe your mother took an instant dislike to your father, while he was always indifferent to her. I spent enough years around them to know that much."

Jasper took in the weariness which blanketed the earl and asked, "And what of your own marriage, my lord? Were you also unhappy with Lady Darrow?"

He shrugged. "Unhappy is such a callous word. I would call what we had tepid. We were never interested in one another.

Perfunctory would be the best way to describe our relationship. We lacked any enthusiasm toward one another and merely fell into a dull routine over the years. Yes, we were polite toward one another. She gave me a son I cherish and a daughter I adore. But we were never close."

Lord Darrow leaned forward. "It is the way of our world, my boy. Now for you, things might be different. You have come into your dukedom as a bachelor. The family fortune is solid. You will be the one who makes his own choice in a bride and not have to bow to the wishes of a parent."

"Does anyone in the *ton* wed for love?" he asked, thinking of the strong emotions he already felt toward Shelby after kissing her.

Smiling ruefully, Lord Darrow said, "Rarely. I actually was in love myself with what I believed to be the loveliest creature in all England. Sadly, her parents had other plans for her." The earl brushed his hands together. "At least I wed a woman who brought a large dowry and gave me two beautiful children. I have been fortunate that my country estate has thrived and that I had such a good friend in your father for all these many years."

Darrow turned to Shelby. "Look all you like, Miss Slade—but I will tell you now that there is nothing dubious about these recent deaths." Glancing back to Jasper, he said, "I know you are floundering a bit, my boy. It is only natural after losing loved ones close to you and taking on a mountain of responsibility which you never anticipated carrying."

Lord Darrow stood. "Shall we go to White's now? I have nothing more I can share with Miss Slade, while you and I have things to do."

Jasper rose. "Very well. Thank you for sharing what you did with us. I suppose there wasn't anything to look into, after all."

Shelby shot to her feet. "You are putting an end to my investigation? Why, I haven't even spoken to the servants yet. And there's still the matter of Lady Fanny." She paused. "And something I must discuss with you privately, Your Grace."

He turned to the earl. "Go to your coach. I will be there shortly, my lord."

Lord Darrow shot him a questioning glance and then said, "All right, Your Grace. I will see you momentarily."

The moment the door closed and they were alone, Shelby said, "The two deaths aside, I am making progress with your niece. I believe I have gained Lady Fanny's trust. Please, give me more time to see if I can get her to speak. To share with me what she heard and saw in regard to her father's death." She paused. "And there is the matter of Her Grace."

"I heard. Bowen told me you intervened when she was reprimanding him for not sharing with her about us bringing Della into the household."

"She was quite vindicative. Bowen cowered before her. I shudder to think how she treats your other servants." She hesitated a moment and then added, "And how she might treat Lady Della."

He had not thought of that. "You believe she would bring harm to the child?"

"Not physical harm," Shelby said swiftly. "But you yourself told me of the extreme favoritism she showed you. It must have affected your relationship with your two brothers. If Lady Della is made to feel small and not as good as her half-sisters, that emotional abuse could be harmful. And lasting."

"I will speak to Mama," he said.

Shelby snorted. "I doubt *speaking* to Her Grace will do much good. She would have to listen first—and then respond accordingly. I don't think she has it in her."

Jasper sighed. "You are a crusader, Shelby. Seeking to right the wrongs of the downtrodden and those who cannot fight back," he observed. "Tenacious. Headstrong. Never one to back down from a fight or challenge."

Her chin went up a notch. "I had to be that way," she told him. "I have always felt a need to set the world right from the time my own world was turned upside down."

"I promise I will have a heart-to-heart talk with my mother. And she will listen. I will make certain of that. I have already threatened to send her back to Edgehill and have her miss the Season. She may be dressed for mourning now but made it perfectly clear to me that she will partake in all the social events once the Season begins. *That* is my leverage over her. If she does not walk a straight and narrow path in the future—both with the servants and Della—then I will upend her world and send her to the country, a place she loathes. Rest assured that I will care for the servants. They are my responsibility now. Not hers. The same goes for Della. I have already told my mother that she is my niece as much as Fanny and Sylvia are."

"If you say so," she said, doubt laced in her words.

"I am the Duke of Edgehaven now. I will always use my power and authority for good. It also guarantees that my word is law within this household. Mama will obey me. Or she will regret it."

Shelby swallowed. "Might I stay? At least another few days, Your Grace?"

"You may. Talk to the servants you wish to interview. Do what you can to bring Fanny out of her darkness. But I tend to agree with Lord Darrow. The deaths of Father and Sutton are not peculiar in any way. There is nothing to be found."

"Then I will complete my investigation and file my case notes with Mr. Franklin," she said stiffly. "I should be able to wrap up things in another three days."

"I agree."

Jasper hated the formality between them but thought the sooner this investigation ended, the sooner he would no longer be her client—and be able to act on that fact.

A knock sounded at the door and Bowen entered. "Mr. Roberts is here, Your Grace, along with a chaise lounge."

"Miss Slade can see to that matter," he said. "I am off to White's with Lord Darrow."

He passed Mr. Roberts in the foyer and welcomed him, telling the secretary to go to the study for instructions from Miss Slade.

With that, Jasper left his house and entered Lord Darrow's carriage, knowing within a few days' time he could share his true feelings with Shelby.

And hope to begin a new life with her.

CHAPTER FIFTEEN

SHELBY QUICKLY DASHED off a note to the tailor, inquiring when the next fitting was for Jasper. Instead of summoning a footman, she rang and asked for Mr. Watson to come and speak with her. He was the servant closest to the previous duke, and she wanted to talk to him now since her time in the household would be cut short.

When the valet arrived, she asked him to have a seat. He did so warily.

"I have a favor to ask of you, Mr. Watson. I know we have not been properly introduced. I am Miss Slade, His Grace's new secretary. I know we both take care of His Grace in different ways. Because of that, I wanted to get to know you a bit."

The valet relaxed. "Oh, yes, Miss Slade. I know all about you. Your arrival set the household abuzz, His Grace hiring a woman and all." He stopped. "Not that you can't do the job," he said quickly.

She laughed. "I take no offense, Mr. Watson. People have been questioning whether I can do what I do for a good number of years now."

He looked at her curiously. "How long have you been a secretary, Miss Slade?"

"I have held other posts than secretary," she told him. "In fact, I have taken care of myself for twenty years or so."

She fibbed a bit, of course. While she had taken to the streets over twenty years ago, Mr. F had removed her from that life fifteen years ago. Still, that early education in street smarts was what made her so successful as an agent for Bow Street. And she had gone to work for the agency almost a decade ago.

Surprise filled Watson's face. "You don't say, Miss. Why, you had to be a wee tyke."

Leaning in, Shelby lowered her voice, sharing a confidence. "I was orphaned at an early age, sir. I had to learn to do a little bit of everything in order to survive. I have worked at honest positions for many years now, but I will admit that I did what I had to in order to survive on the streets for a good number of years."

His eyes widened, and she quickly corrected any misconception he had, not wanting him to think she had catered to those with a taste for children and wanting to hide her past as a pickpocket and thief.

"Oh, I did it all, Mr. Watson. Sold flowers and meat pies. Made deliveries. Swept up at inns. Worked as a chimney sweep until I grew too tall." She smiled. "Whatever work I could get, I took it."

The valet visibly relaxed. "I am sorry you lost your parents so young, Miss Slade, but it is a testament to them and your own perseverance that you have come up so far in the world. To think, an orphan—and female—who is secretary to a duke! I quite admire you."

Her parents had nothing to do with the burning drive within her to escape her past and better herself. That was best left unsaid, however.

"And I admire you, Mr. Watson. To serve as valet to first one duke and then another. How did you get your start?"

Shelby listened as the man walked her through his career, and she said, "It is obvious you held the previous duke in high esteem and were most devoted to him. Did you nurse him through his illness? I heard it was a lingering one."

"Oh, it started small, Miss Slade. So small none of us—least of all His Grace—thought anything of it, especially since he had been hale and hardy his entire life. It started with a bellyache here and there. Some nausea and diarrhea. A little tingling in his toes." The valet paused, sorrow crossing his face. "Then it grew worse over several months. Headaches. Confusion. Blood in his piss. Muscles that cramped, especially in his belly. His heart racing. Oh, it was terrible. The doctors said by the end that nothing could be done. That most likely it was something eating away at His Grace's insides."

She clucked her tongue sympathetically. "I am sorry you had to witness that, Mr. Watson. Did His Grace have to have a special diet? I know some doctors order one for patients."

"Dr. Davies—and then Dr. Barton—recommended a bland diet." Sorrow filled the valet's face. "By the end, His Grace had trouble swallowing."

"Did you fetch his meals and help to feed him since he was so weak?"

"Usually, a tray arrived from the kitchens. A maid or footman would bring it. I did my best to spoon something into the duke's mouth but . . ." His voice trailed off as his head shook.

With different servants bringing the trays, it could have been someone in the kitchens lacing the duke's food with arsenic and then handing it off to a servant to bring upstairs. Or a pair of people working in tandem, sprinkling some in his food. With different servants delivering the food, it would be hard to narrow it down to a single suspect. And Watson, whose eyes now filled with tears, seemed so upset over the duke's passing that she doubted he had anything to do with the death.

"I am so sorry to have upset you, Mr. Watson," Shelby apologized.

"No, it's not your fault. I simply miss His Grace."

"You must have spent quite a bit of time together," she said, taking a different tact.

"We did," he said, removing a handkerchief and wiping his eyes. "His Grace was the best person I ever knew, man or woman. He always had a ready smile for others, despite the fact he was unhappy."

"Unhappy?" She waited a beat, not wanting to pounce on what Watson had just said. "Did he not enjoy being a duke?"

"Oh, he liked it just fine." The valet paused. "I shouldn't say anything."

Shelby saw he *did* want to say more and encouraged him by saying, "I promise to keep anything you say in confidence, sir."

"It's just that His Grace had been forced to marry Her Grace. *She* made life miserable for him. He tried to spend as little time around her as possible."

"Did he seek companionship elsewhere?" she prodded gently.

Watson sighed. "He did. Most gentlemen do. But no long-lasting affairs. Just the occasional tumble at Mrs. Martin's or some such place." Watson froze, realizing he had gone too far. "I shouldn't be talking of such things, Miss Slade. You'll be thinking me a terrible gossip."

She touched his sleeve. "I am glad you trusted me enough to do so. I wish I could have known His Grace. He sounds like a fine man. The new duke also seems a good man."

"Oh, he is. Used to go every Sunday and hear his sermons when we were in Hertfordshire. His Grace was so proud of his son. I have every faith in His Grace becoming a fine duke."

She knew this was her chance to steer the conversation once more and said, "Well, I have a letter for His Grace's tailor. He couldn't recall when he was to return for a fitting and neglected to tell me, so I have nothing recorded in his diary. I hoped you might deliver the note personally to His Grace's tailor, Mr. Watson."

The valet smiled. "I'd be happy to do so, Miss Slade. His Grace certainly needs to start dressing more like a duke and not a man poor as a church mouse."

She chuckled and he joined in.

After Mr. Watson left, Shelby spent the rest of the morning talking to a servant here and there, even going to the kitchens and sitting with Cook to have a cup of tea. She was skilled at questioning others without them realizing what she was doing. By the time she finished, she had no firm suspect in the duke's poisoning. She still believed he was poisoned but knew it would be hard to determine who might be involved.

She left a note for Edgehaven, telling him she would return tomorrow morning, and spent the rest of the day and much of the night looking into several of the household's servants. While she learned of a groom and a parlor maid who were sweet on one another and of the recent death of Bowen's mother, she found the reputation of the staff spotless. No gambling debts. No one dismissed with cause.

Yet *someone* had to have doctored Edgehaven's food. That is, if he truly had succumbed to arsenic poisoning. Perhaps she was wrong and that had not been the case, after all.

As for Lord Sutton's fall, his tumble down the stairs might be the accident that it appeared to be. He both gambled and drank lightly and other than his affair with Adele Simmons, the earl had not had any longtime mistresses. With his father lingering between life and death, it seemed Lord Sutton had merely succumbed to drowning his sorrows in drink, his only mistake trying to go downstairs in such a drunken state.

That led her to question *why* he had gone downstairs. What was the reason Lord Sutton, so unsteady on his feet and his head swimming from drink, had decided to leave his bedchamber?

Shelby decided she needed to establish when Lord Sutton had left the house and when he had returned. If any servant had seen him and noticed his condition. The best person to speak with would be his valet. She would need to learn the name of the servant—and where he now was. There would have been no need for him to remain with his employer dead and Watson to serve the new duke.

She fell into bed, determined to find the answers she sought tomorrow.

And to hopefully spend time with Lady Fanny Lincoln.

JASPER WENT TO the waiting carriage, nodding to the footman who stood next to the stairs. He allowed the servant to open the vehicle's door for him and then climbed inside. For a moment, he caught Lord Darrow unaware. The man seemed lost in thought and extremely worried, judging by the look on his face.

Once the earl became aware of Jasper's presence, however, his demeanor changed, and he smiled brightly.

"There you are, my boy."

As he seated himself across from the earl, Jasper asked, "Is something wrong, my lord?"

"No, nothing at all."

"I couldn't help but see you seemed to be anxious. You have been so helpful and supportive to me since Father's death. Comforting me. Advising me. It just struck me how little I have given back to you. Yes, I may have lost a beloved father—but you lost your closest friend of many decades. I realize that I have been selfish. I should have offered you comfort, as well. Especially losing Lady Darrow so recently, you must be feeling out of sorts with both these deaths."

"At least Lady Darrow was not struck down quickly. I had time to prepare for her death, as she grew ill over several weeks."

"You never truly mentioned what was wrong with her. I only know from Mama that you left the Season early last year, due to the countess feeling poorly, and that she passed in October. I should have done more than merely write you a condolence letter. I should have come to see you."

The earl shrugged. "My wife saw more than one doctor, and they spouted gibberish at her. Sometimes, I think physicians know only a little more than we laymen do. Lady Darrow always loved the country. Because of that, I took her home to spend her last days there."

He flicked a piece of lint from his sleeve and then said, "Her death did not affect me to the extent your father's did. I told you that most of the *ton* weds for convenience. To strengthen ties between families. Men, for large dowries to bolster their own wealth. I married Lady Darrow because it was expected of me. She was a pleasant sort, a bit of a fluffhead. For the most part, we led very separate lives. In the end, her passing was sad but affected me very little.

"On the other hand, I have spent many more hours in your father's company over the years. Edgehaven was like a brother to me, even more so than my actual brothers. They were several years younger than I was, born less than a year apart, and thick as thieves to this day. They were also jealous that I was the one who inherited everything. I rarely see them. Edgehaven, on the other hand, was a man I saw daily for months at a time."

"I know you and Lady Darrow always returned to town at the beginning of the new year, the same as my parents always did. That is unusual for members of the *ton*."

"It is," Lord Darrow agreed, "but your mother has always enjoyed the conveniences of town. As close as I was to your father, I did not mind returning early, before the crowds came. Sometimes, it was as if we had London to ourselves for a short while each year."

"Since it is January and long before the Season begins, will there even be anyone at White's?" Jasper asked.

Lord Darrow chuckled. "There is *always* someone at White's. Not every member chooses to retreat to a country estate or if they do, they may only go for a few weeks a year. Then there are members who are gentlemen yet to come into their titles and keep rooms in town year-round. It won't be crowded today, but I can assure you that we will not be the only patrons to stop in for a cup of tea and a look at the newspapers."

"Is that what men do at White's?"

"Women are known to be gossips, but I will tell you, my boy, men do just as much talking as women do when at White's. We merely keep that fact to ourselves. Especially during the Season,

White's is busy. Filled to the brim. Every seat taken and then some. Yes, many a lord comes to have his morning tea or coffee and peruse the newspapers, as well as move from group to group to gossip with the membership present. You may also dine at White's, and they have rooms available for their members to stay in overnight."

"I did not know that. Of course, I will never need to do so, now that I own one of the largest townhouses in London."

"Ah, but you never know," the earl said mysteriously, and then glanced out the window. "It looks as if we have arrived."

Moments later, the carriage began to slow and then came to a full halt. A footman opened the door, and Jasper allowed the older man to exit the carriage first before following him to the pavement. They went inside the building, where he was introduced to several of the staff and taken on a tour of the facilities. Jasper saw both the billiards and card rooms, along with the dining facilities and a coffee room.

They returned to the ground floor to a morning room filled with half a dozen men, a few reading their newspapers and others chatting amiably.

"I will introduce you to those members present, and then I must be off," Lord Darrow said. "I have an appointment with my solicitor which I must keep."

"Thank you for bringing me to White's and smoothing the way, my lord," Jasper said. "Your friendship to my father was invaluable, and I appreciate the same myself."

The earl smiled fondly at him. "You—and your brothers— were always like sons to me. It is wonderful to see the man you have become. You will also grow into your role as the Duke of Edgehaven. I have no doubts about that."

Lord Darrow then took Jasper about the room, introducing him to the handful of members present, and then left for his appointment. Jasper sat in a chair, wanting some time to himself to reflect on things. A staff member came and asked what he might bring, and Jasper asked for a cup of tea and any of the morning newspapers to read. The tea appeared quickly, as did the newspaper, and he settled into the chair, sipping his tea, lost in thought.

He knew he was making the right decision in asking for Shelby to bring her investigation to a close. He believed now, especially after talking with Lord Darrow, that there was nothing foul regarding the deaths of his father and brother. Father was ill over several months, exhibiting signs that two physicians had diagnosed. Since neither man had given a thought to arsenic poisoning, he wouldn't either. Simply because the symptoms of arsenic ingested by a human mimicked those of a very ill person did not mean someone had murdered his father. The thought was simply too fantastic and would have been difficult to pull off, especially in two different households.

As for Jarrod, Jasper realized he truly hadn't known his brother. Yes, they had been close growing up, but not as close as Jarrod and Jude had been. Besides, Jasper had seen little of his oldest brother since they had reached adulthood. Yes, Jarrod had brought his family to Edgehill every Christmas but beyond that, Jasper had rarely seen his brother. The conversations between the two of them had been few and far between, especially since Jarrod spent so much time in London at the Season, while Jasper had remained with his parishioners at Edgewood. In fact, he had spent more time with Mary and his nieces during their visits to Edgehill than he had Jarrod. It seemed he hadn't known much about his brother as an adult. He would never have guessed Jarrod to be unfaithful to his countess, much less producing a bastard child.

At least that was one good thing which had come from inviting Shelby to investigate matters. If he had not gone to Bow Street, he never would have known about Adele Simmons and her unborn child. Miss Simmons had been a tiny thing, so delicate and fragile. With her not surviving the birth of her daughter, he shuddered to think what might have become of Della. Her other uncle had washed his hands of the babe, and Jasper did not want to think what might have happened to his niece.

Now, though, he knew of her existence and had been able to take her into his household. He didn't care about his mother's protests regarding Della. Those fell upon deaf ears. It wasn't as if Mama were even close to Sylvia or Fanny. She seemed to barely tolerate her role as a grandmother, and Jasper couldn't recall seeing any true affection shown by her to her grandchildren.

He knew now that his brother had been disappointed he'd only sired females and doubted Jarrod had spent much time with his girls. Mary, on the other hand, had seemed to be a good mother, always affectionate and kind to her daughters whenever they were present. He would do his best to help them grow into wonderful young ladies. Sylvia would turn ten soon, and he thought in the blink of an eye, she would be preparing for her come-out.

"Is this seat taken?" a voice asked.

Jasper looked up and quickly came to his feet. The man standing before him looked to be an even six feet and was lean yet muscular. His brown hair had golden highlights, and his hazel eyes reflected a bit of mischief.

"I hope you do not think me too bold to come up without an introduction." The man smiled. "You were the only gentleman younger than fifty years of age in the room, so I was eager to make your acquaintance." He held out his hand. "I am Bradford. The Duke of Bradford."

He couldn't help but smile as he shook another duke's hand. "It is delightful to meet you, Your Grace. I am the Duke of Edgehaven. Please, join me."

Bradford sat in the other chair, and Jasper resumed his seat.

"I must give my condolences to you, Your Grace. I knew your father. All of Polite Society knew him. He was one of the most jovial, kind men in the *ton*. I read of his passing in the newspaper. We've just come to town from Marblebridge, our country estate in Surrey, my duchess, daughter, and I."

"I gather it is unusual for most of the *ton* to be in town during the bleak month of January. What brings you here, Your Grace?" he asked.

A smile lit the newcomer's eyes. "Ah, it is because of my duchess. She is a most unusual woman. You see, she designs furniture."

"That is remarkable," he said. "I know nothing of that process."

"Remarkable only touches the tip of the iceberg, Edgehaven. Abby draws her designs and then takes them to her cabinetmakers. She owns a rather large building where a group of men crafts the furniture. She also owns the shop in which the goods are transported to and sold from. I could not be prouder of Abby's accomplishments."

"I am duly impressed," he said. "I am new to Polite Society myself and to hear of a working duchess, especially one so talented, gives me hope that I will not be bored by everyone I meet."

Bradford laughed heartily as a servant came and placed a cup of coffee in front of him. The duke thanked him and took a sip of the hot brew. "So, tell me of yourself, Edgehaven. How you came to be an unexpected duke and what you did before you inherited your title."

He related how he was a third son and had held the living at Edgewood for several years, explaining that Jude had recently died in battle and his oldest brother in an accidental fall.

Bradford nodded. "Yes, I do recall reading about Lord Sutton's untimely death. I had met him briefly. I am sorry for your losses. So, being a duke is quite a new venture for you. Do not worry. You get used to it. If I could, anyone can."

"Your words cause me to believe you were not the heir apparent, Your Grace."

His companion burst out laughing. "No, I wasn't. You were kind enough to share your story with me, so I will briefly tell you mine. I was the younger of two brothers. We were twins, born only minutes apart. My father—and I use that term loosely—

married my mother, taking her as his third wife. He was more than thirty years her senior, and his first two wives had only produced females. He was looking for an heir and hoped to get one off Mama."

"Well, he got an heir and a spare, but I assume something tragic befell your brother?"

The duke's face darkened. "Father rejected us," he said flatly. "When my mother began increasing, he thought she had come into the marriage already with child. He banished her to one of his northern estates, far away, in Norfolk. And not to the grand house itself. No, Mama, Eli, and I lived in a one-room cottage in abject poverty. We know now that Mama became large so quickly because there were two of us growing inside of her, but Bradford never believed that and never wished to lay eyes upon us."

"My heart aches for you, Your Grace," Jasper said. "What a cruel thing His Grace did to your mother and his sons."

"I grew up knowing I would never have to be the Duke of Bradford—and glad of it. Fortunately, my mother had a relative who bequeathed to her a sum. We tried to convince Mama to buy a larger, more comfortable cottage, but she insisted upon purchasing army commissions for Eli and me. And so we went off to war."

A shadow crossed Bradford's face, and Jasper knew what came next.

"My twin died during the war. He was a hero. Then I discovered that I had become the Duke of Bradford. I sold my commission and came home to England, collecting Mama, and heading to Marblebridge, the ducal country seat in Surrey. I was determined to do the best job I could as the duke, while still feeling terribly guilty, knowing it should have been Eli in my place. I hated my father so much that I swore I would never wed and have children because I did not want to carry on the bastard's name."

Bradford's features softened. "Then I met Abby. And nothing

has ever been the same."

"Does it strike so quickly?" he asked.

The duke looked at him with interest. "For me, yes, but love matches are rare among the *ton*. Did you leave behind a sweetheart at your parish, Edgehaven? Were you considering marriage while you were still a clergyman?"

"I turned thirty this past Christmas Day, Your Grace. I had decided it was time to take a wife and start a family. Since I have become the duke and come to town, I have met someone. A woman who, in her own way, is as unique as your furniture-designing duchess."

"Does this woman have a name? And how did the two of you meet? Especially since so much of the *ton* remains in the country."

Jasper chuckled. "She is far from a member of Polite Society, Bradford. In fact, she is the antithesis of most women of the *ton*. She actually works for her living. I met her because I hired her when I went to Bow Street recently."

Bradford smiled broadly. "Then you must be referring to none other than Miss Shelby Slade."

Surprised filled him. "You know of her?"

"I know her—not of her. She handled a delicate matter for me. I would recommend Miss Slade to anyone who needed a satisfactory conclusion to a matter troubling them." Then the duke paused, understanding dawning in his eyes. "It is Miss Slade you referred to. The woman you have met."

"Yes," Jasper confirmed, hoping since this duke had hired Shelby, he might be willing to share what he knew of her. "What do you think of Miss Slade? I am curious about her."

"Whatever you have hired her to do or discover, she will never quit until she accomplishes her task. Miss Slade is committed to solving her cases and setting your world right again. She champions those who seek justice. She has an innate compassion for the downtrodden."

"Obviously, you were satisfied with the outcome of your case. But do you know anything more personal about her?"

Bradford studied him thoughtfully. "I have come to know Miss Slade fairly well because she and my Abby are friends now. Miss Slade is courageous. Persuasive. Headstrong." He chuckled. "And most opinionated."

Jasper smiled. "Yes, I am learning that for myself."

"Her background is most humble," the duke continued. "I am not comfortable sharing her story with you. That is for her to reveal to you if she chooses to do so. I will say this, Edgehaven, you seem most interested in someone who will only be in your employ for a short while. I will warn you to be respectful to Miss Slade. I would not see her abused in any way—or you will answer to me."

He liked that this man was standing up for Shelby. It told Jasper a good deal about Bradford's character.

"Have no fears, Your Grace. My intentions toward Miss Slade are honorable." He paused. "She doesn't know it yet—but I plan to make her my wife."

CHAPTER SIXTEEN

JASPER EAGERLY AWAITED Shelby's arrival the next day. He had been disappointed to find her note when he returned to his townhouse yesterday after his very interesting talk with the Duke of Bradford.

Before going downstairs, though, he stopped in the school-room, as was his custom, and spent a quarter-hour talking with his nieces as they breakfasted. Or rather he and Sylvia talked, while Fanny listened. The girl was always alert, however, listening to the conversations around her. She would even nod her head to answer one of his questions, but she still hadn't spoken directly to him, at least not a real conversation. As he left, he told Miss Hall that he didn't have time today but wanted to take his nieces to the park sometime tomorrow. The governess readily agreed, telling him how happy both girls were after spending time in his company.

"And if Miss Slade could come along, that would be most welcomed," Miss Hall continued. "She is already a favorite with your nieces."

"I will make certain that we adjust the schedule so that she might accompany us," he told the governess.

Downstairs, he sipped on his coffee and perked up when Shelby arrived.

"Good morning, Miss Slade. I took the liberty of ordering

breakfast for us both."

"Thank you, Your Grace," she said, slipping into her usual seat.

He informed her that he had received a message from the tailor's shop and would go this morning for a fitting. She had encouraged him to also see a bootmaker and shirtmaker and had arranged for him to go to both places this morning.

After they had finished breakfast, they went to his study, where Shelby said, "Since you will be at fittings all morning, I will take that time for a bit of sleuthing."

"You have new avenues to pursue?" he asked, certain that she couldn't.

"No rock must remain unturned," she said cryptically.

"I will need you to return here no later than half-past one."

Her eyebrows arched. "You have business for me to attend to? Or will you want to hear a report from me regarding my progress?"

"Neither. We have been invited to tea."

She looked at him blankly. "Tea? Someone invited *both* of us to tea?"

"Yes. I went to White's with Lord Darrow yesterday, as you know, and he introduced me to the gentlemen in attendance there. After he departed, a friendly chap came in, and we spent a pleasant hour together. He was the Duke of Bradford."

Jasper was a bit jealous of the smile that came to her face at the mention of the duke's name.

"Ah, yes. Bradford. He and his duchess are lovely people. It was a pleasure to help His Grace with his case."

"He had quite nice things to say about you, as well. He and his wife are in town for a few days before they return to the country."

"Her Grace must have finished another round of her drawings," she said. "She designs furniture and is said to be quite talented."

"Yes, His Grace told me about her endeavors. I would like to see her shop and view what is there."

"You will not be disappointed. I have heard it said that Her Grace has a rare talent."

"And the support of her husband," Jasper noted. "I would say that would be important in the eyes of the *ton*."

She sniffed. "The *ton*. They have an opinion on everything, usually not a good one. Yet the Duchess of Bradford is a kind, intelligent woman. I know some frown upon her continuing her design work after her marriage, but I fully support a woman who goes after what she wants."

"You do not have a favorable opinion of Polite Society," he stated.

"If you had been assigned to some of the cases I have worked on their behalf, you would see that all that glitters is not gold, Your Grace. In fact, there is an ugly underbelly to all of English society, no matter where you look."

He sympathized with her, knowing she'd had a difficult past. But it was in her past. He was interested in the present.

And a future with her.

"As I said, I wish for you to return so that we might visit this shop before we go to tea."

Shelby frowned. "I will accompany you to the shop if I must, but I will not be going to tea, Your Grace. I am your employee, whether people think it is your secretary or the fact that I am the agent on your case. It is not my place to socialize, especially with those who rank at the highest level of Polite Society."

"I won't take no for an answer, Shelby. His Grace specifically asked for you to come to tea and was eager to tell his wife you would be joining us."

"How did my name even come up?" she asked sharply. "I doubt you were discussing your secretaries while at White's."

She had him there. Her name had come up because Jasper had seen the look on Bradford's face as he talked about his wife. His gut had told him they were a love match—and he had asked the duke if love struck quickly. Then he had declared he planned to make Shelby his wife.

Naturally, the duke had been both elated and curious. They had spent the next half-hour talking about why he had gone to Bow Street and how he had met Shelby before he'd even set foot inside the agency's headquarters. Bradford had assured him that Shelby was quite good at what she did and that becoming a duchess would simply be a new challenge which she would face with ease.

Jasper had begged the duke not to mention his intention to offer for Shelby, explaining that she seemed to have a disdain for members of the *ton*. He revealed his plan was to let her complete her investigation and then when he was no longer a client, pursue her with a tenacity that would convince her she was the only woman for him.

Bradford had thought the plan solid but said it would be good if they could be thrown together in a social situation. He had suggested afternoon tea, saying Abby would be delighted to meet him and renew her acquaintance with Shelby.

He hated lying to her but said, "Actually, we were talking about secretaries, and I mentioned how competent mine was. When I mentioned your name, the duke eagerly jumped on the information."

Doubt shone in her eyes. "And so you told him I was merely pretending to be your secretary while working my case? You outed me when my role was to be kept in secret?"

"I have kept your mission a secret and your true purpose in my household quiet," he said defensively.

"You blabber it to a man you just met?" she asked defiantly.

"He knew who you were, Shelby. And His Grace was most pleased with your work on his behalf. He explained how his mother had been in love and run off with Paul Baxter, her father's steward, and how she was forced to return home in order to wed the ancient Duke of Bradford after her father caught up with them. That Baxter was dismissed without references and how she had thought fondly of him over the years."

She let out a long, slow breath. "Yes, I was able to locate Mr. Baxter for Her Grace. Unfortunately, Mr. Baxter was on his deathbed. They were so happy to see one another, even though they knew it was for a final time. It gave Her Grace the closure she needed—and Mr. Baxter went peacefully."

"Bradford mentioned that his mother had wed Lord Ladiwyck, who had acted as guardian to the current duchess after she was orphaned. That it was Lord Ladiwyck who gave her the funds to start her furniture business. I know both the duke and duchess would be happy to see you again."

"All right," she said begrudgingly. "I will go to tea with you. But—"

"Thank you," he said, relieved that she would go to both the furniture shop and tea with him.

"For now, I have a few loose ends which I am trying to tie up." She rose, and he did the same.

"I did also commit you to one more thing."

Shelby looked at him, not bothering to hide her exasperation. "What, Your Grace?"

"A walk with the girls sometime tomorrow. I told Miss Hall I wished to take them out and she is the one who suggested that you accompany me. That my nieces have grown quite fond of you."

Her face relaxed. "I would be happy to do so. I still want to unlock the door Lady Fanny hides behind and help her return to speaking again."

Placing his hands on her shoulders, he said, "If anyone can bring her back to us, it is you."

They gazed at one another a long moment, the air charged between them. He was weighing the idea of kissing her again when she broke away. He cleared his throat, glad she had done so, not wanting his bold action to push her further away.

"Then I will see you back here in a few hours," Jasper said.

"I will be here, Your Grace."

SHELBY LEFT THE house, pulling her cloak tightly about her. The late January wind was sharp today. She left the square and hailed a hansom cab, giving the address of the boardinghouse Adele Simmons had resided in as her destination. She hoped because it was so early in the day that she would find Adele Simmons' half-brother at home. Since he worked as a card dealer at Mrs. Martin's, she knew he was probably sleeping at this time of day but didn't care. Her time was running out and answers still needed to be discovered. Already, Jasper had limited her time and wanted this case closed. She had a feeling that he had already given up on the idea of his father being poisoned.

She almost had herself. The symptoms the previous duke had displayed had not alarmed either physician the duke had seen. In her judgment, Dr. Barton was knowledgeable and competent, and the thought of arsenic poisoning had never occurred to him. Perhaps she had been reaching beyond her grasp, desperate to uncover some kind of conspiracy against the dead Duke of Edgehaven simply because his son was wary about the circumstances of his father's death, along with Lord Sutton's. Her conversation with Mr. Simmons should clear up some of the hesitation she felt.

Arriving at the boardinghouse, she was granted admittance by its owner, who recognized her.

"How is the babe doing?" the woman asked anxiously.

"I am happy to report that she is thriving. Both a wet nurse and nursemaid have been hired to look after her, and His Grace will raise her in his household, along with his other nieces."

"Ah, that is a happy end to what might have been a sordid story. But what brings you back, Miss Slade?"

"I have a few questions I need to ask Mr. Simmons." Shelby did not explain further, letting the woman think it had something to do with Lady Della.

"Mr. Simmons is most likely asleep. He works until almost dawn."

"I would not ask if it were not important. After today, Mr. Simmons need never see me again."

Fretting, the woman said, "While Miss Simmons was sweet, Mr. Simmons has a bit of a temper. I suppose it is all right if you go on up then."

"Then let him take it out on me."

Shelby went upstairs to the room where Adele Simmons had died. She rapped on the door and waited. Nothing happened. Knocking again, she did so more sharply and for a longer amount of time, meeting with success as a disheveled Simmons opened the door.

"What do you want?" he asked grumpily, recognizing her.

"I need but a few minutes of your time, Mr. Simmons," she said, pushing past him and entering the room. Looking about, she could see Adele had been the one to keep the place neat. Now, it looked like a pigsty, with clothes strewn about and a foul smell permeating the room.

"I said, what do you want?" Simmons asked, more awake now—and angry at the intrusion.

Opening her reticule, she handed over a pound note. He glanced at it and then pocketed the note, still studying her warily.

"You said you were here when Lord Sutton called upon Miss Simmons that final time. What was his condition? Did he appear to have been drinking?"

"No," he said guardedly. "Why?"

"Do you keep any strong drink here?"

Simmons shook his head. "No, Adele didn't like it. I would stop at a tavern sometimes for a drink or even grab a whisky before I left Mrs. Martin's."

"Do you know how long Lord Sutton's visit to your half-sister was?"

He cocked his head and looked up, thinking a moment, and then glanced back at her. "Several hours. That's what she said. I was only here for part of it because I needed to go to work. When I left, they were still sitting in the parlor downstairs. I stopped in and said my goodbyes. His lordship seemed sober to me."

Shelby had gotten the information she'd come for. "Thank you, Mr. Simmons. I won't be bothering you again."

She moved toward the door, and he said, "Wait."

When she turned, she saw he struggled. "What is it?"

"How . . . how is the babe?"

"Lady Della is well," she told him, glad that he had asked after the child.

"*Lady* Della?"

"Yes. She is His Grace's niece, even if Lord Sutton and Miss Simmons were not wed. His Grace means for her to be treated with the utmost respect."

"So, the servants call her Lady Della? And others?"

"Well, there are only a few who are not staff who reside in the household. His Grace has two other nieces. He introduced Lady Della to them, saying she was their cousin. Children that age don't often ask questions that adults do. The girls are young and have accepted the babe as their cousin. Have no fears, Mr. Simmons. His Grace will be a kind, loving guardian to Lady Della. He understands that you did not have the means to care for her and is happy to do so. She will be raised alongside her half-sisters and educated as they are. One day, she will even make her come-out in Polite Society."

"She'll marry a swell?" he asked.

"Only if she wishes to. His Grace's goal will be for Lady Della to be happy."

"Well, I'll be jiggered."

Her attitude toward the man softened. "If you ever wish to see Lady Della, you may call upon His Grace. I can provide the address for you."

"No, no," said Simmons quickly. "She's one of them now. She doesn't need to have anything to do with the likes of me." He hesitated. "Don't tell her about me. I don't want her coming to look for me. She's in a better place now."

"She is loved and will be well provided for," Shelby agreed.

Though Simmons seemed happy for his niece in this moment, she thought she should issue a final warning, just in case he got any ideas he shouldn't.

Meeting and holding his gaze, she said, "One last thing, Mr. Simmons. Never seek out His Grace and demand payment to keep this matter quiet. It would not go well for you if you did."

Without hesitation, the dealer said, "Understood."

"Then good day, Mr. Simmons."

Hailing another hansom cab, Shelby made her way back to Mayfair. When she arrived, she first went to the stables and found the groom on duty when Lord Sutton had returned that final time. He confirmed that the earl had not appeared drunk in the least bit. She thanked him and went inside the house, asking to see Bowen and Mrs. Bowen in private. They agreed to her request and met in Mrs. Bowen's office, where she prepared the weekly menus with Cook and went over the household's accounts.

Closing the door, Shelby said, "I am speaking to you in confidence, Mr. and Mrs. Bowen. I am here in this household at His Grace's request. I am not a secretary."

"You're not?" Mrs. Bowen said, appearing alarmed.

"No. I work for Bow Street. I would appreciate you not sharing this with the rest of the staff."

"You're a runner?" Bowen asked, clearly surprised. "Well, you could knock me over with a feather. A female runner." He paused. "Why are you here, Miss Slade?"

"I would rather not get into the particulars of my investigation, but I do have a question for the two of you."

"Ask away," the butler said, clearly intrigued.

"Did either of you see Lord Sutton after he returned to the household after he had gone riding?"

"I didn't," Mrs. Bowen said.

"I did. We spoke briefly," Bowen said.

"Did he appear to be in his cups upon his return?"

The question seemed to startle the butler. "Why, no. Now that you ask, his lordship was quite sober. Although, he did tell me he was going to the library for a brandy and asked that the fire remain lit until he left. I could check and see how long he was there."

"Who refills the bottles of brandy?"

"Why, I do," the butler said.

"Did you notice a bottle missing? Or rather empty?"

"Not really, Miss Slade. I replace what has been drunk each week. Only one bottle of brandy was in the library and not much was missing from it. His Grace—that is, the previous duke—had not touched a drop since he came from the country. He had been much too ill to consume alcohol. And Lord Jasper, His Grace now, doesn't touch strong spirits."

"What of Her Grace?"

"No, she only drinks sherry. I know Lord Darrow and His Grace used to drink quite a bit of brandy or whisky during their times together, but Lord Darrow has not been in the library since last Season, I suppose." He paused. "Is any of this helpful, Miss Slade?"

"Yes, it certainly is. Thank you for your time."

Shelby left the office and went to the duke's study, which was empty at the moment. She now knew that Lord Sutton had not arrived home drunk, and he had not drunk to excess once he arrived here. In fact, according to the groom, Lord Sutton had arrived home only an hour before he supposedly fell to his death. She might never know why the earl was returning downstairs, but she did know that Lord Sutton's death was not caused by a drunken, accidental fall.

Someone had pushed him—and then most likely dabbed his clothing with a bit of brandy to make it appear as if he'd been drinking heavily.

And if Lord Sutton had been murdered, the likelihood of the Duke of Edgehaven being murdered went up exponentially.

CHAPTER SEVENTEEN

JASPER ARRIVED HOME, hoping Shelby would already be present. He had told his coachman to wait in front of the townhouse, saying he would soon be leaving again, and giving the driver the address of the Duchess of Bradford's furniture shop, which the duke had provided for Jasper yesterday during their chat.

He entered the foyer and handed his coat to Bowen, saying he was only here for a short time and to keep it available for him.

"Miss Slade is waiting for you in your study, Your Grace," the butler informed him.

"Thank you, Bowen."

Going to his study, he opened the door, finding Shelby gazing out a window, unaware of his presence. He studied her for a moment, her height tall compared to so many women of the day. He was looking forward to the time he could undo her lustrous hair and run his fingers through the heavy, rich brown locks. He closed the door behind him, and she must have heard it click because when he turned again, she was facing him.

Immediately, he could tell something was wrong. Already, he could read her so well. She held many things in, but he knew something had occurred which had upset her.

Thinking it best they leave the house and her to share whatever was wrong in the carriage, where they had privacy, he said, "Are you ready to leave?"

She came toward him. "You look quite dapper, Your Grace."

He realized she meant the clothes he now wore. "I do not resemble a clergyman anymore?" he teased. "Yes, I have come directly from my tailor's, where I had a final fitting on many garments. These were finished up while I was still in the shop. What do you think of the new me?"

A smile tugged on the corners of her mouth. "I think you make for a fine duke but then again, I always knew you would. You certainly now are dressed for your station in life."

"We can talk more in the carriage," he told her and they left, returning to the foyer.

He claimed his greatcoat again, and Bowen offered Shelby the cloak she always wore. It was a dark, nondescript garment and when she became his duchess, he wanted her to dress in finery. Then again, she might not wish to give up the practical, wool cloak. Jasper didn't want becoming a duke to change his core, and he realized even when Shelby became his duchess, her essence must remain. She would need to be true to herself, above all else.

He handed her up into the carriage and sat opposite her. Encouragingly, he said, "Tell me what is on your mind. I can see something is troubling you."

"Is it that obvious?"

"No," he said truthfully. "I think you do a good job of hiding your feelings from the world. In fact, you would make for a most formidable card player. No one would ever be able to read in your eyes or body language the hand you held."

"I will take that as compliment, Your Grace. I do play cards at times when I am working in the gaming hells."

"Working?"

"Yes. You heard me refer to myself as Mr. Andrews' sister when we went to see Adele Simmons and her half-brother. There are times in my investigative work when I dress the part of a man. Mr. Andrews has a mustache and a dapper way of dressing. I will play a few hands of cards at the tables dressed as him, as part of my sleuthing, before I move on and talk to those who work at the establishments."

"There is still so much I do not know about you."

"Why should you?" she challenged.

He wanted to tell her how he longed to know everything about her, including every sweet curve of her body. Instead, he said, "Tell me what you have discovered."

"I still have not completely convinced myself that your father was not poisoned by arsenic, but I am willing to concede—for now—that his death could have been from natural causes." She paused. "On the other hand, after speaking to numerous people, I do not believe Lord Sutton was drunk on the night he took his fall."

"How did you reach this conclusion? Several remarked how he reeked of brandy."

Shelby walked him through everyone she had spoken to, from Mr. Simmons, one of the last outsiders to see his brother after he came to the boardinghouse, to the groom who took Jarrod's horse when he returned that night.

"I even spoke to Bowen and Mrs. Bowen," she said. "Lord Sutton arrived home—sober—and went to the library for a snifter of brandy. Since Bowen is the one who replenishes the decanters, I asked him what amount was missing and if it were enough to mean Lord Sutton was deep into his cups. He told me how your father had not had anything to drink since his return to town because of how it upset his stomach. That Lord Darrow had not called recently, and they were the ones who usually consumed the spirits in the library. That your mother only partakes of sherry and that you do not touch a drop of strong drink. What was missing from the brandy decanter was enough for Lord Sutton to have had two drinks at most."

Her gaze met his. "Yet Lord Sutton smelled strongly of brandy when discovered. I believe he did have one snifter of brandy before he retired and that someone dabbed his clothes with brandy so that the strong scent would still be coming off him when his body was discovered."

Horror filled Jasper.

"I still have not established why he came back downstairs since he was dressed for bed. Yes, Lord Sutton might have tripped on his dressing gown, but at this point, I do not believe in any form or fashion that his lordship had had too much to drink, making him careless."

Understanding filled him. "You think he was pushed down those stairs, don't you? That the brandy was placed on his clothing so that others would believe Jarrod was drunk when he fell."

"I do, Your Grace. The question now remains who would do such a thing—and why?"

"You still believe their deaths are linked," he said flatly. "We are back at the beginning with both Edgehaven and Sutton."

"No, I told you I am willing to accept your father was getting old and despite his lifetime of good health, he had become ill over several months. That is an established fact. As to Lord Sutton's death? I find it more suspicious than ever."

Everything Shelby had said troubled him. It pointed to someone in his household that committed murder.

"Who would have wanted to kill my brother? It makes no sense. I am the only one who would have profited from the deaths of both my father and brother."

"The entire household knew after calling Dr. Barton frequently and your vigil at the duke's bedside that his time drew near. It was why you had sent for Lord Sutton and your nieces, to allow them to say their goodbyes to His Grace. So yes, it was obvious to whoever did this that you would become the new duke. But that seems *too* obvious. You certainly did not do this or you would never have asked Bow Street to look into it. Once again, I can only venture to think it is someone who had a grudge or complaint against Lord Sutton himself that is responsible for his untimely death. Going on the theory that Lord Sutton's death had nothing to do with His Grace's, it was someone who wanted Lord Sutton to suffer. For Lord Sutton to die. Whether he became the new Duke of Edgehaven might be irrelevant."

Shelby sighed, leaning back against the cushion. "I have looked into Lord Sutton and the places he frequented in London, including some of the gaming hells. From everything I learned, Lord Sutton drank and gambled lightly. His gambling was more for entertainment with friends and not a madness which possessed him, as is often the case. I may need to go to wherever his country estate is located and ask a few questions there to see if I can uncover the link I seek."

Jasper shook his head. "That makes no sense. Because whoever pushed Jarrod down those stairs was already inside *this* household. I don't think a trip to Sutton's estate would be profitable or have you gain any additional or valuable knowledge."

He raked his fingers through his hair, frustration filling him. "The only person who might have done so would be his valet. Obviously, this servant came from the country with my brother when I called him and the girls to London."

"Who is it? I have yet to meet him."

"I dismissed him with a good reference and a healthy bonus. I inherited Watson from my father and had no need of a second valet. I asked if he wished to hold another position within my household, and he said he preferred leaving and finding work as a valet to another lord."

"Do you know what employment agency he was associated with?"

He shook his head. "I'm sorry. I don't."

"Then I need his name. I will track him down and question him. I know you wished for me to wrap up my investigation in the next day or so, but I believe whatever this valet could tell me might be critical."

"Shelby, I do not want you going after this man on your own."

She gave him a knowing smile. "You don't believe I can take care of myself, do you? Let me tell you this, Your Grace. Long before I became an agent of Bow Street, I lived on the streets of London for years."

He gasped. "I had no idea. You are so . . . refined."

She gave him a steely smile. "I learned to fight—and fight dirty. If this valet tried to lay a finger upon me, that finger would be broken, along with a few other choice bones. I am fast with my feet and fists and because I am a woman, men always underestimate me. I also received training on how to defend myself when I first came and trained at Bow Street."

She smiled. "I could probably take *you* in a fight, Your Grace, and you are much larger than I am. I carry a blade and could slice open your gut before you knew I had done so. Not to brag, but I am also an excellent shot."

"I wonder about that childhood of yours," Jasper said. "It could have hardened you, Shelby, yet you are one of the kindest people I have met, too. You must have been schooled at some point. Taken off the streets and turned into the lady before me."

"I did have someone act as a savior to me after years of living and learning on the streets. Actually, two someones who are dear to me. They took me in. Cleaned me up. Gave me a home and an education. They served as surrogate parents to me. I look upon them as my true parents since I never knew my father and my mother was not much of a mother to me."

He leaned forward, taking her hands in his. She tried to pull away but he held her firmly.

"You came from a nothing and have made quite a life for yourself. I believe I admire you more than anyone I have ever met, Shelby Slade." He squeezed her fingers and then released them, sitting back, his heart beating rapidly.

She licked her lips, causing desire to shoot through him. Before he could act upon it, though, the carriage came to a stop, and he knew they had arrived at their destination.

They entered the furniture shop and a man met them.

"Good afternoon, my lord, my lady. I am Mr. Hogan, the manager of this shop for Her Grace, the Duchess of Bradford."

He indicated another man who joined them. "And this is Mr. Nix, our most knowledgeable clerk. Are you searching for a particular piece today or merely preferring to browse?"

"I am the Duke of Edgehaven and met His Grace yesterday at White's. In fact, we are having tea with Their Graces when we leave here. His Grace was effusive in his praise of his wife's designs, and we wanted to see them firsthand."

"Yes, His Grace is Her Grace's biggest supporter. Then allow me to guide you around the store and tell you about our inventory."

"Thank you, Mr. Hogan. That would be most kind of you," Jasper said.

They spent over an hour going through the shop. The manager was interesting, and Jasper couldn't help but admire not only the designs but the craftsmanship of each piece. Mr. Hogan told them about the different kinds of woods used, such as oak, walnut, and birch. Shelby was drawn to a secretaire of cherry veneer.

As she lingered behind, he gestured to Mr. Hogan to follow him and asked about another piece. Then quietly, Jasper asked, "Is the secretaire available?"

Mr. Hogan said, "It is, Your Grace. I see Her Grace is taken with it."

He did not bother to correct the manager. "I want it for her. It is to be a surprise. Could you have it delivered to my townhouse early tomorrow morning, say seven o'clock? I do not want her to see the delivery wagon or its arrival."

Hogan smiled. "That can easily be arranged, Your Grace. I merely need your address."

He provided it and then said, "Send the bill to my solicitor," and also gave Hogan that address, as well.

Turning, he saw Mr. Nix had joined Shelby and was telling her about the secretaire. She moved her hand along the wood a final time and said, "Let's see what else is here."

They spent another quarter-hour with the pair, who told

them about the lines of several pieces and why it made that item so aesthetically pleasing.

When they had seen everything in the shop, Jasper thanked Mr. Hogan for his time and said, "I most certainly will return and purchase a few items from you. I need to look about my house and see what I might replace. I have recently inherited my title and still am not totally familiar with every room in my residence."

"I understand, Your Grace," Mr. Hogan said, leading them to the shop's entrance and opening the door for them. "I wish you a most pleasant afternoon. Farewell."

Jasper gave Bradford's address to his coachman, and they settled themselves inside the vehicle for the short ride to the duke's townhouse.

Shelby sighed. "I cannot imagine the talent it would take to visualize a piece of furniture and capture it on paper, seeing it brought to life."

"I am sure we can ask Her Grace about that process. Changing the topic of conversation, you seemed quite taken with that secretaire."

She smiled wistfully. "It is one of the most beautiful pieces I have ever seen. I asked Mr. Nix its cost." She shook her head. "Something that fine is not available on an agent's salary. Sometimes, I am paid a bonus by a client for work well done but even then, that secretaire is far beyond my means."

Then she sucked in a quick breath. "Oh, I am sorry, Your Grace. I did not mean to mention a bonus to you. Please, do not feel I did so, hinting for you to provide one to me at the end of my investigation."

"I had not thought to do so, but it is an excellent idea," he declared.

Her mouth set stubbornly. "I will not accept one from you. Keep it."

He wished to smooth things over with her, but the carriage halted, and he knew they had reached the Bradford's townhouse.

Jasper climbed from the vehicle and handed down Shelby, and they made their way to the door.

A butler answered their knock, one who might be all of thirty years of age. It surprised Jasper because butlers were usually much older.

"Good afternoon, Your Grace. It is good to see you again, Miss Slade."

He noted the warm smile Shelby gave the butler. "Hello, Nelson. How are you and Mrs. Nelson?" she asked as they were admitted into a grand foyer.

"She is well, Miss Slade, as am I. Thank you for asking. Let me take you to Her Grace's sitting room. It is where tea will be served this afternoon."

As the butler moved ahead of them, Shelby tugged on his sleeve and quietly said, "This is a great honor. His Grace must have been quite impressed by you. Most entertaining by the *ton* is done in drawing rooms alone. For you to have been invited to Her Grace's private sitting room indicates how highly His Grace thinks of you."

"Or *you*," he countered.

They arrived, and Nelson had them wait a moment, announcing them and then gesturing for them to enter. They stepped into the room as the duke and duchess came to their feet, both smiling.

"Good to see you both," Bradford said affably. "Especially you, Miss Slade. I told Mama you were coming to tea today, and she was sorry she and Lord Ladiwyck already had plans, else they would both be here now."

Bradford turned to Jasper. "I am happy to introduce you to the light of my life. Darling, this is His Grace, the Duke of Edgehaven."

The duchess, who possessed dark blond hair and bright blue eyes, had a willowy figure and the soft scent of jasmine clinging to her.

He took her hand. "It is an honor to meet you, Your Grace.

Especially since we have come from your furniture shop and seen your creations on display. You are incredibly talented."

A genuine smile lit her face. "Oh, I wish I would have known you were going. I would have met you there."

"Mr. Hogan and Mr. Nix were excellent guides," he said. "But Miss Slade and I are still curious about your process."

The duchess turned to Shelby and took her hands. "I am so happy to see you, Miss Slade. Come and sit. We can talk of furniture." Her eyes lit with mischief. "And our new babe. Well, she isn't exactly new. She will be a year old come March."

"It is our favorite topic of conversation," Bradford said, grinning.

"I would be delighted to hear about her—if you are willing to hear me brag about my nieces."

"Oh, we have so much to discuss!" the duchess proclaimed. "And possibly, if His Grace doesn't mind, we might talk about how Miss Slade is helping you out. Of course, if you wish for the details of the case to remain private, we certainly understand. If so, I will merely bore you with details regarding my designs and how they come to fruition."

They settled themselves as the teacart arrived and once the maid left, Jasper said, "We definitely wish to hear about your babe and your design work, Your Grace, but we could use fresh eyes regarding details Miss Slade has recently uncovered.

"You see, I believe my father—and brother—might have been murdered."

CHAPTER EIGHTEEN

J ASPER ACCOMPANIED SHELBY to his waiting coach. A good feeling ran through him. The Duke and Duchess of Bradford had been delightful. They had listened to everything he had to say about the deaths of his father and brother, Shelby filling in details along the way. While the couple didn't have any insight to offer at this point, both promised to think over what had been shared. Jasper also said he would continue to keep them up to date regarding the investigation. Though Lord Darrow had thought there was no case at all, Jasper believed he should keep Bow Street on the job.

Then a nursery governess had brought the couple's daughter down for a visit at the end of teatime. Jasper had held the babe, much as he had done with Della. As he did so, he had told the Bradfords about her and his other two nieces. Throughout their time together, the conversation continued to flow with ease. If the Duke and Duchess of Bradford were a good example of what members of Polite Society could be like, then he might not mind being a duke, after all.

Especially with Shelby as his duchess.

Once inside the carriage, she said, "You liked them, didn't you? The duke and duchess."

"They were most amiable. I cannot recall when I have been around a couple so warm and friendly. Bradford wishes to meet with me again. He suggested we go riding early tomorrow morning."

"You are in need of a friend, Your Grace. I think the Duke of Bradford would make for a fine one. After all, he is a bit like you. An unexpected duke. A second son who always assumed his brother would take on the title."

"You are right," he agreed. "Neither of us was meant to play the role we do." He smiled. "Perhaps that is why I liked him so much. Her Grace, too."

Shelby nodded. "She is lovely. And I don't mean in appearance alone. Her Grace has a sweetness about her. A calm and creative nature, as well."

"It was fascinating to hear about her process. When she took up a sketchbook and from thin air created a beautiful chest on the page, I was amazed. The work I saw in her shop convinced me I need to purchase several items from her. Perhaps you and I can go through the townhouse when we get home and see . . ." He stopped. "It is late, though. I should see you home instead of having us return to my residence."

He raised a hand to rap on the roof, but she took his wrist and lowered it. Just her touch caused his heart to beat wildly in his chest and his lips to itch, wanting them on hers.

"That is unnecessary, Your Grace. We are almost to your townhouse now. I will take a hansom cab home."

Anger surged through him. "Why are you so stubborn all the time, Shelby?"

"Miss Slade," she prompted primly.

"*That* is what I am talking about."

She sighed. "We have been over this before," she chided. "I am the agent on your case."

"Yes—and my friend," he insisted. "I know you better than anyone in London. After sharing the details with the Bradfords, I believe you should remain on the case longer."

Shelby pursed her lips. "And what would Lord Darrow think of your decision?"

"It is not his to make!" Jasper said, losing his temper. He took a calming breath. "Darrow has been a good friend to me, especially since my father's passing. But I was wrong to let him convince me nothing is wrong. My gut tells me there is—and that you are the one to find the truth."

The carriage slowed and then came to a stop, the door opened by a footman. Jasper bounded down the steps and held out a hand for Shelby to take, wanting his fingers wrapped around hers for even the briefest of time.

When she reached the pavement, she said, "Good evening, Dr. Barton."

"Good evening, Your Grace. Miss Slade," the physician said.

"What are you doing here?" Jasper asked worriedly, realizing Barton was coming from his house. "Are the girls all right?"

"I am certain they are fine, Your Grace. I came at the insistence of Her Grace. Another megrim." Barton shook his head. "Forgive me for being frank, but I believe she is using them as an excuse to summon me. I don't think she had one at all this visit."

"Why would she do that?" he asked, confused. "Do you give her medication for them?"

"Sometimes. I did not see the need to do so tonight, however. If you will excuse me, I still have one more patient to see before I head for home. Have a pleasant evening."

Dr. Barton's words troubled him. "If Mama lied about her megrim, I want to know why. Would you come inside with me?"

"If you wish," Shelby said.

Bowen admitted them, not meeting his gaze as he said, "Welcome home, Your Grace. Miss Slade. Allow me to take your coat."

As he shrugged from his greatcoat, Jasper said, "Look at me, Bowen, and tell me why Her Grace needed Dr. Barton to visit her."

His butler flushed. "Her Grace had one of her megrims, Your Grace. She insisted I summon Dr. Barton."

"What brought on the megrim?"

Fidgeting, Bowen said, "Her Grace became upset over something."

"She shouted at someone again?" he pressed, anger building within him. "The truth. Now."

Bowen winced. "Yes, Your Grace. It was a small matter. A maid who was dusting knocked over a figurine by accident. I sent it out to be repaired. Her Grace missed seeing it on a table and asked about the piece. When she learned it had been damaged, she became most upset, saying it had been a gift, and she treasured it."

"Did she yell at the maid?"

The butler nodded in confirmation. "And several others, Your Grace. There was no calming her."

"Thank you, Bowen. I will go and see her now and discuss the matter." His hands had bunched into fists, and Jasper felt like punching something himself. Looking to Shelby, he asked, "Will you go with me, Miss Slade? I do not trust myself not to murder her."

Alarm filled her face. "Perhaps you could wait until tomorrow morning to address the matter, Your Grace. It would be wise to have both time and space occur before you confront Her Grace."

"No. I will do so now," he said stubbornly. "Please accompany me."

He turned to mount the stairs, assuming she would follow. She did so because he sensed her presence behind him. Jasper counted as he ascended the stairs and kept counting each step until they reached Mama's rooms, hoping to get his temper under control. He opened the door without knocking, going through an empty sitting room. He did have the presence of mind to knock on the door that led to her bedchamber, however.

"What now?" he heard her say through the door. "Go away. I need nothing else."

Opening the door, he marched into the room, seeing Mama seated at her dressing table. Their eyes met in the mirror, and she whirled, coming to her feet to face him.

"Edgehaven! What on earth are you doing here? And with this—"

"I warned you, Mama. I told you to behave yourself. To conduct yourself as the lady you supposedly are. You have not. Instead, you have once more allowed your temper to rule. Because of it, I am sending you to the country. I will give you tomorrow to pack, but I expect you to be gone by the day after."

She slapped him, the sting causing his face to burn. When she raised her hand to do so again, he caught her wrist, forcing it down to her side.

Rage filled her face. "You are abusing your power, Edgehaven. I gave birth to you—and this is how you treat me?"

He removed his wrist and coolly said, "If you learn your lessons, perhaps you might be able to return for next Season. This one should be spent in mourning for Father, not gallivanting about as if you haven't a care in the world."

"I will *not* pretend to mourn for a man who caused me nothing but misery for years and years," she bellowed at him. Then she turned her gaze on Shelby. "You want me gone so you can be with her. I know I am right."

"What if I do want that?" he countered. "What business is it of yours?"

"You are a duke, by God. This woman? She is nothing."

Jasper held his temper. "She is nothing short of brilliant, Mama. Miss Slade is intelligent. Polite. Kind. She looks after others. She is, in every way, your complete opposite. You only think of yourself. Because of that, it is time you learned a lesson in humility. Edgehill is the perfect place. In fact, I think I shall send you to the dower house."

Shock filled her face. "I am no dowager duchess, Jasper. I *am* the Duchess of Edgehaven." She glared at him. "I will tell Lord Darrow of this. *He* will convince you to let me stay."

"While I have always admired the earl and am quite fond of him, I do not take orders from Darrow, Mama. Goodnight."

He turned, and she shouted, "Do not walk away from me."

Facing her again, Jasper said, "That is exactly what I am going to do—else I might regret what I say next. Pack your things tomorrow." He paused, feeling the need to issue a final warning to her. "And if you abuse any servant—even a single time—I will remove you from the dower house and Edgehill." His gaze bored into her. "And you would not like where you were sent next. Let that be warning enough."

She looked at him, stunned, her jaw falling open, though no words of protest were uttered.

"I bid you goodnight."

He wheeled, quickly moving past Shelby, who fell in behind him as his mother raged at the top of her lungs. Jasper moved down the corridor, needing to escape the sound of Mama's voice. Finally, when he could no longer hear her, he stopped and turned.

Shelby collided with him, having hurried after him. He grasped her elbows, steadying her.

"That woman would drive a man to drink," he declared.

Then sliding his hands down her arms, he took her hands in his, bringing them to his lips and tenderly kissing her fingers. "Thank you for being there. For keeping me from doing violence against my own mother."

She stared at him, her lips moving, no words coming out. He gazed down at her, yearning filling him. Then he started pulling her along the corridor.

"Where are we going?" she managed to get out.

"Where we can have some privacy."

He moved rapidly down the corridor until he reached the door to his rooms. Flinging open the door, Jasper rushed inside, quickly closing it behind them.

"We are in your ducal rooms," she hissed.

"It is the only place I can talk to you privately. Besides, in your line of work, I am certain you have been in far more precarious places than a duke's rooms. There are things which have been left unsaid which must be addressed between us. Now, Shelby. Not later. Before I lose my courage."

Confusion filled those golden-brown eyes, and he led her to the settee, easing her down. He slipped her cloak from her shoulders and took both her hands in his.

"I never would have met you if I hadn't been suspicious of the deaths of my father and brother. I still believe one—or both—may have been murdered. Whether or not you will be able to tie them together—or ever learn the truth—remains to be seen. What will always remain, however, is my deep affection for you."

She startled and tried to pull away, but Jasper only gripped her hands more tightly.

"I know how you feel about having a personal relationship with a client. That is why I have tried to keep my true feelings quiet. Until now." He swallowed. "I cannot help myself, Shelby. You are the light in my day and the guiding force in my life. Once this case is closed, I need to keep you in my life. Not as my secretary. I want you as my duchess—and all that entails. I want to be your everything, as you are to me. I see us as friends. Companions. Lovers. Husband and wife. Duke and his duchess."

He paused, allowing his words to sink in, seeing tears well in her eyes.

"Tell me there is no one else who claims your heart. Tell me that you feel what I feel every time I look at you, Shelby. Touch you. Tell me you can see a future together with me."

A lone tear escaped, cascading down her cheek. He leaned in and kissed it away, feeling her shudder.

"Jasper, I do not know what to say. I am, at heart, an orphan from the streets. There is so much you do not know about me."

"I know all that I need to know, my love. And the rest? It will be the adventure of a lifetime, coming to know all of you. All the secrets you hide within you, but only those you are willing to share with me, Shelby. If you wish to keep your past a mystery, go ahead. I know you. I know your character.

"I love you."

Her tears began to fall rapidly now, and she tried to blink them away. "What would others say? A duke marrying a woman such as me."

He noted with satisfaction that she was not turning him down. If she didn't have feelings for him, she was frank enough to have told him to hold out no hope. Instead, she worried about his peers' reaction to a marriage between them.

"Do you think I care what the bloody *ton* thinks? I might have been born into it, but I have never truly been a part of it. A duke may do as he chooses and blaze his own trail through Polite Society. I want to live my life with you in it, Shelby Slade. With you by my side always. Will tongues wag? Of course, they will. But the *ton* always has to find something to gossip about. They will rake us over the coals for a short while, as if we care, and then move on to other, juicier scandals. We will find others like us. Those whose company we enjoy. People who accept us for who we are."

Through watery eyes, she said, "You mean those such as the Duke and Duchess of Bradford?"

He squeezed her fingers. "Exactly. It is obvious that they are deeply in love with one another. They are unconventional but sometimes, those types can even become the darlings of Polite Society. If they are the only friends we ever made, I would be happy, knowing I had you and their friendship. Bradford has told me, though, that he has others to introduce us to."

"Us?" she questioned.

He brought her hands to his lips and smothered them in kisses. "Yes, my love. I have told His Grace that I intend to wed you."

"Jasper! When did you do that?"

He grinned shamelessly. "When I met him at White's yesterday. You asked how your name came up? When I heard in Bradford's voice the love and pride he held for his duchess, I asked him how he had known he loved her. Because I had met someone I, too, loved."

Gazing at her solemnly, he added, "I have never been in love, Shelby. Yes, I had a fine time sowing my wild oats during my university days. I have walked an extremely narrow path since that time. In fact, you are the first woman I have even kissed since those days. I want to kiss you now, Shelby. I want to do more than kiss you—but I can stop at kisses. For now."

He saw she had come to a decision and held his breath, waiting for her to tell him whether he would be miserable for the rest of his life or be the most joyous man who walked this earth.

"I may be a fool myself, Jasper, but I love you. I *love* you. If you don't kiss me, I shall be the one to kiss you." She smiled. "Thoroughly, I might add."

He beamed at her. Releasing her hands, Jasper said, "You are the one driving this carriage, my love. Take us where you wish to go."

With that, Shelby thrust her fingers into his hair and pulled his mouth down to hers.

CHAPTER NINETEEN

S HELBY COULDN'T BELIEVE how daringly she now acted—but hearing that Jasper loved her had emboldened her. She could list a thousand reasons why it would be foolish for them to wed but one glaring reason outweighed them all.

She loved him . . .

Shelby kissed him. Not a gentle kiss. There would be time for those later. For now, she wanted to consume Jasper. Inhale him. Crawl inside and be a part of him.

Her fingers tightened in his hair as his arms came about her, bringing her flush against him. Then somehow he maneuvered her onto his lap and tilted her head back, giving him better access to devour her. That was the best word she could think of in the haze of desire that rose within her. She loved this man with all her heart. With every fiber of her being. And by some miracle, he returned her love.

They kissed for an eternity. Each kiss branding her as his and him as hers. She never knew that a kiss could communicate so much. Love. Need. Joy. Possession. She only knew she never wanted him to stop.

One hand cradled her nape, his thumb moving along her neck, stroking her as his tongue did the same in her mouth. His other hand now moved to her breast, palming it, kneading it. His fingers playfully tweaked her nipple, and heat shot through her.

She shivered in delight.

Her reaction must have told him not to stop because he slipped his hand inside her bodice and somehow freed her breast. His fingers caressed it lovingly, and desire poured through her. Suddenly, his mouth engulfed it, his tongue and teeth working some kind of spell, bewitching her. Fire spread through her limbs and down to her core, which began pulsating in need.

"Jasper!" she gasped.

He lifted his head, their gazes connecting. "Yes, my sweetest love?"

"I need . . . I need more than kisses. I need you . . . inside me."

A slow smile lit his handsome face. "I would like nothing better than to bed you, my love. Are you certain that is what you wish?"

When she found herself incapable of forming any words, he filled in the gap. "Never mind. We can do so later. After we speak our vows."

"No! I don't want to wait," she told him, her breathing ragged. "I . . . well, I am more worried about you. After all, it wasn't that long ago that you were a man of the cloth."

He smoothed her hair. "And you believe that is the reason we should now refrain from joining together?"

She nodded.

"Let me say two things, love. First, many clergymen are not religious in the slightest. They are simply third sons who are encouraged—if not forced—to go into the church, and they have the morals of an alley cat. While my own personal moral code tends to be stricter than others, I have no internal dilemma when it comes to making love with the woman I love. So, what say you, Shelby Slade?

"I want you. Now," she admitted.

"Sweeter words have never been spoken," he murmured, his mouth returning to hers, ravaging it.

Shelby felt him rise and clung to him as he carried her into his bedchamber. Gently, he placed her on the large bed and took a step back. She saw the heat in his eyes, desire glowing within them. His fingers went to his cravat, slowly untying it, his gaze pinning hers. Her mouth grew dry as he pulled it from his neck. Then he removed the garments he wore. His coat. His waistcoat. His fingers unbuttoned his starched, white shirt, and he reached for its hem, pulling it over his head and tossing it to the ground.

She sucked in a quick breath.

He was magnificent.

Her eyes roamed his torso, seeing the muscles. She had to touch them.

Pushing off the bed, she went and stood before him, placing her palms on his chest. He felt on fire, a great heat emanating from him. Slowly, her hands glided down his torso, and she felt the muscles bunch and spring to life at her touch.

Her gaze returned to his face, and she said softly, "I never knew a man could be so beautifully formed."

She pressed her lips to his chest and kissed it, feeling the shudder run through him. Emboldened now, Shelby wrapped her arms about him. Her mouth went to his nipple, and she flicked her tongue across it. Hearing his groan of pleasure made her smile, the allure of her feminine power being awakened for the first time. She used her tongue and teeth as he had, delighting in every sound he made.

Jasper took her face in his hands and raised it, his mouth seizing hers again, the kiss hot, wet, and long. When he finally broke it, his breathing was ragged as he asked, "I will need your help getting these boots off. I refuse to make love to you wearing them."

"Then sit, you silly goose," she teased.

He did so and raised a leg. She clasped the boot's heel in both hands and yanked hard. It took three tries before she got it off, and then she removed the other one. Jasper stood, and she said, "Let me," proceeding to remove his tight breeches. When she was done with them and his stockings, he stood before her, gloriously naked.

And hers. All hers.

She licked her lips in anticipation, and he said, "You look like a cat who has discovered the unattended bowl of cream." Then his voice dropped, growing raspy. "I would see you naked, Shelby."

Tingles spread throughout her. "Then help me shed my garments, Your Grace."

He might not have coupled with a woman in a good number of years, but Jasper had skill as far as undressing her went. His fingers were as nimble as any lady's maid, and he unclothed her quickly.

A slow smile spread across his face as a hand skimmed the curve of her hip. "Mine," he said hoarsely. Possessively. "All mine."

A wicked gleam danced in his eyes, and Shelby knew she was in the hands of an expert.

His hands began to roam her body, his fingertips surprisingly rough. Then she remembered he had mentioned his garden and pulling weeds. This was no soft-handed duke. This man, with his hard muscles and hungry eyes, had never been meant to be a leader of the aristocracy. Fate had a way of surprising others, though, and Jasper was now near the highest level of English society.

For a moment, panic set in. Could she truly stand by his side? Become a duchess? She was a former pickpocket. A Bow Street Runner who haunted some of the worst places in London.

Jasper framed her face with his long, lean fingers. "I know what you are thinking, love. It has struck you that being my duchess means being a duchess for all of Polite Society."

He kissed her tenderly. "You will make for the greatest duchess of all because you will be *mine*. Mine, Shelby, and no other man's. Together, we will lead the lives we wish to lead, the *ton* be damned." He brushed his lips softly against hers again. "Now, come back to me. Quit thinking so much about what is to come during the weeks and months ahead. Your focus should be in this moment—and all the pleasure I am about to give you."

With those words, he covered her mouth again with his, kissing her deeply, his tongue stroking hers even as his hands caressed her body. Soon, he had worked her into a wildness of want and need as she writhed beneath him.

He parted her folds and slid a finger inside her, causing her back to arch as he stroked her deeply. She couldn't help but moan aloud, the sensation making her feel so incredibly alive. Another finger joined the first, and soon his movements had driven her into a frenzy. Then something began building within her. Something unknown. Something exciting and thrilling and mysterious.

When the explosion came, she thought she was prepared for it—and wasn't. Her body hummed and then erupted with sensations new and volatile. She rode a wave of pleasure so great that she thought she might die from it as she clung to Jasper. Slowly, slowly, it subsided, causing her to go totally limp.

Then something pressed against her. She knew it to be his cock.

"Have you a French letter?" she asked.

"You know of those?"

She gave him a wry smile. "I am a Bow Street Runner. I have seen the seamier side of life. I have been exposed to things no future duchess would dream of knowing."

He kissed her lightly. "I do not have one. I told you, this is the first time I have coupled with a woman in years. I will end this now if you wish me to. I can understand if you do not wish for a babe."

She could hear disappointment in his voice but knew he would be the gentleman he always had been and stop.

But she didn't want him to stop.

"It doesn't matter," she told him. "If a babe is the result of our coupling, then it is meant to be." Shelby grinned. "After all, you have promised to wed me. I think we can arrange for a marriage license before nine months have passed."

Jasper smoothed her hair and gently kissed her brow. "I have been honest and told you that I have been with other women, but this feels different. *You* are different. Coming together with you will be what I have waited for my entire life."

He began kissing her deeply, even as his cock pressed against her core. Then with a strong thrust, he was inside her. The pain was minimal. She wondered if that had anything to do with the fact that she rode a horse astride as a man did. Pushing all thoughts aside, Shelby concentrated on Jasper. On his scent. His feel. She ran her hands along his broad, naked back, reveling in the feel of him.

Then she caught the rhythm of his movements. It was like a dance, one so sensual and pleasurable, that she had to join in. Becoming a participant changed everything. She moved with him. They moved together as one. That incredible pressure built within her again and erupted as he drove deeply into her, his seed spilling inside her.

He collapsed atop her, his breathing irregular, his body pressing her into the mattress. She welcomed his weight, feeling still a part of him, their bodies still joined. Then Jasper rolled to his side, his arm going about her, pulling her flush against him.

"You are amazing," he said, his hand lazily drawing circles against the small of her back.

He continued kissing her leisurely, and Shelby thought this moment was the best of her life.

Gradually, their bodies cooled. He kissed her swiftly and rose from the bed, returning with a basin and cloth. Gently, he bathed her.

"Did you enjoy our lovemaking?" he asked.

She reached up and stroked his cheek. "So much that I would ask you to do it again. I know it takes a man a bit of time to recover, though."

Jasper kissed her throat. "It might not take that long. Just touching you—kissing you—I feel myself growing hard again." He paused. "You are tender now, though. We need to give your body time to rest." He cradled her cheek. "We should dress now."

Shelby had no idea how long they had been upstairs and began to worry what the servants might think.

"I can see you are already worrying," he said.

"You know me so well. But I have much to tell you about myself, Jasper."

He kissed the tip of her nose and then offered his hand, helping her rise from the bed. "I told you. Tell me what you wish. Keep as much of your past in the past as you want. I am only interested in our present and future together."

With Jasper's help, Shelby was able to dress quickly. She returned the favor, and soon they both looked presentable. She retrieved her cloak, and he took her hand, leading her from his bedchamber and down the stairs. When they came close to the last landing before they reached the foyer, he stopped them.

"Wait here. I will send the footman on duty at the door on a brief errand. That will allow you to slip out of the house.

Jasper rounded the corner and called the footman's name. She heard the servant respond and Jasper telling the servant to go to the kitchens and get him something to eat.

"Bring it to my study," he instructed.

Half a minute later, she heard him call her name softly. Shelby scrambled to the landing and then down the last of the stairs. He kissed her again, his arms going about her.

Breaking the kiss, he said, "I don't want to let you go."

"We will see one another tomorrow morning. Remember, we are to take your nieces for a walk in the park. And then I need to see what path to follow to find your brother's killer."

His brow furrowed. "I don't like the thought of you in danger. I almost wish you would drop the entire investigation."

"Don't you want justice for your brother? Besides, if you do have a murderer in your household, no one is safe until he is exposed. Let me do what I do best, Jasper."

He kissed her again hungrily. "I think what you do best is kiss me."

"I cannot stay." She pushed him away. "I will see you tomorrow morning."

Frowning, he said, "I hate you going out into the dark. I should have my carriage take you home."

"Much of my work occurs at night. I know how to blend into the shadows. I have also told you I can defend myself as well as any man."

He clasped her shoulders. "I trust you. I just worry about you." He kissed her again swiftly. "Go, before I drag you back up the stairs and make love to you all night long."

"Goodnight, Jasper. I love you."

He caught her hand and raised it to his lips. "I love you more than I ever thought possible. The thing is, I believe I will come to love you more each day we are together. Can you imagine how much you will be loved when we are old and gray?" he teased.

She lifted their joined hands and kissed his hand. "It will be a lifetime filled with love." She released it and hurried to the door, opening it and slipping outside before she allowed temptation to keep her in his arms.

Walking through the square, her heels sounded in the quiet of the night. She turned and soon found a hansom cab, instructing it to take her home. It would not be home for much longer. She would soon live wherever Jasper lived. Her husband. Her one, true love.

Placing her key in the lock, she turned it and entered the house, going straight up the stairs to her bedchamber. She slowly undressed, reliving each moment with Jasper, touching her fingertips to her lips, thinking of his mouth on hers.

As she climbed into bed and snuggled beneath the bedclothes, Shelby hoped that she could solve this case. Her final one. She didn't think it would be appropriate for a duchess to also be a working agent of Bow Street, slinking through the night and interviewing rough types, dealing with criminals and bringing them to justice.

Would it be enough for her, being a duchess?

She told herself it would because she would have Jasper as her husband. Giving up Bow Street and all that entailed would be worth it if it meant a life with the Duke of Edgehaven.

CHAPTER TWENTY

SHELBY ENTERED JASPER'S townhouse the next morning and noticed the flurry of activity. She supposed it had to do with packing up Her Grace's things for her trip back to Edgehill. While she supposed she should be sympathetic to the duchess, who had lost her husband, she found she couldn't muster any pity for the woman. From the little she had seen of Her Grace, the duchess was a terrible person. She didn't seem the least bit affectionate with Jasper, whom she claimed as her favorite, and Shelby had never seen the woman with her grandchildren. Those two young girls had lost both parents in a short amount of time and needed all the love and attention possible. At least they had Miss Hall, who seemed to dote on them, as well as Jasper, who was quite good with his nieces.

Going into breakfast, Bowen stopped her and said, "I must warn you to stay out of Her Grace's way, Miss Slade. She is verbally slicing everyone who crosses her path and is most angry with His Grace—and you, in particular."

It didn't surprise Shelby. The duchess would have guessed Shelby was the one who had complained of her behavior to Jasper. Even though Jasper had been the one to issue his mother the ultimatum regarding her poor behavior, the duchess would blame Shelby.

"Thank you, Bowen."

The butler looked upon her with gratitude. "No, thank *you*, Miss Slade. Those who have remained in this household over the years only did so because of their fondness for His Grace. Once he passed, even Mrs. Bowen and I were considering going elsewhere. Good positions are difficult to secure, however. I only hope those at Edgehaven will be able to live through the nightmare of waiting upon Her Grace."

She entered the breakfast room and found Jasper sipping his usual cup of coffee. He nodded to a footman, and the servant left. She assumed he was to fetch their breakfast from the kitchens now that she had arrived.

Joining him, she asked, "Have you written to your staff at Edgehill?"

"About what?" He smiled at her lazily, his eyes undressing her. She felt her cheeks grow warm under his gaze.

Taking her napkin, she placed it in her lap, saying, "You need to send a note immediately to Edgehill. Even if your mother will not be staying in the main house, I'm certain they'll need to prepare the dower house for her." She leaned in. "And draw straws, I suppose, as to who might have to wait upon her."

He laughed. "You are absolutely right. In fact, though I am loath to leave you, I should travel there today and see things are ready for Mama."

"How far away is Edgehill?" she asked, already missing him.

"A little more than two hours if nothing goes wrong. I suppose it would be prudent to hire a post chaise to take me there this morning and return me to London by late afternoon. That way, Mama could have use of the horses and carriage tomorrow morning when she leaves and they would be fresh."

Shelby sniffed. "I hope she will remember to have them returned to London and not keep them for her personal use."

Jasper reached for her hand under the table. "How are you today?" he asked quietly.

"I am well," she replied. Then realizing what he referred to, she added softly, "A bit sore. But it was worth the slight discomfort. How are you?"

"Not regretting a single moment," he said honestly. "And I enjoyed a ride early in Rotten Row with Bradford before I visited with my nieces." He paused. "Dining with you now, however, is by far the highlight of my day."

Their breakfasts arrived, and they ate quickly. He asked her to accompany him to his study and once there, said, "I will have to forgo our walk with the girls since I should get to Edgehill."

"I have an idea. Why don't you take Lady Sylvia with you? She would enjoy the special time with you. It would give me several hours with Lady Fanny. I feel if I can get her alone, I will be able to somehow break through the wall she has erected around herself."

"That's actually an excellent idea. Come with me, and we'll tell them now. I think I will offer for them both to come with me. If they say yes, then you should plan to come, as well. If Fanny chooses not to, then you may stay with her."

They went to the schoolroom, where the girls were working on their lessons. Jasper explained that he had business to attend to at Edgehill and would be gone for the day.

"I'll return before nightfall, but I wondered if either of you might like to keep me company on the trip."

"I do!" Sylvia proclaimed, leaping to her feet. "I like to ride in the carriage." She glanced to her sister. "Fanny gets a bit sick when riding, though." She sat again, taking her sister's hand. "I don't have to go, Fanny. I can stay here with you instead."

The younger girl shook her head.

"Perhaps Lady Fanny would care to spend the day with me," Shelby interjected. "Since Lady Sylvia will be gone for the day, it would allow Miss Hall to have a holiday today for herself. Lady Fanny, we could go for a walk in the park as we had previously planned and then perhaps to one of the museums or bookstores I told you about."

Fanny's eyes lit with excitement, and she nodded eagerly.

"Then it is settled," Jasper declared. "Miss Hall, don't think a bit about schoolwork today. Go visit a bookstore or do a bit of shopping for yourself. I shall leave a few pounds with Bowen. Collect them from him so you can make a day of it and enjoy yourself. Sylvia, fetch your cloak. We will be off on our adventure, while Fanny and Miss Slade will have one of their own."

"Yes!" Sylvia cried out, scampering from the schoolroom and passing through the door to the room she shared with her sister.

"This is a bit unorthodox, Your Grace," the governess said.

He smiled at the woman. "I think spontaneity is underrated, Miss Hall. Go enjoy the time to yourself. I promise to take good care of Sylvia. We should return by teatime today, so if you wish to do your scheduled reading with my nieces, please be home by five o'clock."

"And I will make certain Lady Fanny and I return by teatime, as well," Shelby promised.

"See Bowen before you leave," Jasper told her. "He will also provide funds for your outing. You can have lunch somewhere or even treat yourselves to an ice at Gunter's."

Shelby smiled at him, great tenderness in her eyes. "That is most thoughtful of you, Your Grace." She looked to Fanny. "If you still want to walk in Hyde Park, go and collect your cloak. We will make a day of it, my lady."

A pleased smile touched Fanny's lips, and she left the schoolroom, although much more sedately than her sister had.

Within minutes, they were all ready, standing in the foyer, ready to face the chilly day. The four left the square together, with Jasper and Sylvia hailing and boarding a hansom cab, which would take them to an office where they might rent a post chaise. Shelby and Fanny remained on the pavement, waving as the driver flicked his wrist and drove away.

"I know Lady Sylvia will have a special day with your uncle, but we, too, will have our own fun today, my lady," she promised the young girl.

"Fanny." It came out softly. When Shelby didn't react, the girl tried again. "Fanny," she said, a bit louder this time.

"You wish for me to call you Fanny? But you are a lady. It wouldn't be proper for me to address you in such a familiar fashion."

Fanny's bottom lip thrust out in a pout, and Shelby laughed. "Very well. For today, you may call me Shelby and I shall call you Fanny."

The girl nodded her approval and tested it, saying, "Shelby."

"That is right, Fanny. I am Shelby. Shelby Slade." She grinned cheekily. "Your guide for today."

Fanny giggled, the sound touching Shelby's heart. Without prompting, Fanny slipped her hand into Shelby's, and they walked toward Hyde Park. They reached the park, and Fanny led them down to the Serpentine again.

"I like walking beside the water," Shelby said.

"Me, too," Fanny told her.

They spent a good two hours strolling the park, Shelby doing most of the talking, but Fanny always replied when asked a direct question. Since they had all day together, Shelby decided not to rush things. If she pressed too hard or too fast, she worried that Fanny might withdraw again.

"I find I am hungry. Do you think we should stop for a pie? Or we could even go for a bite to eat at Gunter's."

Fanny nodded. They left the park, and she led them to a hansom cab, asking the driver to take them to Gunter's in Berkeley Square. The establishment was known for its ices and sorbets, but it also served sweets, sandwiches, and tea. They arrived and were seated, a dark-haired woman coming to wait upon them.

"We have been out walking and could use something to warm up," she told the server. "Fanny, would like you like some hot chocolate?" When the girl nodded, Shelby added, "And tea for me. We could also do with a sandwich each. What are you serving today?"

The woman described what was available, and they made their choices.

After the server left, Shelby said, "Be sure you save room for something sweet at the end of our meal. Gunter's has some amazing sorbets and ices."

Fanny frowned. "What are they?"

"Have you never been to Gunter's before?" she asked.

"No. We never go anywhere."

"Did you come to town with your parents for the Season?"

"What's that?"

At six, Fanny would have no idea about the social swirl that occurred each year in London, so Shelby said, "Did you travel to London when your parents came each spring?"

"Sometimes. But we always stay with Miss Hall. We didn't see Mama or Papa much." She paused. "Papa went to London without us, too."

Of course, she knew that was so Lord Sutton might see Miss Simmons.

"Well, your uncle is eager for you to see the city. I believe he will be arranging outings for you and your sister to go on."

"Will you go, Shelby?"

Knowing she would wed Jasper, she said, "I will if you want me to come along with you."

"I wish you would live with us. We could go for a walk every day."

She vacillated before saying, "I would like that very much," thinking it was up to Jasper to tell his nieces about their upcoming marriage. Especially since they had not discussed a wedding date, she had no idea when the marriage might occur. If she told Fanny about it, she knew the small child would spill all she knew.

Their food arrived, and they ate with gusto before taking their time to discuss what sweet to top off their meal with. Fanny finally decided on a maple ice, while Shelby decided to try a *fromages glacés*, one of the rich custard ices frozen in molds in the shape of cheeses. When their desserts arrived, they allowed each other to sample what the other had ordered. Fanny declared while she liked the custard ice of Shelby's, she preferred her maple concoction.

They ate in contented silence, other tables around them filling up. She didn't ask any questions of Fanny. The girl had talked plenty already. Shelby wanted the conversation to unfold naturally and not be forced, and she certainly did want to wear the girl out after she'd stayed quiet for so long.

At some point today, she did want to broach the subject of Fanny's father.

After Gunter's, they went to Piccadilly Arcade, which had only been open for a few years. Fanny had never been window shopping before, so they went through the arcade, looking in the windows of the various shops. The girl had never done anything like this and became a chatterbox, which warmed Shelby's heart.

Finally, they stopped at a bookstore and spent a leisurely hour, combing the shelves. Fanny found a book of Aesop's fables, and Shelby told her fables were some of her favorite tales. When she saw how Fanny looked longingly at the book after she replaced it on the shelf, Shelby removed it again.

"I think we need a reminder of this day. I would like to buy this for you, Fanny."

"Would you, Shelby? I'll share it with Sylvia. She's a really good reader. She could help me with the words that are hard."

They purchased the book, and then Shelby said, "We should go home now."

Fanny frowned. "I don't like it there."

"What don't you like?" she urged.

They began walking slowly along the pavement, hand-in-hand. Fanny didn't speak anymore so Shelby hailed a hansom cab. She gave the driver their Mayfair address, and the horse began trotting along.

"I like Uncle Jasper," the girl finally said. "He's nice. He comes to see us at breakfast and asks us questions. And he listens to what we say." She paused. "Papa never talked to us."

"Sometimes, fathers are very busy."

Fanny sighed. "Papa was always busy. He didn't talk much to

Mama or us."

Shelby let that lie a moment and then said, "I am sure you miss your parents."

"I miss Mama," Fanny said, her eyes growing bright with unshed tears. "She was nice. But she was sick a lot. It's because she kept trying to have a boy. Papa said she had to have one." She shook her head sadly. "I don't think he liked girls."

She hid her disgust. Most men of the *ton* had no use for girls. It was what made Jasper and the Duke of Bradford stand apart. Watching the duke with his babe at tea yesterday had warmed her heart, as did hearing Jasper brag to the couple about his nieces. She knew no matter what children she birthed, Jasper would love them wholeheartedly.

"Grandmama doesn't like us either."

"What makes you say that?" she asked carefully.

Fanny shrugged. "She . . . she just doesn't."

"Maybe if you spent more time with her, you could get to know her better," Shelby suggested.

"No!" The vehemence in Fanny's voice startled Shelby.

"Do you not like your grandmama?"

The girl's face hardened, making her look far beyond her tender years. She shook her head but clammed up and said nothing more for the rest of the ride. They arrived, and Shelby paid the driver. She led Fanny inside the townhouse. The footman on duty greeted them, and she asked for tea to be sent up to the schoolroom as she handed him her cloak.

Leading Fanny up the stairs, she said, "Miss Hall will be back after teatime for you to read together. Perhaps Lady Sylvia and your uncle Jasper will also be home by then, and you can read from your new book."

When they turned on the landing of the second floor, the Duchess of Edgehaven stood there. Fanny gasped, clinging to Shelby's skirts, burying her head in them. Shelby could feel the girl trembling and wondered why she was so frightened of her grandmother.

Handing Fanny the wrapped book they had purchased, she said, "My lady, take this book to the schoolroom and wait for tea. I will be there shortly."

Fanny released Shelby's skirts and accepted the book. She glanced at the duchess and then scurried by her.

"Your Grace," Shelby said.

The duchess' eyes narrowed. "You scheming strumpet. You think you have my son wrapped about your little finger. I know it is you who put in his head to send me to the country."

Coolly, she said, "I merely informed His Grace of your abominable behavior. It was he who decided your fate. Actually, you did that yourself. His Grace gave you the chance to improve upon your actions, but you reverted to your cruel self."

Anger blazed in the older woman's eyes. "How dare you speak to me in such a manner!"

"I merely speak the truth, Your Grace. You have looks and wealth. A lofty title. But you are unkind. Why, even your granddaughter is frightened of you."

The woman's eyes widened. "Why do you say that?"

"She told me that you didn't like her. And I could feel her quivering as she clung to me just now, after she spotted you. You have three beautiful grandchildren, Your Grace. You should appreciate them. Love them. Spend time with them."

"I cannot believe you think to tell *me* what to do. You will pay for having me banished to the country, Miss Slade." The duchess sniffed haughtily. "And just so you understand, I only have *two* granddaughters, Miss Slade. That . . . creature is not one of them. I will never recognize her as a part of *my* family. Not coming from the mother who birthed her."

She refused to lower herself to this woman's level. Tamping down her anger, Shelby calmly said, "Lady Della will be better off not being around you, Your Grace," Shelby told the older woman. "So will your other granddaughters. Your influence upon them could have been great, and you could have shared abundant love with them. Instead, you are a vile woman who deserves no pity."

The duchess looked aghast at having been spoken to so bluntly. "Good day, Your Grace," Shelby said, ending the conversation and continuing up the stairs, glad to escape from a woman who had everything and chose to throw it all away out of spite.

She arrived to find Fanny sitting at the table in the schoolroom, still shaking after the encounter. Scooping up the small girl, she cradled her in her lap.

"There, there," she comforted. "You are safe. You will not be seeing your grandmama for a long time. Her Grace is leaving for Edgehill tomorrow."

"Good," Fanny said. "I don't like her."

A maid arrived with a tray. It contained a cup of milk for Fanny and a small teapot for Shelby's tea, as well as a few biscuits.

She moved the young girl to a chair and thanked the maid. Handing the milk to Fanny, she poured tea for herself and began sipping it, trying to calm herself. The tea was hot but terribly bitter. She usually took it plain but added both sugar and milk to it, hoping to improve upon the taste. After two more sips, she realized even that did not help make the brew palatable, so she set it aside, still half-full. They sat in silence, both she and Fanny lost in thought for some minutes as they ate their biscuits and Fanny finished up her milk.

Then out of nowhere, Fanny said, "She pushed him."

Shelby stilled. She turned and looked at the young girl, who gazed up sadly at her, her eyes bright with tears.

"What did you say?"

Fanny's mouth trembled. "It was Grandmama. I saw her. She pushed Papa down the stairs."

Cold fear pooled in her belly. "You saw this, Fanny?"

The girl nodded sleepily. "I'm tired, Shelby."

She also felt weary but stood. "Why don't you lie down for a bit, Fanny? I'll stay with you. I can even tell Miss Hall that you can wait and do your reading tomorrow."

Helping Fanny to her feet, she led the girl from the schoolroom into the bedchamber. Fanny climbed onto the bed and curled into a ball, falling asleep immediately.

Shelby gazed down at the young girl, horrified by Fanny's words. She would have to tell Jasper the minute he returned from Edgehill.

But she, too, was so sleepy. Perhaps if she lay next to Fanny and just rested her eyes for a few minutes, she would get over being so drowsy.

Then she heard something and turned.

The Duchess of Edgehaven stood in the room. "I know you coupled with my son," she accused. "I went to his rooms. To beg him to change his mind." Disgust filled her face. "I heard the sounds coming from his bedchamber." Her eyes narrowed. "And I knew *you* were the one with him."

Fear filled her, even as her limbs grew heavy. Then, in a moment of clarity, Shelby said, "You put something in the tea."

The duchess smile enigmatically. "And the milk. I am always thorough."

Shelby fought to keep her eyes open, knowing she was in danger, as was Fanny. She dug her nails into her palms, fighting to stay awake, and then lifted Fanny from the bed. Though her legs felt like lead, she rushed past the duchess, the child in her arms, and made it to the corridor.

She had to get away. She had to take Fanny. She needed help.

Her vision grew blurry. Then she spied Lord Darrow. She did not question his presence. No words would come out. It was as if her lips were frozen and numb.

"Miss Slade?" he asked, concern filling his voice. "Is something wrong?"

Her arms grew weary with Fanny's weight. "Take her," she said, thrusting Fanny toward him. "Keep her . . . safe."

Shelby leaned against the wall and sank down it, hitting the ground. She fought to keep her eyes open and saw the duchess appear. Lord Darrow handed the sleeping child to her.

A sound came from Shelby, one of protest, but it wasn't a

word at all. The duchess carried Fanny back into the room as the earl came toward her. He managed to get her to her feet.

"You are ill, Miss Slade. Here, let me help you."

He put an arm about her and somehow got her down the stairs. They reached the foyer, and she fought to keep her eyes open as nausea roiled through her. She heard Lord Darrow call for her cloak.

"Miss Slade has taken ill. My carriage is out front. I will take her to Dr. Barton."

Her cloak was draped about her shoulders, and then she felt the cold as the door opened and the earl maneuvered her toward his carriage.

This was wrong. All wrong. She couldn't leave Fanny. The duchess had drugged her. Them. She had to tell Lord Darrow they couldn't leave.

Then she felt the motion of the carriage beneath her and knew she was inside it. She fought to keep her eyes open.

And lost.

CHAPTER TWENTY-ONE

JASPER LOOKED OVER at Sylvia, who stared out the window at the heavy London traffic. He was glad his niece had accompanied him to Edgehaven today. The post chaise had gotten them to the country before eleven o'clock, and he was able to notify his staff of his mother's arrival the next day, specifying that he wanted the dower house prepared for her. He made it perfectly clear that she was to remain there and not be allowed to set foot inside the main house, at least until he returned to the estate.

He had taken Sylvia down to the stables because during their journey to Hertfordshire, she had talked of her desire of learning how to ride. They had met with his head groom and found a mare which she and Fanny could learn to ride upon once they returned to Edgehill. The groom assured Jasper that the horse had a tough mouth and gentle spirit and would be just the mount for young girls to learn upon. Jasper thought it a good idea for Shelby to also learn how to ride. Being the city girl she was, he doubted she had ever been given the opportunity to do so and knew she would take to the saddle with ease.

They had returned to the main house and walked through it together. Jasper allowed Sylvia to pick out a room for herself and Fanny once they returned to Edgehill. Surprisingly, Sylvia asked if she and her sister could share again, saying she needed to be close to Fanny and take care of her. He then told his housekeeper which bedchamber had been chosen and she assured him all rooms would be readied for their return. Jasper also quietly told the servant to have the duchess' rooms in good order, only saying he was ready to take a bride and would do so soon. He wanted Shelby to be officially his and had decided he would purchase a special license in Doctors' Commons tomorrow once his mother had vacated the house. He didn't care for her to be a witness to the ceremony. He would send a note to the Duke and Duchess of Bradford, though, asking if they would be willing to act as witnesses to the marriage vows. Of course, he would want his nieces present at the ceremony. They already seemed to like Shelby a great deal. He would tell them of the upcoming marriage at tea today.

Two hours later, they left Edgehill to return to the city in a new post chaise. Even though it had been a quick trip, it had been good to see Hertfordshire again. They even passed through Edgewood, and he pointed out to his niece the church he had served for several years, wondering whom the bishop had chosen to take his place.

It had taken them a bit longer to reach his London residence, thanks to the heavy traffic in the city, but it was a little past four, according to his watch. Knowing he had told Miss Hall not to return until five o'clock this afternoon in time for the girls' reading, he assumed Shelby and Fanny were taking tea together. He hoped they had enjoyed a day on their own and that his niece had opened up to Shelby.

The post chaise pulled up in front of his townhouse, and he thanked the driver. As he helped Sylvia from the vehicle, he spied Lord Darrow's coach pulling away. He supposed his mother had summoned the earl to her side, complaining bitterly about her son exiling her to the country for the next several months. It was considerate of Lord Darrow to come and tell Mama goodbye.

A footman admitted them, and he had no doubt that his mother was keeping Bowen busy.

Jasper handed his coat to the footman as Sylvia said, "Come

on, Uncle. Let's go to the schoolroom. I want some tea, and I want to tell Fanny all about what we did today. She will love knowing we have our own pony to ride."

He looked to the footman. "Have more tea sent up to the schoolroom if you would," and then followed his niece, who raced up the stairs with the energy only the very young had.

They arrived at the schoolroom, and he saw a small teapot, along with a cup and saucer and an empty cup which he assumed contained milk at one point. Two biscuits remained on a plate. A book of Aesop's fables also rested there. But where were Shelby and Fanny?

Then he heard a voice coming from the girls' shared bedchamber, the door ajar. It wasn't Miss Hall speaking.

It was Mama.

He had never known his mother to visit the schoolroom, much less spend time with her granddaughters. An odd feeling came over him.

Just then, Sylvia cried, "Miss Hall! I have ever so much to tell you about today."

He turned and saw the governess smiling at Sylvia.

"That is why I returned early, my lady. To hear about all your adventures."

Trusting his instincts, Jasper told the governess, "Take my niece to the kitchens and have tea there if you would, Miss Hall."

She gave him a quizzical look but then smiled at her charge. "Come along, Lady Sylvia. We will see if we can wheedle a biscuit or two out of Cook."

He waited until they had gone and then moved through the threshold. He saw Fanny lying on the bed, sound asleep, his mother perched beside her granddaughter. In her hand, she held a letter and read from it. She stopped, however, when she became aware of his presence.

"Why, hello, Edgehaven. As you can see, poor Fanny is worn out from her outing today."

He moved toward the bed, and his unease deepened.

"What are you reading to her, Mama?" he asked, spying an open casket on the bed beside her. It was stuffed with letters.

"Just a little something. Poor Fanny is so tired after such a long day. Why, she fell asleep during tea."

"*You* had tea with Fanny?"

When she only smiled at him, Jasper turned back to his niece and gently shook her shoulder. "Fanny, wake up. It is Uncle Jasper. I want to hear all about your day with Miss Slade."

The girl did not stir. Concern filled him, and he clasped her shoulders, lifting her to a sitting position. "Fanny? Wake up, little love."

Jasper shook her again, harder this time, but her head only drooped to one side. He scooped her into his arms.

"Something is wrong with Fanny, Mama. I cannot wake her."

His mother's expression was serene. "I am certain she will be fine, my darling. The girl simply needs to sleep. Put her back in her bed so that she can rest."

"No," he said firmly, and then snatched the page in her hand.

Jasper began skimming it and realized that it was a love letter. One written to his mother. It was not in his father's hand, one which he would have easily recognized. He glanced to the end and saw a single letter.

D.

Raising his head, his gaze met Mama's. "Who wrote this to you?" he demanded. "And when was it written? I see no date upon it."

She smiled at him.

"Mama, tell me who wrote this letter."

"Why, my lover, of course," she said matter-of-factly. "The only man I have ever loved." She indicated the casket next to her. "He has written me many such love letters over the decades. I hope he will continue to do so after we are wed. We are finally free of them, you know."

"Free? Free of whom?" his gut already telling him the answer.

"Why, your father and Lady Darrow. You see, Lord Darrow

and I were to be married until my father put down his foot," she calmly explained. "An earl wasn't good enough for my father. No, he wanted nothing less than a duke for his daughter. Actually, not for me—but for the family. For the prestige of being able to say he was related to a duke by marriage."

"Darrow? You were in love with Lord Darrow?"

She smiled brightly. "We have been in love all these years, my boy. Soon after I wed, I found myself with child. I did not know if the babe belonged to Darrow or Edgehaven. Once Jarrod came out of me, he favored me in looks. But he was too carefree. Too much like Edgehaven in every other way.

"Jude was the image of Edgehaven. At least, Jude did not get Edgehaven's casual, free spirit. Jude was more serious, taking after me."

With dread, Jasper asked, "And what of me, Mama? Whose son am I?" he asked softly.

"Why, you are most definitely Darrow's son. Once again, you took your looks from me, as well as your solemn nature, but you received the best of Darrow as well."

"Did Father know this about me?" he asked hoarsely, his belly in knots.

"He didn't—until the very end. Though he could barely walk, I found him snooping in my rooms. He found the letters, you know. Recognized Darrow's hand immediately. Even in his poor, weakened state, he railed against me, wanting to know how long the affair had gone on. I told Edgehill I had coupled with Darrow before I had even come to the marital bed—and that I had continued to see the earl over the years."

What a betrayal of his father. And Lady Darrow. Jasper didn't recognize the woman before him. Working up his courage, he asked, "Did you poison Father? With arsenic?"

She smiled benignly. "How clever of you to have finally guessed the truth. You always were the brightest of the three of you. You took that after me, as well. Yes, I have always used arsenic in small amounts. I learned when I was a girl during my first Season that it enhanced a woman's complexion." She patted her cheeks. "See? They are still unlined, even at my age."

"You gave it to Father, didn't you? You had him ingest arsenic. Why?"

She shrugged and then said, "Lady Darrow was dying. She received the diagnosis in the middle of last Season and asked Darrow to take her home to die. I thought as long as we would finally be rid of her, we might as well remove Edgehaven, as well. It would give you the chance to become the duke and me to finally live with the man I adore."

Horror filled him. This woman had given birth to him. And yet he—no, everyone—had not known the true depths of her evil nature.

"So, you decided to help Father along?"

"It was so easy," she purred. "I did have a little help from my lady's maid. She has been with me for many years and knew how I felt about Darrow, often covering for us so that we might be together."

"She is the one who put arsenic into his food?"

"Yes, Jasper. Have you grown thick in the head or are you not listening?"

Then it struck him that she had mentioned him becoming the duke, and he asked, "Did you have anything to do with Jarrod's death?"

Mama waved a hand dismissively at him. "He was always so affable and yet so weak. He would have made for a terrible Duke of Edgehaven."

Pinning her gaze, he asked, "Mama, did you push Jarrod down the stairs?"

She smiled slyly. "Well, Edgehaven *was* on his deathbed now, wasn't he? I could not have Sutton inherit the title. The title I wanted for you, my darling boy."

His voice unsteady, Jasper's final question was, "Did Fanny see you do so?"

Her nose crinkled in disgust. "I think she must have. I went to the library and brought a tumbler of brandy with me. I dribbled it down the front of Sutton's dressing gown. I wanted others to think that he had been deep into his cups and had fallen. When I returned, the girl was next to him, weeping."

Her eyes narrowed. "I told her to keep silent—or the same would happen to her."

The ominous words hung in the air. No wonder Fanny, a frightened six-year-old girl, had not told anyone what she had seen. Because she had been threatened with death.

From her grandmother.

He knew there was no possibility that his mother would ever hang for her crimes. Why, if word got out what had occurred, scandal so huge would color the entire Lincoln family. It would follow Sylvia and Fanny as they made their come-outs and even haunt his own children in the years to come.

He gazed down at his niece, still sleeping in his arms, and them back to his mother.

"Did you give Fanny something in her drink, Mama? Have you killed her, too?"

"No, of course not, Jasper. I am not that cruel. Besides, she has kept quiet as I asked. I merely gave her a touch of laudanum to help her rest."

"Where is Miss Slade, Mama?"

Anger flared in her eyes. "She grew ill. I asked Darrow to take her to a doctor."

"Mama, did you also give Shelby something in her tea?" he asked, thinking of the teacup and milk cup sitting on the schoolroom table.

She looked innocently at him. "I have no idea why Miss Slade grew ill."

"You are mad," he told her. "You murdered your husband and your firstborn. You must pay for what you have done."

She laughed sharply. "A duchess would never hang, my sweet boy. And you cannot afford for word to get out. Just think of the enormous scandal it would cause. No, you must wed a beautiful, graceful woman. I have a few in mind for you to meet during the upcoming Season. Let's forget this silly notion of sending me to mourn in the country."

"You are not going to the country anymore, Mama."

Her face lit with relief. "Oh, Jasper, I am glad you are finally seeing things my way. I will guide you through this Season and find you the wife of your dreams."

He took a step back from her, his arms fast about Fanny. "You are going to a madhouse," he said bluntly, naming the most famous asylum in England.

Shock filled her face. "You cannot *mean* that, Jasper."

"Oh, I mean it, Mama. I do not trust sending you to the dower house at Edgehill. You are going to pay for your crimes for the rest of your life as you rot in an asylum."

He wheeled and hurried from the schoolroom, racing down the stairs. He came across Bowen and said, "You are to have two footmen escort Her Grace to her room and lock her inside it. She is not to leave under any circumstances. Is that understood?"

"Yes, Your Grace," Bowen said and hurried away, running down the stairs.

When Jasper reached the foyer, the footman on duty hurried toward him.

"Is Lady Fanny ill, Your Grace?"

He nodded, and the footman said, "I hope it is not what Miss Slade came down with."

"Tell me about her," he barked out.

"She left here with Lord Darrow helping her, Your Grace. Miss Slade was as white as a ghost and could barely walk. I helped Lord Darrow place her into his carriage. He told his driver to head to Dr. Barton's."

"Thank you," Jasper said and went outside, knowing it would take a quarter-hour to have his horses harnessed and his carriage readied.

He took off running through the square and reached the street. Continuing along the pavement, he flagged down a hansom cab, giving Dr. Barton's address to the driver. The driver saw Fanny was unconscious in Jasper's arms and promised to get them to the doctor as soon as possible.

Jasper settled against the cushion, praying Fanny and Shelby would both be all right.

CHAPTER TWENTY-TWO

As THE HANSOM cab started up, Jasper knew if he were to help Shelby, he would not be able to do so with Fanny in tow. As the girl's guardian, he must protect Fanny above all else. Her breathing was even and regular. He did not think his mother had given too strong a dose in the girl's milk. He needed to find a safe place for her but did not know where to turn.

Then it occurred to him. The Duke and Duchess of Bradford lived nearby. He could entrust Fanny to them.

He called to the driver and changed his destination. Within five minutes, the hansom cab pulled up to the Bradfords' residence.

Descending from the vehicle, Jasper told the driver, "Wait here. I will return, and we will go to the first address I gave you."

The driver didn't question the additional stop, merely saying, "Yes, my lord. I'll be waiting."

He hurried to the door, pounding on it fiercely. It opened, and he recognized Nelson, the butler, from his previous visit here with Shelby.

"Nelson, I must see Their Graces at once," he said, pushing past the butler into the foyer.

"They are still at tea, Your Grace. If you will follow me."

The butler led him upstairs, and they entered a library, where he heard the duchess laughing. Her laughter died, though, the minute she spied him. She and the duke sprang to their feet as he hurried toward them.

"What's this?" Bradford asked.

"I don't have time to explain. This is my niece, Fanny. I am entrusting her with you. She has been given some laudanum and is only sleeping. Would you summon a doctor to look at her, though? Just to be certain all is well with her."

"We would be happy to do so, Your Grace," the duchess assured him.

He thrust Fanny into Bradford's arms. "Protect her," he said and turned.

"Wait," the duke called, and Jasper turned back. "This is about your case, isn't it? Where is Miss Slade?"

"I fear she is in danger," he revealed, tears stinging his eyes. "I have an inkling where she may be. I must hurry if I am to save her."

Determination filled Bradford's face. "Well, you aren't going to do that alone. You will need help. My help." He turned to his wife. "I'll have Nelson send for the doctor, my darling. Stay with little Fanny here. We will be back soon, hopefully with Miss Slade."

The duke pressed a soft kiss to his wife's mouth and then handed Fanny over to her as the duchess said, "Be safe, Elijah."

Bradford looked to Jasper once more. "Let's go."

The two men left the library and hurried down the staircase. Nelson lingered in the foyer, and Bradford told his butler to send for the doctor at once.

Nelson said, "A footman can go for the doctor, Your Grace. I believe I am needed with you, wherever you are going."

"Very well," Bradford said.

They moved to the door, and Nelson told the footman standing beside it to leave immediately and fetch the doctor. The three men spilled out onto the pavement, where the hansom cab was still waiting. They piled into it.

"Hurry, Man," Jasper ordered, and the vehicle took off.

As they traveled down the London streets, Bradford said, "Tell us all you can so that we might be prepared for what is to come."

A deep shame filled Jasper, but he knew he had an ally and did not believe Bradford would judge him for the actions of others.

"I went to my country estate today in Hertfordshire with Sylvia, my other niece. It was strictly for the day and to inform the staff that my mother would arrive tomorrow and take up residence in the dower house. Mama has been quite difficult. Not recently, either. It is a common thread throughout my life."

Sighing, he said, "When Sylvia and I returned, I found Shelby missing and Mama sitting with Fanny. Mama was reading a letter to her, even though she slept. I was able to draw out that Mama dosed Fanny's milk with laudanum and must have done the same with Shelby's tea."

Bradford frowned. "Why would your mother do such an odd thing?"

"Because she is mad. Years ago, she fell in love with Lord Darrow, but her father put an end to their relationship, forcing her to marry my father since he was a duke. She is the one who has engineered everything. Mama gave Father arsenic over time, causing him to fall ill. She admitted doing so once Lord Darrow's wife was diagnosed with something terminal. Mama wanted the two of them to finally be together."

Nelson gasped. "That's horrible!"

"Oh, it grows worse. I was always Mama's favorite," he admitted. "I hated the favoritism that she showed me—and now I know why she did. Most likely, I am Lord Darrow's son."

He fell silent, allowing the two men to absorb what he had just revealed.

"So, your mother is the one who caused Lord Sutton's accident?"

Jasper nodded. "It was no accident. She pushed him down those stairs. She just admitted to me that she never knew if he were Father's son or Lord Darrow's because he resembled her so closely. But Sutton's nature was similar to my father's. With Sutton out of the way and Jude killed in war, it cleared the way for me to inherit the dukedom."

"Do not feel any guilt, Edgehaven," Bradford said. "This is all the doing of a madwoman."

"Either she is mad—or as clever as a fox," he said flatly. "Either way, I cannot stand the sight of her, knowing she murdered my . . . her . . . husband. And my brother."

The duke placed a hand on Jasper's shoulder. "Edgehaven *was* your father, Your Grace. Legally—and in every sense of the word. He loved you, and you loved him. Nothing will ever change that."

"I saw red," he admitted. "I wanted to kill her. I know, though, if word of this gets out that scandal will taint my family for years to come. I had Mama escorted to her rooms and placed under lock and key. I will send her to an asylum so that she can never hurt anyone else ever again."

"What of Miss Slade? Is that where we go now?" Nelson asked.

"I was told she took ill. I assume from Mama's hints that she also gave Shelby laudanum in her tea. The servants told me Lord Darrow escorted Shelby from the house and was taking her to a doctor. That she appeared very ill."

"We go to Dr. Barton's now. I do not know if Darrow knew what Mama had done to Miss Slade or if he is in on the scheme and trying to dispose of Shelby. I have no idea if Mama acted alone or if she and the man my father called his closest friend plotted Father's murder so they could finally be together. I hope to catch up to them at Dr. Barton's."

"Barton? We use him," Bradford said. "He is Lord Darrow's nephew."

Fear almost paralyzed Jasper upon hearing this. "I had no idea," he said, trying to understand the implications. "Lord Darrow was as a father to me and my brothers growing up. He told me how jealous his two younger brothers were that he was the one who inherited the earldom, instead of them. If Barton is his nephew, then I wonder what lengths he might go to in order to please his uncle?"

"We will find Miss Slade, Your Grace," Nelson said fervently.

They rounded a corner, and the hansom cab traveled half a block south before slowing and then stopping in front of a house. Bradford stepped from the vehicle first and tossed a coin to the driver, who caught it and grinned.

"Thank you, my lord," he said as Jasper and Nelson spilled from the cab.

"Be ready for anything," Jasper told his companions. "And if one hair has been harmed upon Shelby's head, I will be out for blood."

The trio moved quickly to the door, and he pounded upon it until a servant answered.

⟫⟩⟨⟪

SHELBY FELT HERSELF coming around. She had only drunk half of the tainted cup of tea and supposed the full dose would have knocked her out cold. She was lying on a settee and kept her eyes closed as two men spoke. She recognized Lord Darrow, who was speaking, but she was familiar with the other man's voice and racked her brain until his identity came to her.

Dr. Barton . . .

"I cannot do what you are asking, Uncle," the physician said. "I swore an oath. I am to protect—not harm—others."

"I do not care about any bloody oath," the earl said tersely. "I am in an impossible situation, Nephew. I need you to get rid of this woman. Tonight."

Fear rippled through her. Shelby didn't know the extent of Lord Darrow's involvement in the deaths of his friend and Lord Sutton. If the Duchess of Edgehaven had acted on her own—or if the lovers had schemed together. Whatever the case, Shelby would not go down without a fight. Not when she had just found love and a new life with Jasper awaited her. She bit her tongue as hard as she could, pain running through her, as she tried to awaken more and not slip back into a deep slumber. She began clenching and unclenching various muscles as she continued to listen to the pair discussing her fate.

"How would I even accomplish that?" Dr. Barton demanded.

"Dump her into the Thames, for all I care. She has been dosed with laudanum and will be pliant. I promise you, she will not awaken. Miss Slade will simply slip beneath the waters. It is winter and already dark enough, but you should wait until traffic dies down some. I will leave my carriage with you since you do not have one of your own. That way, you can transport her without arousing any suspicion."

A harsh laugh sounded. "And what am I to tell your coachman?" Dr. Barton challenged. "Oh, my good man, drive me to a bridge and help me pull an unconscious woman's body from your employer's carriage, so that we might dump her into the water and then drive merrily away, thinking nothing of having murdered a poor soul."

"I do not want my servants involved, especially if Bow Street comes around, looking for their agent. What they do not witness, they cannot discuss. I will take them with me. *You* will drive the carriage yourself. You alone are to take care of this nosy troublemaker."

A loud gasp sounded. "I simply cannot do this, Uncle."

"You will do as I say!" shouted the earl. "Who paid for your education? And all of your medical schooling? Who helped set you up in this house and your practice? I did. That is who. I recommended you to my friends, and now many of the *ton* uses you for their aches and pains. Your father is weak and worthless and never did anything for you. I saw the potential in you. *I* am the one you owe your allegiance to. You will do as I say—or I will destroy you."

Shelby sensed the shift in the air and knew that Barton would capitulate to Lord Darrow. Weak men such as Barton always would whenever a wealthy, powerful man of Polite Society threatened them, despite their feeble attempts at protest. While she had liked the doctor, she understood that his entire life and livelihood had been thanks to his uncle. If forced to make a choice between Lord Darrow and her, Dr. Barton would choose family—and his own continued success ministering to members of the *ton*—over the life of a woman he owed no allegiance to.

Thank goodness that while she was still a bit drowsy, she was throwing off the effects of the laudanum. She moved her leg slightly, making the blade in her boot easier to reach. Yet in her weakened state, she could not fend off both these men. She needed Darrow to leave. She would have a better chance at survival if only Barton were the one trying to murder her.

"All right." Resignation was obvious in the physician's voice. "I'll do as you say."

"That's a good lad," the earl praised. "You will not regret it. And when Bow Street comes knocking on your door—and they will, I warn you—you are to say I brought Miss Slade to you because she was ill. Think of whatever diagnosis you made, and then tell them you summoned a hansom cab for her and she left here alive. You are the man of medicine. Think of the details that will make them believe you. Whatever you decided troubled her. Whatever medication you gave her. Use that education of yours. Throw a bunch of fancy words at them."

A long pause occurred. Shelby tensed.

"Be clear that I left before you even examined her. That you placed her in a hansom cab and sent her on her way. If she didn't reach home? Well, she was in a weakened, vulnerable state. It would not be unheard of for a driver to take advantage of that situation. Rob her. Dump her body. If it washes up, that is. Whatever happens, stick to the story you tell. Do not budge from it. Bow Street will press hard, with one of their own gone missing. But it is a violent profession. And a woman doing a man's job?"

Lord Darrow laughed. "I'll wager most of the runners will think Miss Slade got exactly what she deserved."

Shelby wanted to rise from the settee and kick the man in the balls. She kept herself from doing it, though. She needed to reserve the strength she had. She would deal with Dr. Barton first.

And then handle the treacherous Lord Darrow.

"I'm off," the earl said. "Remember, wait for the streets to be clear."

"How much laudanum did she receive?"

"I have no idea. If she begins to stir, pour more down her gullet. Or you must have something you can give her to keep her quiet. If you think it will be easier, just slit her throat." Darrow chuckled. "She won't give you any trouble then. If her body does come ashore, it would then appear she was robbed and murdered."

She marveled at how cold-blooded the man was.

"I'm off," Lord Darrow said. "My carriage will be waiting for you. I'll have the coachman stay with the horses. I will instruct him to leave the moment you appear. Return the horses to my mews when the deed is done. I will alert my head groom so you will be expected. Stop by for tea tomorrow, Nephew. You can tell me then all about your little adventure."

"Little adventure?" echoed Dr. Barton, his voice wavering.

Opening her eye a slit, Shelby saw the earl place a hand on his nephew's shoulder.

"You will do as you've been told—and then forget about this night. You have the rest of your life ahead of you. A thriving career. You are a decent-looking fellow. I say it is time you wed. I will arrange a bride for you." Darrow paused. "Just take care of our little problem—and keep your mouth shut."

Quickly, Shelby closed her eye again. She sensed Lord Darrow moving toward her. He came and stood next to her as she breathed evenly.

"A pity," he said. "You were quite lovely to look at, Miss

Slade."

And then a noise sounded. Someone was banging on Dr. Barton's door loud enough to wake the dead. Hope sprang inside her. Her heart told her things would be fine.

Jasper was here . . .

CHAPTER TWENTY-THREE

JASPER PUSHED PAST the woman who had answered the door. Bradford and Nelson raced inside, as well. The servant sputtered something unintelligible.

"Where is Dr. Barton?" he demanded.

"W-w-with . . . with his uncle," she stammered. "And the young lady who's so ill."

Relief poured through him.

Shelby was here.

"Take us to the examination room at once!"

"They're . . . they're in the parlor, my lord." She pointed to closed doors just off the left of the small foyer. "There."

His eyes narrowed. "It is His Grace. And if I were you, I would make myself scarce."

The servant fled, and he strode to the doors, finding them locked. With a strong kick, he remedied that problem.

The three men rushed into the room. Jasper spied Dr. Barton, looking flummoxed. A quick scan and he caught sight of Lord Darrow standing next to a settee, Shelby sprawled on it.

The earl's eyes went wide, darting about.

"There's nowhere to run, my lord," Jasper said evenly. "Step away from Miss Slade."

Instead, Darrow did the opposite. He wheeled, yanking Shelby to her feet, one arm going about her waist, the other pressing against her neck, forcing her head back.

Her eyes went straight to Jasper. He saw calm in them. No panic on her part.

And then she winked at him.

"Stand back—or I will snap her neck," the earl warned.

"You'll do no such thing, my lord," Shelby told him, her right wrist twisting by her side.

Jasper realized while Lord Darrow had her body pinned against his, he had left her arms free. Then he caught sight of the blade in her right hand. In the blink of his eye, her left arm flew up, her fingers grasping her captor's hair. As she thrust her right arm upward, Shelby tilted her head to the side, leaving the earl's face unprotected. The knife slammed into his cheek with great force, buried to the hilt. Then Shelby jerked her arm down, the blade slicing through skin and bone until it reached Darrow's chin and was free again.

The earl screamed to the high heavens, dropping to his knees, his hands going to his face as blood spouted everywhere.

Shelby, the blade still in her hand, turned to Dr. Barton. "Sew him up. Give him nothing for the pain. I want him conscious during the interrogation."

She looked to Nelson. "Go straight to Bow Street. Ask for Mr. Franklin. Tell him that I sent you. He is to bring two agents with him and a secretary to record Lord Darrow's confession. By the time they arrive, I am certain Dr. Barton will have his lordship's bleeding under control and his wound stitched closed."

"Yes, Miss Slade," Nelson said, hurrying from the room.

Darrow blubbered loudly as Shelby turned to face him. "You suggested Dr. Barton slit my throat. How does it feel, my lord? To be cut open?"

"You bitch," he managed to say.

Glancing to Barton, she said, "If you have an examination room, carry him there. If you don't, I would place him on the kitchen table." She looked to Bradford. "Perhaps you might help Dr. Barton carry Lord Darrow, Your Grace?"

The duke nodded grimly. "I can do so, Miss Slade. Come, Barton."

Bradford grabbed the earl's arm and brought him to his feet. The physician took his other elbow as the earl continued weeping, his hands pressed to his ruined flesh. They left the room, and Shelby finally looked at him.

"I am sorry you had to see that, Jasper," she said softly. "I was limited in the places I could stab him, thanks to his hold on me."

"You were magnificent," he declared.

She cocked her head. "You aren't horrified by what you saw?"

He closed the gap between them, wrapping her in his arms. "I am amazed at your skill. At you."

She yawned sleepily, giving him a lopsided grin. "I might have done better if I weren't so tired. Fighting that bloody laudanum has worn me out."

Leading her to the settee, he eased her down on it. He took a seat beside her and tilted her until her head rested in his lap.

Shelby gazed up at him. "You aren't afraid of me? You don't find me revolting?"

"I find you utterly enticing," he said huskily. "And I plan to purchase a special license tomorrow so that I can have you in my bed sooner rather than later."

She sighed. "It will take a while for Nelson to rally the troops. And Barton to repair the earl's face." Her eyelids began to flutter. "Let me sleep until Mr. F arrives. I should have . . . my senses . . . about me by . . ." Her voice trailed off, and she fell asleep.

Jasper sat with her in his lap, smoothing her hair, until Bradford appeared.

"Lord Darrow's face has been stitched up, and the bleeding stopped," he said cheerily. Gazing down at Shelby, the duke added, "You have yourself quite a woman there, Your Grace."

"I do," he agreed. "I told her I would purchase the special license tomorrow. Would you and Her Grace be interested in witnessing our ceremony the day after tomorrow?"

Bradford beamed. "Abby and I would be delighted to attend.

In fact, why don't you let us host the wedding breakfast?"

"There will be only two guests," he said. "My nieces."

"An intimate ceremony and breakfast then," the duke declared. "And as long as we are coming to your wedding, you should call us Elijah and Abby. I have the feeling we are going to be quite close friends."

He smiled. "Then it is Jasper and Shelby inviting Elijah and Abby to our wedding."

Nelson appeared in the doorway, Mr. Franklin and two Bow Street Runners accompanying him.

"Ah, Mr. Franklin," Jasper said. "Thank you for coming so quickly. Lord Darrow has been seen to by Dr. Barton and should be ready to speak to you now."

The older man flicked his wrists, and the two agents disappeared. Franklin came into the room and gazed down at Shelby's sleeping form.

"She is all right?" he asked softly.

"Better than all right," he said. "She single-handedly brought down Lord Darrow, even though she had been drugged with laudanum."

"She is our world," Franklin said.

Jasper frowned. "Beg pardon?"

The old man reached out and smoothed Shelby's hair. "I found her on the streets, years ago. She agreed to come with me for one night. Mrs. Franklin and I opened our home and our hearts to her. Shelby is the child we were never able to have."

"Then I must ask if you have plans for the day after tomorrow, Mr. Franklin. You see, Bradford here is hosting a wedding. Our wedding. Mine and Shelby's."

Franklin beamed. "Does Shelby know about this?"

"I told her that I was going to purchase a special license. I will do so tomorrow. She does not yet know I have already picked out the date for the ceremony."

"Mrs. Franklin and I will be there with bells on our toes, Your Grace."

The Bow Street Runners entered the room, escorting Lord Darrow and Dr. Barton.

"If Nelson and I are no longer needed, I think we shall return home. Abby will have preparations to make for your wedding," Bradford said. "Come along, Nelson. It seems we are hosting a wedding breakfast."

The butler grinned cheekily. "Yes, Your Grace."

"Thank you both for your help," Jasper told the two men.

Bradford shrugged, biting back a smile. "What are friends for?"

Looking to Nelson, he added, "The value of your assistance cannot be overlooked. I plan to award you a healthy sum for your brave assistance today."

"That is most generous of you, Your Grace," the butler said. "I am most grateful."

"I wish to do more than that, Nelson. The Duke and Duchess of Bradford will be invited to our wedding, but I wish to extend an invitation to you and your wife, as well."

The butler's eyes widened, and then he smiled broadly. "Mrs. Nelson and I would be happy to attend the ceremony, Your Grace."

"Come along, Nelson," Bradford said. "We have things to do. And I need to get you out of Edgehaven's sight before he tries to hire you away from me."

As they left the parlor, he gently shook Shelby. She came to and smiled up at him.

"Mr. Franklin and his men are here. Bradford and Nelson have left to inform the duchess that we will be married at the Bradford's townhouse the day after tomorrow."

A radiant smile graced her beautiful lips. She looked to Mr. Franklin. "Do you like him, Mr. F? Do you think he will do?"

"He'll do nicely, Shelby. Now, let us conclude this case."

She sat up and swung her legs to the floor, becoming all business now. Jasper merely sat and observed the proceedings.

"The sooner we get our answers, the quicker Dr. Barton will

be able to give you something for your pain, Lord Darrow," Shelby said crisply, once more the Bow Street professional.

Darrow cursed softly, and Jasper wondered if he had ever truly known the man who was, in all likelihood, his father.

One of the agents removed parchment from his satchel and quickly set up, ready to record the proceedings. When he was ready, he nodded at Shelby, who began her interrogation.

"Did you conspire with Her Grace, the Duchess of Edgehaven, to murder her husband, using arsenic?"

The earl looked startled by the question. "No. I did not."

Shelby looked grimly at Darrow. "Did you know Her Grace was slowly poisoning her husband?"

"Not at first," he admitted. "I think she got the idea after my wife was diagnosed with a terminal illness. We left London in the middle of the Season so she could be at home in the country when she went. Our son and daughter came, along with their families. It was . . . actually a pleasant time." He paused, staring off in the distance. "Possibly the best of my marriage."

Shelby cleared her throat, drawing Darrow's attention. "When did you learn of Her Grace's actions, my lord?"

"She wrote to me upon my wife's death. I had notified her and Edgehaven of it."

"This was mid-October, correct?"

"Yes, Miss Slade," the earl said wearily. "In her note, the duchess informed me of her husband's ill health. At that point, I had no idea what scheme she had hatched. I only learned of it when I came to London, shortly after Christmas." Darrow shuddered. "Edgehaven looked like a cadaver. The last I had seen him, he'd been hale and hardy, but that was six months ago."

Shelby thought a moment. "Did His Grace not write to you of his poor health?"

"No. We were bosom friends during the eight months or so when we were in town, but we rarely if ever corresponded when we were apart. I asked him what was wrong." Darrow swallowed hard. "He told me he never wished to see me again. It was then I knew that *he* knew. About . . . us."

"You mean about you and Her Grace's longstanding affair," Shelby said sharply.

Darrow winced. "Yes. We had wished to wed during her come-out Season, but her father denied my suit. He wanted his daughter married to a duke. We became lovers shortly before her wedding." The earl looked at Jasper. "We continued our love affair until last summer."

The earl shook his head, wincing again from the pain. Shelby looked to Dr. Barton and said, "Give him a brandy to take the edge off."

Quickly, the physician went to the decanter and poured a healthy amount of brandy into a snifter, taking it to his uncle. Lord Darrow sipped at it, his eyes closed.

"My lord," Shelby continued, "what did Her Grace tell you when you came to London? After His Grace refused to see you ever again?"

"That Edgehaven had found the letters I had written to her. They went back decades," he admitted. "Then she shared that she had begun having arsenic added to his food. She used it on her face, of all things, but she had her lady's maid cozy up to a footman. Between the two of them, they sprinkled the arsenic into His Grace's food and drink. Small amounts at first and then larger portions as time went on, causing His Grace to fall deeper into illness."

He named the footman. Jasper already knew the lady's maid, who was the only servant who had been in the household for a good twenty years or more.

Wearily, the earl sipped his brandy and said, "Her Grace told me that she got the idea from my wife's illness. That if we were rid of both our spouses, we could finally be together."

"What about Lord Sutton's death?" Shelby asked.

Darrow shook his head. "I had no idea she would go so far. She always thought Jarrod too pleasant. Too weak to be a duke." His eyes flicked to Jasper and then away again. "She wanted her youngest son to be the Duke of Edgehaven upon her husband's death."

"Because he was your son?" Shelby prodded gently.

"She thought so. I . . . I am not certain that I am his father, though. Jasper was born on Christmas Day. Her Grace and I were definitely together during that spring, but I was out of town when I believe he was conceived. My wife's father had a heart attack, and we left London for a good two weeks to visit him in the country. Her Grace and I did not couple until at least ten days after our return to town. Jasper favored his mother in looks. His nature was more serious than that of his brothers. Despite my misgivings, she convinced herself he was our child."

Darrow shrugged helplessly. "I just do not know. I am sorry. So sorry. I loved her. I have always loved her, despite all she has done. That love has caused me to act in a most dishonorable fashion. I am ashamed of my actions—and I will rectify matters immediately."

Lord Darrow stood. He came to Jasper, who rose. The men gazed at one another a long time.

"I do love you as a son," the earl said softly. "But I am not nearly the man your true father was. I believe you to be his, Jasper. I will go now. I have an heir. He will take the title."

Jasper's heart was breaking as he saw a man he had trusted—even idolized at times—standing before him, totally broken. Yet at the same time, the earl had conspired to kill the woman Jasper loved. Darrow must be punished to the full extent of the law. Unfortunately, peers in England rarely were charged with crimes, even ones as heinous as Lord Darrow had committed.

"What will you do?" he asked, knowing his own actions would be weighed and then executed once he knew what Darrow planned.

The earl's lips thinned. "The honorable thing. I will be cleaning one of my guns this evening. It will accidentally discharge. My son will become the new Lord Darrow." He placed a hand on Jasper's shoulder. "Please. Tell him none of this."

"I won't," he promised.

With that, the Earl of Darrow left the room without another word.

Shelby turned to Dr. Barton. "I know his lordship is your uncle. I was conscious. I heard him tell you how to dispose of me." She paused. "And I know you would have done as he ordered."

Tears welled in Barton's eyes. "My uncle did everything for me. I . . . I did not know how to refuse him."

"You are to leave London," she told him. "You are a good doctor. I think a good man, albeit a weak one, is inside you. Go to some country village. Establish a medical practice there. Never return to London. Is that understood?"

Tears ran down the physician's face. "Yes, Miss Slade. Thank you."

"Leave us," she instructed. "We still have a few things to discuss."

The doctor made himself scarce. Only after he left, did she speak.

"There is still the matter of your mother, Your Grace," she said formally.

He cleared his throat, his emotions raw. "I have her sequestered in her rooms. She has been told that she will spend the remainder of her days in an asylum."

Shelby moved to him, touching his sleeve, pity in her eyes. "Are you certain that is what you wish? I have been inside one of those madhouses, Jasper. They are a living hell on earth."

Resolve filled him. "She murdered my father *and* my brother," he said through gritted teeth. "If I could see her hanged, I would do so. You and I both know that would never happen. No, I will send her to one in the morning. Or as soon as I can find a place for her."

Mr. Franklin spoke up. "We can handle that for you, Your Grace. My agents here can accompany you to your home and remove Her Grace this evening." He paused. "Would you care to say goodbye to her first?"

"No," he said firmly. "I must go to the Duke of Bradford's. It is where I left Fanny, my niece. She is who is important to me. Fanny and her sister, Sylvia. I am their guardian. I did not protect Fanny as I should have."

Shelby protested, saying, "No one could have known that Fanny would be out of bed at that time of night and see what she saw. You weren't even her guardian at that time, Jasper."

She was right. But he must do what was best, moving forward. That was taking care of his nieces. Never seeing his mother again.

And marrying this woman.

"See that you have come and gone by the time I return home," he said sharply.

"I will go myself and supervise things, Your Grace," Mr. Franklin said. "I will let you know which asylum she has been placed in. With your permission, I can discuss with your solicitor how to pay for her care." He looked to his agents. "Come along."

The three men exited the parlor, leaving him alone with Shelby. No words passed between them. She merely stepped into his arms, and he held her to him for the longest time. Her warmth flowed from her into him, taking away all the cold and darkness, giving him courage to face whatever came their way in the future.

Jasper kissed her softly and then said, "I hired you to find the truth, never knowing how much it would sting."

"I am so sorry, my love."

"I'm not. We know what happened now. We will be able to help Fanny heal. She is young. She will recover from this trauma." He smiled. "She has us."

Shelby smiled up at him. "And we will always have each other."

Jasper kissed her deeply, knowing wherever Shelby was, that was where home would be.

CHAPTER TWENTY-FOUR

JASPER AND SHELBY left Dr. Barton's residence and slowly moved down the pavement, arm-in-arm. Within a block, they were able to hail a hansom cab and gave the address for the Duke and Duchess of Bradford to their driver. They climbed into the vehicle, and Jasper slipped an arm about Shelby. She rested her head against his shoulder and immediately fell asleep.

He wished he could do the same, feeling completely drained by the events of this day. At least Jasper believed, based upon what Lord Darrow had said, that he was his father's son and the true Duke of Edgehaven. Still, he was wounded emotionally by the betrayal of Darrow. The man had been a second father to him and his brothers all these years, but a false friend to the Duke of Edgehaven. He supposed the depth of love between Darrow and Mama ran deeply. A small part of him did feel sorry that they were forced apart so many years ago by his grandfather. He also knew members of the *ton* engaged in extramarital affairs regularly. His brother was a good example of that practice.

Yet it was the actions of his mother which stung the most. Not only had Mama lain with another man for decades, but she had murdered her own husband and then her firstborn child. She had waved away her despicable behavior, justifying her actions because she wanted to wed Lord Darrow and for Jasper to become the Duke of Edgehaven.

If he could give away the title, he would. He would do anything to bring back his father and brother but knew it was impossible. How betrayed Father must have felt when he learned his good friend of a lifetime had been falsely playing him for more than thirty years.

Weariness blanketed him as they pulled up to Bradford's townhouse, but he thrust it aside. He had others depending upon him—and that began with Fanny. The horrors the girl had seen had driven her to become almost mute. Jasper only hoped in time, with love and attention, that Fanny's terrible memories would recede and finally fade into oblivion.

The hansom cab driver pulled in behind an elegant carriage, and Shelby opened her eyes as they came to a stop. The love he saw in them as she looked up at him nearly broke him. No, it would be this love which would help put him back together, piece by shattered piece.

They exited the vehicle, and a footman leaped to the pavement from the ducal carriage, heading toward them.

"Your Grace, you are to dismiss your driver. His Grace wishes for you to take his carriage home this evening. We will be ready for you when you wish to depart."

"Very well."

He turned and paid their driver, and then he and Shelby went up to the door, where Nelson answered their knock.

"It is very good to see you both," the butler said.

"I cannot thank you enough for coming to my aid this evening, Nelson."

"Come to the winter parlor. Their Graces are waiting there for you."

They followed the butler and found the duke and duchess waiting for them. The duchess enveloped Shelby in her arms as the duke took Jasper's hand and shook it.

"Come and sit," the duchess said. "A substantial tea is coming. You have had a long day and missed your supper."

Servants rolled in the teacart, and the duchess poured out for them. Jasper found he was starving and for several minutes, they ate in silence. Finally, he sat back and asked, "How is Fanny?"

"I had sent a footman to Dr. Barton's house since he is our usual physician," the duchess began. "He returned here, saying a servant had turned him away at the door. Of course, now I know why. Thankfully, our footman took the initiative to bring back another physician. He looked over your niece, and Fanny is well, Your Grace."

He breathed a sigh of relief. "Thank you for looking after her while we attended to the business at hand."

"Elijah told me everything that happened when he arrived home." Sympathy filled her blue eyes. "I am so very sorry, Your Grace."

"At least we now know all the truth," he said, his voice tinged with sadness.

"I know you and Elijah have bonded this night." The duchess smiled at Jasper and Shelby. "My husband also shared that we are to host your wedding breakfast. We will be honored to do so. Only if you will call me Abby from now on. I insist upon it."

"We would be happy to do so," Jasper replied for the both of them.

"Would you like me to go with you to Doctors' Commons tomorrow?" Elijah asked. "I have experience in obtaining a special license." The duke took his wife's hand and kissed her fingers tenderly.

"I would be happy for your company," he said. "You have been a good friend to us, and I hope our friendship will grow in the coming years."

They went upstairs to retrieve Fanny from a bedchamber. A maid sat beside the bed, watching over the small girl. Jasper thanked the servant and then scooped Fanny into his arms.

Fanny opened her eyes and sleepily asked, "Uncle Jasper?"

"It is I, my little love. Close your eyes and go back to sleep."

She did so, and he carried her to Bradford's waiting carriage. He thanked his new friends again and climbed into the vehicle after Shelby. Minutes later, they arrived home.

A worried Bowen met them and said, "Your Grace, a Mr. Franklin is waiting to speak with you in the drawing room."

Jasper frowned. Franklin had promised he and his men would have come and taken Mama away before he and Shelby arrived with Fanny.

"Let me attend to Lady Fanny first," he said, mounting the stairs, Shelby at his side.

Miss Hall was seated at Sylvia's bedside and quickly stood when she saw them. He placed Fanny upon her bed, and the governess removed Fanny's shoes and pulled the bedclothes over the sleeping child. Jasper motioned for Miss Hall to come into the corridor.

"My niece needs rest. Let her sleep as long as she wishes to in the morning." He looked to Shelby. "Do you think the girls should have lessons as usual tomorrow?"

She nodded. "I believe keeping to a routine would be wise. In fact, after breakfast I will take the girls for an outing in the park. While you are running your errand," she added, smiling up at him.

They wished Miss Hall a pleasant evening and left the governess. As they descended the stairs, his fingers found Shelby's and held them tightly as they made their way to the drawing room where Mr. Franklin awaited them.

He rose as they entered the room. "Have a seat, Your Grace. I must share some distressing news with you."

"Did things not go well with my mother?"

Sympathy filled the older man's eyes. "No, Your Grace, they did not. Have a seat. Please."

Dread filled Jasper as he and Shelby sat on a settee, their fingers still intertwined.

Mr. Franklin sat across from them and said, "When we arrived, I explained to your butler that we were here at your request and that we would be taking Her Grace with us. Bowen led us upstairs to the duchess' rooms. The footmen on duty were dismissed, and we entered after announcing ourselves, using the key provided by Bowen."

Franklin removed a folded sheet and handed it to Jasper, saying, "We found this."

Perplexed, he released Shelby's hand and unfolded the page. Inside, he saw Mama's handwriting.

My dearest Jasper —

I realize now that you will do as you promised and send me away. I cannot live in a world without my darling Darrow.
Be the best duke you can be.

All my love,
Mama

His gaze met Franklin's, a sick feeling washing over him. "What did she do?"

"Her Grace ingested arsenic, Your Grace. Quite a large amount. It must have killed her very quickly."

Shelby's fingers found his, and he drew strength from them.

"Where is she?" he asked hoarsely.

"The duchess is still in her bedchamber. Mrs. Bowen is taking care of the body now. As far as her lady's maid and the footman who were complicit in your father's death, they are gone. Do you wish for my agents to pursue them?"

"No. I want this sordid incident behind us." He hesitated, knowing it would hurt to say the words aloud. "I hope you will not think less of me, Mr. Franklin, but I am going to look to the future. Mine and Shelby's future. I will see Mama quietly buried somewhere tomorrow, and then I plan to wed Shelby the day after as we had decided. I hope to see you and Mrs. Franklin at the ceremony."

"I think you are making a wise decision, Your Grace. It is best to close the door on this ugly chapter. If you would like, I can make arrangements for Her Grace's burial. To ease that burden from you. Would you like her buried at—"

"I do not want her next to my father. She is a suicide and doesn't even belong in hallowed ground. Do whatever you wish with her, Mr. Franklin. I will not be attending any service for her, nor do I wish to even know where she is buried."

"I understand, Your Grace. I will handle matters now."

Franklin rose, and Jasper and Shelby did the same. He offered his future father-in-law, of sorts, his hand.

"I am sorry we have met under such dismal circumstances, sir, but good has come from evil. It led me to Shelby. Let me assure you how much I love your daughter and that I will always put her first."

"I know you will, Your Grace." Franklin looked to Shelby. "Let Mrs. F and me know the time for the ceremony. I will see myself out."

Jasper watched Franklin go and then turned to his betrothed. "I need your strength tonight, my love. Would you stay with me?"

"I will."

They climbed the stairs together and entered his rooms. Slowly, he allowed Shelby to undress him. He did the same for her, and they got into bed. He slipped his arms about her, drawing her into his chest.

"Sleep, my sweetest love," he whispered.

Sometime in the night, she woke him and they made love, slowly and tenderly. Afterward, they lay awake in one another's arms, talking quietly about all that had occurred—and about their future together. He was glad they had made love because it affirmed to him that they were alive and their love was pure and true.

"Go to sleep," she urged. "I will be here in the morning, Jasper. I will always be here for you—and you for me."

As he drifted off, Jasper knew his best days lay ahead with the woman he loved.

EPILOGUE

London—Ten years later . . .

JASPER SAT BEHIND his desk in his study, waiting for Shelby to arrive. They were hosting two events tonight, both annual affairs. The first was a dinner party for their ever-growing circle of good friends. Amazingly, all the men were dukes—and their duchesses were remarkable women. Not ones Polite Society would have expected dukes to wed, but incredible women, all the same. These duchesses led full lives, keeping their husbands happy and being mothers to their respective children. Yet they all forged their own paths through the *ton*. Delaney designed hats worn by members of Polite Society and middle-class women. Margaret painted portraits of people who interested her. Finola trained her Honeyfield spaniels. Fia composed and played music. Willa taught part-time at an orphanage she had established. Nalyssa took men who had inherited titles and turned them into true gentlemen. Abby's furniture designs were heavily in demand.

And Shelby was still at Bow Street.

She was no longer a runner, though. Instead, she had taken on administrative duties at the agency, becoming indispensable to Mr. F. Since Edgehaven was only a couple of hours from London, she came into town two days a week, usually Tuesdays and Wednesdays. She met with new clients, seeing if Bow Street should take on the case or not, and assigned the appropriate agent to each investigation. She also met regularly with agents regarding the progress of their investigations, asking them questions and helping direct them in ways they had not thought to head. She reviewed case files once an inquiry came to a close. One day, Shelby hoped, after Mr. F's retirement, that she might manage the whole of Bow Street on her own.

If so, that would be several years down the line. Besides Bow Street, Shelby was a mother to seven. Their four boys—ages nine, seven, five, and two—had joined Sylvia, Fanny, and Della. Shelby had handled Sylvia's come-out two years ago and would do the same for Fanny when her debut came either next year or the year after. Fanny wasn't certain when she wanted to make it, because she was heavily involved in her art. Art had been Fanny's way back into the world, and they had encouraged her to draw and paint as much as she wanted. It helped that she never had to see her grandmother again. Both girls had accepted that the Duchess of Edgehaven had passed away and was buried. Neither had ever asked a single question about her demise. If they knew she had taken her own life—which was possible, thanks to the gossip of servants—they never mentioned it. Sylvia had been wed for a year and was now increasing, her own child due in early September. They would go to her once they finished off the current Season.

A knock sounded and Jasper said, "Come."

Fanny entered, carrying a frame, and he knew what that meant. It was Fanny who had said on the first Christmas Jasper and Shelby were wed that their joint birthdays got lost in the holiday's happenings. She suggested they celebrate in the summer instead. They had begun to do so that next July.

And each July, Fanny painted a picture for them as a gift.

She had done landscapes. Still lifes. Portraits of each of their four boys. He wondered what this year's picture might bring.

"Is Shelby not home yet?" Fanny asked.

"No," he said, not bothering to hide his smile. "She must be tied up with some important case."

Fanny blew out a long, exasperated breath. "Does she not realize what today is?"

He chuckled. "Oh, do you mean the dinner party we are to host for our friends, followed by the ball we are giving this evening?"

His niece laughed. "She certainly is an unusual duchess, Uncle Jasper. You have to admit it."

"She is—and I wouldn't have her be any other way."

"Nor I," Fanny agreed. "Shelby is the best mother Sylvia, Della, and I could have had. She treated us as her own from the beginning. It is a good thing she did have us and gets to dress us and organize our come-outs, what with four boys. They are certainly a handful!"

"I couldn't agree more. How she gets them to behave is beyond my comprehension. One look—and they snap to attention. And yet those boys love her with all their hearts."

He moved from the desk and glanced out the window, seeing a hansom cab pulling up. Shelby climbed from it. She refused to take the ducal carriage to work, leaving it for his use each day while they were in town.

"She is home," he said, moved as always at the thought of being in her presence. Even after a decade together, Shelby was his everything.

"Then we should go greet her," Fanny suggested. "I have my present for you."

"What is it this year?"

"No peeking!" she declared, holding the painting close to her as they left the study.

They went to the foyer, where Shelby was handing off her bonnet and reticule. Spying them, she said, "Oh, I know I am late. I said I would be home in time for tea, and it is already half-past five. I know our guests will arrive at seven."

"Take a breath, my love," Jasper said. "Fanny has a present for us."

Shelby brightened. "Our picture? I cannot wait to see it. Hand it over."

Instead, Fanny slowly turned it around. Two joined hands had been painted onto the canvas. He recognized the wedding ring his wife wore. Emotion overwhelmed him as he reached for his duchess' hand and entwined their fingers together as seen in the painting.

"You are always holding hands, as if you were still newly-weds," Fanny proclaimed. "Your bond remains strong. I wanted this present to show the love you hold for one another but pictured in a unique way."

"It is absolutely perfect," Shelby said, motioning Fanny to come to them. She wrapped her arm about the young woman and kissed Fanny's cheek.

"Thank you," Jasper said, kissing the other cheek. "You outdo yourself each year."

"I live to paint," his niece said. "I want to be like the Duchess of Westfield and paint whatever I choose." She smiled. "But you need to go and get ready, Shelby."

"I will just say hello to the boys, and then I will bathe and dress."

"I instructed Bowen to have hot water sent up the moment you arrived," he said. "So don't be too long." He claimed the painting from his niece. "I will show this to our guests at dinner. They are always eager to see your latest creation."

Taking the painting to the drawing room, he left it there so he could show it to their friends and brag on Fanny when they gathered for drinks before dinner. Then Jasper went up to Shelby's rooms. The duchess' suite was only used for bathing and dressing. Breaking with tradition, they slept in the duke's bed each night. Their bed.

He arrived as the last of the servants brought the buckets of water necessary for the bath. When her lady's maid lingered, Jasper told the servant Her Grace would ring when she was needed. She laughed merrily and left the room.

Shelby barged into the room out of breath. "Oh, it will be a quick bath, I am afraid. Where is—"

"I dismissed her. Told her you would ring when you were ready for her."

A slow smile spread across her lovely face. "Jasper, I don't think we have time for what you want to do."

He moved to her, bending and slipping his hands under her layers of clothing, removing her stockings and shoes.

"What do you think I want?" he asked huskily.

She grinned. "Exactly what I want."

"Then we better get to it—else we will be late to dinner, my love. Or at least the drinks served beforehand. I will do a rapid yet thorough examination of the body I love so."

Shelby laughed. "I thought investigating was *my* specialty, Your Grace."

He framed her face with his hands and kissed her deeply. Love poured from him into her and flowed back again as they made quick, passionate love.

They were only ten minutes late to the drawing room. Bowen was discreetly distributing glasses of champagne to their guests when they arrived. Jasper caught Nalyssa talking about the latest young man she had taken under her wing, an architect who had unexpectedly inherited an earldom.

"If only he were as fastidious in his dress as he is with his drawings," Nalyssa said and the others laughed.

"Ah, there you are," said Xander. "We placed bets, you know. On how long you would be delayed."

"And I won," declared Fox, checking his timepiece.

"Exactly what do you win?" Shelby asked the duke.

Gallantly, Fox took her hand and kissed her fingers. "Your friendship and that of your husband's is the only gift I need." Fox looked about the room. "The gift we all deserve. Shall we raise a glass?"

The large group—eight dukes and their duchesses—raised their champagne flutes high.

Fox looked to Jasper. "You are the host. You do the honors."

"Very well." Jasper looked across the group, seeing the many friends Elijah and Abby had introduced them to over the years.

Daniel and Margaret
Henry and Fia
Pierce and Nalyssa
Fox and Delaney
Xander and Willa
Cy and Finola

Raising his glass, he said, "To the best group of friends we could be blessed to have. As a whole, we were all men who suddenly became dukes through a variety of unusual circumstances. And most importantly, to the exceptional women who agreed to become our duchesses." His eyes misted with tears as he looked to his beautiful wife. "Especially to Shelby, my light and my life."

Jasper paused and then said, "To friendship."

"To friendship!" said those gathered, enthusiasm in their voices.

He took a sip of the cold champagne and gazed down at his duchess. Quietly, he said, "And here is to another year of blessings. I love you, Shelby."

His wife cupped his cheek. "And I love you even more, Jasper."

Jasper kissed his wife, despite the drawing room being filled with guests. No other couple noticed, though.

They were all kissing their own spouses—and living their own happily ever afters.

About the Author

Award-winning and internationally bestselling author Alexa Aston's historical romances use history as a backdrop to place her characters in extraordinary circumstances, where their intense desire for one another grows into the treasured gift of love.

She is the author of Regency and Medieval romance, including: Dukes of Distinction; Soldiers & Soulmates; The St. Clairs; The King's Cousins; and The Knights of Honor.

A native Texan, Alexa lives with her husband in a Dallas suburb, where she eats her fair share of dark chocolate and plots out stories while she walks every morning. She enjoys a good Netflix binge; travel; seafood; and can't get enough of *Survivor* or *The Crown*.

* 9 7 8 1 9 6 0 1 8 4 3 1 3 *